Fleur McDonald has lived and worked on farms for much of her life. After growing up in the small town of Orroroo in South Australia, she went jillarooing, eventually co-owning an 8000-acre property in regional Western Australia.

Fleur likes to write about strong women overcoming adversity, drawing inspiration from her own experiences in rural Australia. She has two children and an energetic kelpie.

Website: www.fleurmcdonald.com
Facebook: FleurMcDonaldAuthor
Instagram: fleurmcdonald

FLEUR McDONALD

Broad River Station

ALLEN&UNWIN
SYDNEY•MELBOURNE•AUCKLAND•LONDON

First published in 2022

Allen & Unwin
Cammeraygal Country
83 Alexander Street
Crows Nest NSW 2065
Australia
Phone: (61 2) 8425 0100
Email: info@allenandunwin.com
Web: www.allenandunwin.com

Allen & Unwin acknowledges the Traditional Owners of the Country on which we live and work. We pay our respects to all Aboriginal and Torres Strait Islander Elders, past and present.

A catalogue record for this book is available from the National Library of Australia

ISBN 978 1 76087 884 9

Set in 12.4/18.2 pt Sabon LT Pro by Bookhouse, Sydney
Printed and bound in China by C&C Offset Printing Co., Ltd

10 9 8

The paper in this book is FSC® certified. FSC® promotes environmentally responsible, socially beneficial and economically viable management of the world's forests.

To Rocket, our companion of fifteen years, I've never written a book without you. The underneath of my desk is empty and the house too quiet. For a little dog, you took up a lot of space and I miss you.

And to those who are precious and are my world.

AUTHOR'S NOTE

Detective Dave Burrows appeared in my first novel, *Red Dust*. I had no idea he was going to become such a much-loved character. Since then Dave has appeared as a secondary character in fifteen contemporary novels, including *Broad River Station*, and five novels (set in the early 2000s), where he stars in the lead role.

Fool's Gold, *Without a Doubt*, *Red Dirt Country*, *Something to Hide* and *Rising Dust* are my novels that feature Detective Dave Burrows in the lead role. Eagle-eyed readers will know Dave from previous novels and it was in response to readers' enthusiasm for Dave that I wanted to write more about him.

In these novels, set in the late 1990s and early 2000s, Dave is at the beginning of his career. He's married to his first wife, Melinda, a paediatric nurse, and they're having trouble balancing their careers and family life. No spoilers here because if you've read my contemporary rural novels you'll know that Dave and Melinda separate and Dave is currently very happily married to his second wife, Kim.

Dave is one of my favourite characters and I hope he will become one of yours, too.

CHAPTER 1

'Who are you?'

The woman placed her hand on the glass and stared.

There was no answer, just the sound of everyday things. The tick of the clock, the low hum of the TV from the room next door, the muffled conversations of people in the hallway.

'Who are you?' This time she whispered the words, because she knew she was supposed to know the answer.

Her reflection stared back at her. But it wasn't her. Not the way she remembered herself. Who was this elderly lady with hair so white you wouldn't notice snow on her head? Deep lines crisscrossed the image, and the woman's eyes were watery and dull.

The hand touching the mirror seemed to belong to someone else. The skin was paper thin; sun spotted. The gold rings on the left hand were loose.

Confused, the woman shook her head to clear her thoughts.

The door opened silently and a young woman in uniform came in holding a dinner tray.

'Evening, Clara,' she said, placing the tray on the side table. 'How are you tonight?'

She turned at the sound of the voice.

Clara. Yes, that's who she was. Clara, Clara. She silently chanted her name a few times so it would stay in her memory. Clara . . . Worth. Clara Worth.

She smiled gratefully at the woman who'd helped her solve the puzzle. Then she looked at the name badge on the woman's breast. Casey. What a ridiculous name! It made her sound like she was going on holidays.

Another woman entered the room. This one was holding a file.

'Now, Mrs Worth, I've got your medication, which you must take with food.' She put a little white plastic cup on the table next to the food and stood there looking at her.

Clara bristled at her bossiness.

This one's name was Helen. A hard name to go with her hard face.

She regarded both women.

'Come on, Clara,' Casey said gently. 'Come and have your tea. Chef's cooked up one of your favourites: silverside with mashed potatoes, cabbage and white sauce.' The woman smiled in an encouraging way, so Clara moved towards the chair to sit down, ignoring the woman with the file, who had now put her hands on her hips.

The chair was a sandstone-coloured rocking chair with a crocheted rug covering the seat. She couldn't eat there!

What on earth would her mother say if she didn't sit at the kitchen table with her brothers and sisters?

'Where is Brian?' she asked, looking around. 'We can't start dinner without him.'

Brian was her troublesome younger brother, who was probably out in the street playing in the dust or watering the horses that pulled the sulkies for the farmers coming to town to collect their supplies.

Perhaps her mother was serving in the store this evening. That's why she wasn't here.

'Brian?' the one called Helen asked briskly. 'No Brian here. I need to see you take your medication, Clara, and I have many other patients to attend to tonight, so let's get on.' She took a small plastic container of orange juice from the tray and peeled back the alfoil lid, before offering it to Clara. 'Hold out your hand,' she told her.

Obediently, Clara stretched out her hand and watched the white pills tumble into her palm.

Helen shook the drink slightly. 'Open wide,' she said.

Clara frowned but did as she was told. *Insolent woman*, she thought. *I'm not a child.*

'Hello, Nana!'

The bright voice came from the door just as Clara swallowed the pills with the orange juice. She coughed then looked around, covering her mouth with her hand. The familiar voice was accompanied by a recognisable face. She reached to the back of her memory.

'Mia. Hello, dear.'

Helen wrote something on her file. 'Your grandmother has just had her medication, Mia, so if you could supervise dinner then we'll leave you to it.'

'Sure thing.' Mia bent down, kissing Clara on the cheek.

Her granddaughter smelled like sunshine and clean air. A breath of fresh air.

Not like this place which stank of disinfectant and pee.

I shouldn't be here, Clara thought. She grabbed Mia's hand, grasping it tightly, while her granddaughter sat opposite her.

Casey took the plastic lid from the plate. 'Enjoy,' she said and closed the door quietly behind her.

Mia leaned towards Clara and whispered, 'They've gone.' She took out a small bottle of whiskey from her shoulder bag and held it out. 'Here you go, Nana. Just what the doctor ordered.'

Clara brightened. 'You're such a good girl, Nicole.' The name jarred her memory. She took a sip and then corrected herself. 'Sorry, Mia. I know you're not your mother.' She put the bottle on the table. 'It's so confusing. One minute I'm here and the next I'm not.' Tears welled in her eyes. 'I'm frightened, Mia. I can't stop it.' Fingers she didn't recognise, but she knew were hers, picked at the hem of her light blue baggy t-shirt. When did she start wearing these types of clothes? Her figure had been beautiful in pants and shirts, Theo Marshall had told her. Now the grey tracksuit pants she was wearing hid her weakening body. She looked at herself in disgust.

'The doctor said this would happen,' Mia said quietly. 'I'm sorry I can't fix it.'

Clara nodded. 'I know you can't, dear.' She took a breath and reminded herself who she was then took another swig of whiskey.

She was Clara Worth, daughter of Gwen Simpson, the woman who had single-handedly saved the family business and raised four children. Gwen had been strong, determined and tenacious and Clara was made of her cloth. There was no place to feel sorry for herself here.

She knew Mia was doing something today. She racked her brains to remember what it was. 'Did you . . .'

Seeing her uncertainty, Mia picked up the conversation. 'I've unpacked and got the new house how I want it, so I'm ready to start work in a couple of days.'

'Do you like your place?' This was a safe subject.

'It's pretty old. The toilet is off the laundry and the bathroom has a cement floor that's been painted green! But I'm happy. There's a bedroom at the front and another small one that I'm going to make into an office.'

Something tapped at Clara's mind. She closed her eyes. Green. There was something green . . .

Her eyes snapped open. Yes! Her mother's outside verandah had been painted green. She remembered the pots that lined the cracked cement, full of camellias that loved the Flinders Ranges heat, and the grapevine that grew over the railings. Those grapes had tasted so sweet, but they had seeds. Brian and she had spitting competitions.

Her mother had pretended to be horrified at her unladylike behaviour, but Clara knew she laughed about it secretly.

Mia was still talking. 'I'm going to the station to introduce myself first thing tomorrow morning.' She paused. 'I'm a bit nervous.'

'Don't be nervous, dear,' Clara said, trying to work out why Mia would be. Which station was she going to?

As if Mia had read her mind, she said, 'There are five other coppers at Broad River Police Station, Nana, and a detective. All blokes. I'm going to be the only female police officer.'

Clara remembered now. That kind lady from reception had driven her to Adelaide and stayed with her during Mia's graduation service a little while ago. The graduates had reminded her of herself as a youngster. Their wide smiles, enthusiasm and laughter had made her happy. But she'd found it hard. So many words to follow; faces and names that meant nothing to her. She'd been glad to return to the safety of her room afterwards.

'My mother always used to say that, as women, we might be the first one in our family or community to do something and it's our job to make sure we are not the last.' She picked up the whiskey bottle again and took a little sip, enjoying the burn of the alcohol on the back of her throat. 'It's your job to pave the way for other women to become police officers in the bush.' She paused. 'You're a brave girl, Mia. Just like your great-grandmother.'

A flicker of another memory. A key and two thin green doors with glass panelling above the large, tarnished brass handles. Lined, weathered hands putting the key in the large old-fashioned lock. Clara could even hear the loud click as it turned and the doors swung open, almost as silently as the door into her bedroom here in the nursing home.

Mia was talking and indicating the silverside that was on the plate, but Clara couldn't hear her. The memories inside her head were too loud.

She squinted as she heard her mother's voice. 'Now, Clara, here's a rag. You'll need to rub this cedar polish into the dresser to make the wood shine.' She inhaled the smell of bitter almonds as she unscrewed the lid, the amber liquid spilling onto the rag as she upended the glass bottle. Her hands were always oily by the time she'd finished rubbing all the wooden sideboards and furniture.

'Nana?'

Clara blinked, brought back to the present by her granddaughter's voice.

'You need to eat this before it gets cold, otherwise you'll get into trouble with the old dragon.'

Old dragon?

'Helen is so bossy,' Mia continued.

Picking up the cutlery, Clara cut a small bit of silverside. 'She's not very nice. But the other lady—the one who brings the dinner—she's not too bad.'

'Casey. Yeah, she seems very nice.' Mia took a sharp breath. 'I'm sorry, Nan. I'm sorry you have to be in here.'

Clara found the lump in her throat too large to speak around, so she shrugged and cut another piece of meat.

'What did you do today, dear?' she asked. Had Mia already told her? She couldn't remember.

'I finished unpacking.'

Ah, that's right, they'd already had this conversation.

'Where is the house?' Clara asked cautiously. She wasn't sure if she should know that answer.

'Two streets back from the river.' Mia gave a quiet laugh. 'Not that Broad River is really a river, is it? Just an expanse of still water that breeds mozzies and ducks and grows reeds.'

'Do the ducks still cross the road at the little dip as you come into town?' Clara asked. 'There was a mother duck who used to herd her ducklings across the road, stopping all the traffic.'

Mia nodded. 'They were there this morning when I walked downtown to get a coffee. Six of them. They're really cute.'

'I guess their mothers taught the ducklings where to cross the road because they've been doing it for years now.' Clara was pleased with that sentence. It was quite long, and she was sure it made sense. She pushed her fork into the mashed potato and tried to shovel it into her mouth. Instead, it fell onto her lap.

Mia leaned forward with a napkin, picked up the splodge and put it in the bin.

Clara tried again. Then she remembered something. 'I've got something for you,' she said.

'Do you?' Mia asked. 'What is it?'

'I've forgotten, but I know it's important.' Pushing her dinner aside, Clara stood and waited until she had her balance.

Pacing the boundary of the room, she tried to think. 'Something,' she muttered, 'something to do with . . .' She stopped at her dressing table and looked at the photos on top. There were three: a black-and-white one—her mother and the four children standing out the front of Simpson's Haberdashery; a faded coloured one of her with her daughter-in-law, Nicole; and a new one, in a shiny silver frame—a bright, glossy photo of her with Mia on her graduation day. Mia stood straight beside the old woman in the photo, her police hat perched on her dark hair, her light blue shirt with the police emblem for South Australia on the arm.

'What was . . . Oh, I remember.' Clara looked at the drawers, bewildered. 'I don't recall where.'

Mia was at her side now. 'What are we looking for, Nan?'

'The key.' She gave Mia a watery smile. 'It's for you, dear.'

Mia started to open a drawer and look through it. 'A house key?' she asked.

'Oh no. No, no, no! *The* key. For the shop.'

Mia stopped. 'For Simpson's Haberdashery? No, Nana, the shop was sold years ago. When we moved to Adelaide. Come and finish your dinner before Casey comes back to get your tray.'

Clara felt Mia take her arm, but she shook her off. 'No,' she said more loudly than she intended. 'No, it's here. I saw it and I need to give it to you.'

She shot Mia a look. Sold? She didn't remember selling the shop. Mia must be mistaken. Clara knew she'd only seen the key a few short days ago, and if it had been sold, she wouldn't still have the key, would she? The new owner would.

There were too many drawers to look in. Her heart kicked up a notch as fear flowed through her. Mia was a clever girl, but she didn't know everything.

Gwen had let her play in the shop out of the hot summer sun often, but Clara hadn't played. She'd *explored*! It was a dark and mysterious place that held so many treasures.

'It's got to be here,' Clara muttered, pulling drawers in and out, quickly. So quickly that she couldn't make out what was inside.

'Nana,' Mia said calmly. 'Nana, stop.' She took hold of Clara's small wrist.

Clara shook her off. 'No! I have to find the . . . the . . . thingy.' She could see what it looked like in her mind, but she couldn't think what the object she was looking for was called again.

The door opened and Casey came in. 'Have you finished . . .'

'Where is it?' Clara rounded on Casey. 'Do you know where I put it?'

'Now, Nan . . .'

'It is here, I know it is.' She grabbed her jewellery box from the top of the dresser and opened it. All the tension left her. Yes, it was here. In this box, somewhere. She thrust the box at Mia. 'In here,' she gasped and sat back down on the chair, picking up her fork.

'Everything okay?' Casey asked.

'We're fine.' Mia nodded.

When the door was closed, Mia handed Clara the bottle of whiskey. 'Another sip might do you a bit of good, Nan.' She turned to the jewellery box.

Clara got the feeling Mia was only humouring her. 'It's in there. You only have to find it.'

'Okay. I'm looking.'

Carefully she took out each piece of jewellery and laid it on the table. There wasn't much—a watch, a brooch and a pin for a pair of glasses.

'Underneath.' Clara didn't know where the word had come from.

Mia poked at the floor of the box. It moved. 'Oh, a false bottom!'

'See, I knew it was there.' Clara sat back in satisfaction. 'The . . . thingy.'

Mia drew out a large silver key. 'Why have you still got this, Nana?'

Clara heard the reservation in her voice but ignored it. 'You haven't had the shop in decades. We should give it to the people who own the building. How about I take it to them? I thought I'd like to go for a drive to Barker and have a look around. See what's changed.'

Clara relaxed now. The key was where it should be. With the next generation.

'It is with the owner now,' she said.

CHAPTER 2

Mia tapped the key against her hand. Outside, the wind howled around the corners of her house, causing it to creak and moan, as if the ghosts of past tenants were calling to her. A cup of hot chocolate sat at her elbow and her small bar heater was struggling against the night's chill in the large high-ceilinged room.

Taking a sip of her drink, she wondered why her nan had never spoken of Simpson's Haberdashery since they'd left Barker. Or she'd mentioned it in passing, usually just to share a memory, never in the present tense.

Did she really still own the shop? Mia wasn't sure she could trust what she'd been told. Surely there would have been council rates that needed to be paid and maintenance . . . She knew her grandmother's affairs were taken care of by a solicitor in Port Pirie. George Walker.

Maybe she should make a call to him.

She put the key down carefully and leaned towards the heater, holding out her hands to warm her fingers.

There had been a hard conversation between them years ago in Port Pirie as they parked at the front of George Walker's office.

'There's some things I need to tell you,' Clara had said, her voice wobbly.

Already on high alert—making a trip to Port Pirie had been unusual in itself—Mia had waited.

'I have dementia, my darling girl.' Clara had taken Mia's hands in hers, squeezing for a long moment. The touch she'd been giving Mia since she was a little girl, telling her everything was going to be okay.

Mia's tears had come quick and fast, while her nan had sat stoically in the passenger seat, calmly explaining what was going to happen.

'George is going to take over all my affairs. He will have the power of attorney.'

Mia hadn't understood. Surely it should be her?

'You're young, Mia, I don't want you burdened with any of my problems. George can pay the monthly bills, make sure my care is looked after.'

This time Mia had turned in her seat and stared at her grandmother. 'What care?'

Again, the hand squeeze.

'I'm putting myself in the nursing home in Broad River.'

Her words had been matter-of-fact. Clara wouldn't and didn't change her mind. Mia had been there when all the legal documents had been signed with George Walker. Until Clara's death, George was in charge.

There hadn't been any mention of the shop then.

Now, though, the colours from Mia's TV, set on mute, danced over the white walls of the lounge room. Her grandmother's wooden sideboard, made of walnut and dating back to the 1800s, seemed out of place in the room. It was her most valued possession but it looked strange beside the two cheap lounge chairs and unsteady coffee table she'd bought at a garage sale before she'd left Adelaide.

In the kitchen was a dining table her friends had pooled together to buy her, and the fridge was an Engel car fridge that she'd been given for her twenty-first birthday. The police force had covered her moving costs and would pay her rent. A constable's wage was pretty small and Mia was still paying off her car, so there wouldn't be much money to spare.

When Mia had found out that her application to Broad River had been accepted, she'd been surprised. She'd wanted to be close to her nan and was over the moon that had happened. But would there be people who remembered her from when she was a little girl in Barker? And if they did, would they take her seriously?

Chris, her friend she'd come through the academy with had reasoned that it was more likely the locals could remember Clara than Mia and so what if they did? She had her uniform.

Mia had still been concerned there might be some tough times ahead.

Still, she wasn't a stranger to hard situations. She got up and turned the TV off just as her mobile rang. The Taylor Swift ringtone echoed through the empty house, causing her to jump. She smiled when she saw Chris's name and the photo of the two of them on graduation day that appeared on the screen with his call.

'Hey,' Mia said, switching off the light and heater in the lounge room and walking towards the bedroom. 'How are you getting on?'

'Holy hell, what a first day,' Chris said with a groan. 'Baptism by fire.'

'Why? What happened?' Mia shook out her hair and sat on the edge of the bed, feeling for the electric blanket switch.

'Car accident out on one of the bush roads. Really untidy. Jaws of life and everything.'

'Ah. Fatalities?'

'Two. Local farmer and his wife. Road was wet, and he lost control going around a corner. Rolled a couple of times.'

She softened her voice. 'You okay?'

'Well, shit, we have to be, don't we?' His low voice ached of pain. Or shock. Probably both.

'Not at your first one.'

There was a silence. 'It was pretty awful, but I don't want to talk about it yet.' He paused. 'How'd you go today?'

'I don't start for a few days. Just finished unpacking this afternoon and I think I'll go to the station tomorrow to introduce myself. Should be an experience.'

'Don't let them get to you before you start.'

'I'm not worried. Hang on a sec.' Mia put the phone down and rummaged around in the chest of drawers, looking for her bedtime t-shirt. 'Sorry, back again.' She got changed and climbed into bed. 'I went and saw Nana today.'

'How was she?'

'All over the place. Sometimes she's with it and other times she can't remember her own name. It's horrible. This freaking disease is a thief.' Mia wriggled against the pillows to get comfortable. 'And it's only going to get worse. There's going to come a time when she doesn't know who I am. Sometimes it's like that now.' Mia knew she was only stating the obvious but it helped somehow to put her thoughts into words.

'Do you know how long . . .'

'No. I haven't seen the doctor yet. And from everything I've read about dementia, I don't know if it's possible to tell how quickly the decline will be.' Mia took a breath, trying to ignore the pain that was squeezing her heart. 'What are the crew like in Burra?'

'Pretty welcoming so far. There are five coppers and one detective here, so it's a reasonably big place. It needs to be though because it's the only decent-sized town between Adelaide and Broken Hill. We've got a fair bit of country to cover. Peterborough is about an hour's drive, but the station there is nearly obsolete—not that far from you really.'

'No, might be thirty minutes.'

There was a silence between them. 'Are you going to go to Barker and have a look around your old stomping ground? See if you can remember any of it?' Chris asked.

The key was now lying on her bedside table. Mia leaned over to pick it up and laid it on the doona. The silver sparkled in the light of her bedside lamp.

'Hmm, I think I will.' Her tone was casual.

'Ah, that sounds like you have something up your sleeve.'

'Nan gave me a key today. To the old store in Barker.'

'And that's significant because . . .'

The question hung between them. Mia wasn't sure how to answer.

'She says she still owns the shop.'

Mia could feel the expectation humming down the line. Chris knew there was more to this.

'I'm guessing Nan's forgotten that she sold the building when we left. She must be mixed up about this like she is with so many other things.'

'You should be able to find out who owns it easy enough. A phone call to the shire or something?' Chris paused and when he spoke again there was humour in his voice. 'Now that you've found out this important piece of information are you telling me you're planning on becoming a shopkeeper?'

Mia laughed. 'Idiot,' she said affectionately. 'Of course not! But it's . . . I don't know. The whole thing has made me curious. I haven't been to Barker since I was a kid . . .' Her voice trailed off.

'You'll have to go over and see if the key fits into the lock. Bit like Cinderella but a shop not a shoe!'

Mia laughed. 'Of course, and with any luck there's a prince or a pot of gold waiting for me as soon as I open the door.'

'I'll take the gold. Leave the prince for you.'

When Mia spoke next the laughter had been replaced with wistfulness. 'Guess I'll go for a drive when I can and have a look. Nana says there's something she wants me to bring back to her and I'll know it when I see it.'

'Want me to come?'

'Um . . . Not sure. I might be better off going by myself the first time. It'll be strange to go back after so long.'

'If you change your mind, let me know. We'll just have to see if we can co-ordinate our rosters.'

Mia cleared her throat and looked at the silver watch on her wrist. A gift from a boy who was no longer in her life. 'Guess I'd better go to bed.'

'Yeah.'

Mia knew Chris didn't want to hang up. That was how their friendship worked. They'd talked often enough on the phone to know how each other was feeling by the first 'hello'.

'Maybe you should make yourself a hot chocolate.'

Chris snorted. 'That's not very manly!'

Mia laughed. 'You're a Caramello koala, and you know it. Hard on the outside and soft and gooey in the middle.'

'Shh, don't let my secret out.' Chris laughed before giving a big sigh. 'I'll be okay. I keep seeing the ute, that's all.'

'Totalled?'

'Write-off. The SES dealt with the bodies until the funeral directors got there. I didn't see them. Only held the traffic up and then redirected all the vehicles around the accident site slowly after everything was cleared.' He gave a bit of a cough. 'Didn't do much really. Or see anything.'

'There's nothing "only" about what you did, and you know it. Just like you know what happened there. You know that a family is grieving, and someone had to go and tell them. Don't be too hard on yourself. Sounds like the crew at Burra looked after you pretty well.' Mia spoke gently.

'They did.' She could hear Chris shift in his bed. 'In the long run, this is what we're trained to do.'

Mia smiled at his stoic tone. She made her voice gruff and serious, as if she were the Premier about to make an announcement. 'We're here to keep South Australians safe.'

Chuckling, Chris said, 'Exactly.'

'All right, well, I'd better go to bed. Who knows what tomorrow will bring for both of us.'

'True story.'

After they'd said goodnight, Mia let the phone rest on her chest and looked down at the key sitting on the doona cover. She picked it up, thinking about the times she'd spent in the haberdashery shop when she was very young. Before they'd left Barker. She could see Nana behind the counter, a large smile for anyone who walked through the door. Didn't matter if it was Mrs Holder, who was a couple of months late in paying her account, or little Barbara Jones, who had popped in for a five-cent lollipop. Mr Marshall always got a special smile, and Nana would pretend to slap his hand when he slipped it into one of the jars and picked out a couple of liquorice sticks.

She put the key on the bedside table and switched off the light, rolling over to get comfortable. A memory nudged her.

There had been something under the counter that she wasn't allowed to touch. A curtain that ran along a piece of wire under the counter and usually hid everything from view, but if you lifted it up you could see Nana's lunch and thermos, next to her cup. There was sticky tape, brown paper and scissors. A gun.

Mia sat up. A gun. She could remember it sitting there. Yes! Right on top of a wooden box.

Why did Nana have a gun within easy reach? She thought uneasily. *And where is it now?*

CHAPTER 3

'Yeah, mate, I understand your concern, but there's nothing I can do. You need to bring the gun in to us so we can dispose of it safely.' Jack Higgins ran his fingers over the constable stripes on his police uniform as he listened to the irate farmer on the phone

'They can't make me give up my grandfather's collection. We're not living in a communist country!'

'There's a good reason we have these laws in Australia, John,' Jack said calmly. 'And if you don't bring them in, I'm going to have to come out there and get them. It really would be easier for all concerned if you dropped them in next time you were in Barker, all right?'

'If I find out who dobbed me in . . .' John's voice trailed off but Jack refused to be drawn.

'You're a bunch of bastards,' John continued. 'Don't you understand how sentimental these guns are? Why can't I just register them?'

'That type of rifle is illegal in Australia now.'

'Since when?'

Jack pinched the bridge of his nose and heard the detective he shared an office with snort with laughter. 'Since 1997. Be thankful you're not being charged.'

There was an annoyed silence while the farmer thought about all the implications of that. Then he let out an angry breath. 'I'll get compensated of course?'

'No. That scheme finished a long time ago.'

That brought forth another round of angry accusations and Jack finally lost patience.

'John, if those illegal firearms aren't in at the station by nine am tomorrow morning, I'll issue a warrant for your arrest and come and find you myself. Understand?' He hung up the phone.

Detective Dave Burrows finally laughed loudly. 'Well handled, mate. He's a grumpy old codger, isn't he, that John Manson? Always the first to complain. I often see one of his letters to the editor in the paper, banging on about something that's got his goat.'

'Not that I don't want him to have an opinion, but it would be easier if he complied with the rules,' Jack said, getting up from his desk with uncharacteristic grumpiness. 'I didn't put the laws in place.'

'Nah, but you have to enforce them.' Dave leaned back in his chair. 'I tell you what, if he hasn't brought them in by tomorrow's deadline, let's pull all the farmers' details who have licences that side of town and make a surprise call on them all. Collect John's and check on the others.

Make sure they're all secured in safes. That way he can't say we've singled him out. Not like there's much going on around here.'

While he was speaking, the windows rattled as a strong gust of icy wind threw itself against the side of the building. Somewhere in the police station, a door slammed shut and echoed against the brick walls.

'Thank god for the lack of action,' Jack said. 'Makes a nice change.' He disappeared down towards where the two cells were, and Dave heard the clanging of the second door shutting and a key turning. He glanced over at the email open on his screen and then in the direction Jack had gone. Normally his senior constable would jump at doing something different. But Jack hadn't been himself since the awful tragedy from last year. The investigation into the deaths of Joel Hammond and Steve Douglas had finished, but their deaths had scarred the townspeople, Jack included.

The whole sorry saga had been tragic. A released ex-prisoner, who was about to be exonerated, killed by a paedophile who was trying to save his own arse. Unnecessary and needless. But it had happened and now everyone needed to move on.

Dave knew this better than anyone. The murders of Spencer, his partner from his first station, and Ellen, his former mother-in-law, had been perpetrated by a man seeking revenge on Dave—and those deaths also felt unnecessary and needless. But Dave knew all the guilt and regret and time spent wishing things were different added up to a useless waste of time, because no one could go back and change the past.

The Douglas family had found that out. When the revelations about their son had become public they had up and left Barker overnight, while Jack and Dave had organised Joel's funeral, cleaned up his house and put it on the market. Without a will, the money would just go into the government kitty, but Dave and his wife Kim had hatched a plan. He was going to try to get his boss to authorise the money be used to help people who had just left jail. Joel would have liked that.

Jack came back in and grabbed his police-issued jacket from the back of his chair. 'I'm heading out for a bit,' he said.

'Righto.' Dave nodded. There really wasn't much to say to that.

He heard Jack speak to Joan, the older woman who doubled as their secretary, at the reception desk and then he heard the front door close. Sighing, Dave ran his hands over his face and wondered what else he could do for his friend. He'd suggested counselling, which had been met with a resounding no. Dave had been surprised, considering Jack's girlfriend, Zara, had attended many sessions to help her deal with the trauma of losing her father and brother in quick succession a few years ago. They'd all seen the difference the counselling had made.

Their boss had suggested Jack have a bit of time away from the station but, again, he had refused.

Dave would just have to wait until Jack came to him. Instead of worrying, he instigated the firearms ownership report and printed it off. Pushing his glasses back onto his nose, he looked over the information. Eight farmers with two guns each. Tomorrow they'd check their cabinets and make sure the firearms and bullets were stowed correctly.

He was tracing the map with his finger, working out a route to take tomorrow when Joan popped her head in.

'It's Rhys Martindale on the phone,' she said. 'Something about his crop dying.'

'And what does that have to do with us?' Dave asked, staring at her over the rims of his glasses.

'Line two.' Joan disappeared and Dave looked at the red flashing light.

He put the map and information aside and dragged his notebook towards him as he picked up the phone. 'Rhys. Dave Burrows here. Got a problem?'

'Yeah, mate. Some lowlife has sprayed my crop. You got time to come out?'

Dave pinched the bridge of his nose. 'Sprayed your crop?' Well, this was a new one.

'Bloody oath. The barley is just coming out of the ground and suddenly it's all turned yellow and dying. Jesus, I'm an organic farmer, Dave!'

'Why would someone do that?'

'I don't know! That's why I've rung you.'

'Is it insured?'

'Nope. Got no cover on it at all. You know how much it costs to put a crop in? Diesel and fertiliser prices are through the roof, not to mention how long and costly it is to get an organic certification.' Rhys's voice was hard and angry. 'Can't bloody believe it. Of all the low acts.' His tone turned to disgust now. 'You coming out or what?'

'Yep, sure. Can do. When do you think it happened?'

'Stuffed if I know, mate. I've been in Adelaide for the last week. Took the missus down there for our wedding anniversary. Went to the footy and a few things like that.'

'So you hadn't noticed it before then?'

'Nah, it's only just germinating now and the barley is barely getting through the top of the soil before it's turning yellow and dying.'

Dave snapped his notebook shut. 'I'll be out there in about an hour.'

'Cheers, mate. If I catch whoever has done this they'll wish they hadn't been born.'

Dave nodded, as he put the phone down. The empty threats of blokes who knew the police had to deal with their problems but who were still mightily pissed off. Dave paused at the thought. He hoped that's all it was, an empty threat. Rhys was known to have a bit of a temper.

He rang Jack. 'You around, mate?'

'At the pub.'

Dave's eyebrows shot up. Things must be worse than he'd thought.

'Old Mrs Darby accidentally hit the accelerator instead of the brake and mounted the kerb when she was pulling in,' Jack continued. 'Didn't hurt herself or anyone else but took out the street sign on the corner.'

'Bloody hell. We might have to chat to her family. That's the second time this type of thing has happened. Okay, you stay there and deal with that. I've got to head out to Rhys Martindale's place.'

'What's going on there?'

'Someone's sprayed his crop by the sound of it.'

There was a silence, but in the background Dave could hear crying. Mrs Darby was in a bit of shock, he assumed.

'Shit,' Jack said, 'he's an organic farmer. That'll bugger his certification.'

'Something along those lines.'

A stunned silence stretched out between them. 'Malicious,' Jack finally said. 'Okay, see you later.'

'Going to get Mrs Darby checked out?' Dave asked before Jack hung up.

'Yeah, I'm just about to help her into our car and take her to the hospital. Hopper is going to reverse her car off the kerb, and it can stay here until I get back.'

'Good job. Catch you soon.'

Dave shrugged into his jacket and sent Kim a text message.

Going out of town for a bit. See you tonight.

Kim's response was swift. *I'll be waiting! Xx*

A couple of seconds later, his phone dinged again.

Do you need lunch?

He couldn't help but smile. When Dave had turned up in Barker seven years ago to investigate a car-jacking, which ended up including a murder, he never could have imagined Kim was going to cross his path again. They'd known each other when they were seventeen, and then lost touch, but their romance had been rekindled on the first day he'd walked into her roadhouse.

That long-remembered smile had captivated him all over again.

Kim adored cooking for the people she loved and her offer of food wasn't unusual.

No, I'm all good.

Getting into the driver's seat of his four-wheel drive, Dave thought about popping back home to give Kim a quick kiss, but it wouldn't be long before he'd be back in their warm kitchen, the smell of dinner floating across the brisk evening air to greet him. For now he had work to do.

Flicking on his blinker, he drove out of Barker and made a turn towards the south. Rhys Martindale lived about fifty kilometres towards Port Augusta, down a dirt road that was lined with purple gravel, native pine trees and large lichen-covered rocks, with hills that rose to meet the sky.

Dave kept an eye out for kangaroos; the recent dry times had caused them to migrate from the northern Flinders to the south, chasing feed. There were days he'd be on the road and the whole countryside alongside him would look as if it were moving because the roos were bouncing along the fence line, looking for grass of any kind. Not the green variety though, because that wasn't there.

He followed the winding road down through deep, dry creek beds and over rocky hills, listening to the radio as he went. But he wasn't really listening, he was thinking about Jack.

Maybe Jack needed a new challenge. Get out of Barker and do something else perhaps. Although being a copper was what his partner lived and breathed. Dave understood what it was like to be committed to your job. He'd given up his first marriage to keep doing what he loved. There had been little understanding from Melinda as to why he did what he did.

A plume of dust caught his attention, just as a small Suzuki Swift came flying over the hill in the middle of the road.

'What the . . .' Dave reefed on the steering wheel to drag his car further to the side of the road, while the other driver did the same, to their left. His car thudded over the rocky verge, and the noise of stones kicking up under the chassis was loud. The steering wheel shook as he brought the wagon to a stop.

A glance in the rear-view mirror showed the white Suzuki was still on its wheels, although halfway up an embankment, and had come to a stop too. He reversed back until he was level with it.

The woman in the driver's seat was gasping, her hand to her chest.

'You okay?' Dave asked, getting out. He walked towards her, hoping there was nothing wrong.

'You maniac!' She threw her car door open and charged towards him.

Then stopped.

'Ah, sorry.' She dropped her eyes downwards but not before Dave saw she'd registered his police car.

'Maniac, huh? Guess you're referring to yourself.' He drew himself up to his full height—just over six foot. Dave knew he cut an imposing sight. With his face deadpan, his blue eyes could go from being warm and friendly to ice-cold in a split second. They were in between now and which way they went would be based on the woman's reaction.

'Sorry,' she said again, backtracking towards the vehicle. 'It's just the shock.'

'I'm sure. Got your licence on you?'

'Yeah, I'll get it.' She turned and fiddled inside the car, getting her purse out of her handbag.

'Where were you off to in such a hurry?' Dave asked, noting the numberplate. He should do a check on it, but he wanted to see her licence first.

'Here.' The woman waved the plastic card at him, and he took it, watching her.

Her pale face was framed with curly black hair and her figure was slim. Wearing jeans, a jumper and mid-calf working boots, she could have been a station owner or farmer from this area, but her face wasn't familiar. The car was tidy—no rust or dents from Dave's quick inspection—and the bull bar boasted two round spotlights and a bar one. A two-way and phone aerial were perched on the back bar of the tray.

She looked early to mid-twenties. Her hand was shaking as she handed over her licence.

'I'm heading to my mother's. She rang needing me.'

'Well, Jayde Tonkin, I don't think I have to tell you, but you were driving a little fast. Coming over a hill in the middle of a road like that also isn't a good idea.'

Jayde looked at the ground. 'I know. Sorry. I know the road well and I was being complacent.'

'What's wrong with your mother?'

'Hopefully nothing. I just got a garbled message saying she needed me. Could be anything from the dog being bitten by a snake to her having a fall and breaking her leg. She's never one on details, is mum. But she's by herself and I'm the closest help she has so—' the woman gave a wry smile and hoisted her shoulders in a shrug '—Muggins here comes running.'

Dave thought about Mrs Darby and the uncomfortable conversation Jack and he were going to have with her family about her giving up her driver's licence. He was concerned about being in that position himself when he got older. Losing independence by not being able to drive was one of his worst nightmares.

'Where does she live?' He handed back the driver's licence after noting the address. Even though the town was perhaps one hundred and fifty kilometres away from Barker, Jayde could still be classified as local. He'd bet she'd been driving these roads since she was old enough to legally drive. If not before!

'On the way to Broad River. Just got a house on the side railing about twenty ks from there. Minbarra.'

'Oh, that's where Emily Rose lives. She's your mum?'

'Yeah. I married a farmer down towards Mount Remarkable. Kenny Tonkin.'

'Your mum is pretty capable, though. I've seen her striding down the main street of Barker. Fit as a fiddle.'

'Yeah, she's been fortunate with her health so far. And the fact she can still live by herself.' Jayde glanced at the ground, then back up again. 'Hoping she'll stay like that for a long time.'

'We all hope that about our parents.' Dave scratched the back of his head. 'It's your lucky day that I didn't have the speed camera on. Don't drive in the middle of the road, Mrs Tonkin. It's not good for your health.' He gave her a severe stare. 'And if needs be, I'm happy to drop in on Emily anytime. Just give me a call at the station.'

'Thank you, and I'm sorry again. I didn't mean to get angry. I just had a fright.'

'Good to hear. I won't be as lenient if I run into you again. Pun intended! Have a good day.'

Dave walked back to his car and wrote a note in his book, which he always carried with him. He'd check when he got back and find out if there had been any reports around Emily Rose. See if he needed to add her to the list of community calls he or Jack made once a week. Then he'd ring the hospital and see if there were any new admissions.

In his rear-view mirror, he watched as Jayde got the car back onto the road and drove away a lot more carefully than when she'd driven over the hill.

CHAPTER 4

Mia thought she could control the nerves that were flapping like a kaleidoscope of butterflies in her stomach, but the things that usually helped seemed not to be working today.

She stood out the front of the Broad River Police Station, telling herself that whoever was inside had been through the same academy as her, felt the same nerves and wanted to help the community the same way she did. She and her colleagues would have things in common right from the start.

The station looked like any country cop shop. The large sign out the front told everyone it was the POLICE. The red bricks were pretty ugly, and she touched the light green Colorbond tin that cordoned off the back yard, where the police cars were kept, as she walked towards the front door.

Frosty to touch.

A couple of deeper breaths and Mia opened the scratched flyscreen door, then pushed open the faded wooden one, just inside.

Gosh. How cold the room was. Stark white walls and pin boards displaying pamphlets of missing persons or domestic violence organisations. The floor was lino and the benches in the waiting area plastic.

Police stations had to be like this. When coppers were wrestling people full of booze or drugs, everything had to be unbreakable and easily cleaned. Throughout her training, Mia had done her time in washing out the drunk tanks in Adelaide during her first few months, and it was the lowest of the low jobs in policing.

Behind the thick Perspex shield was an older man looking at her curiously. Mia wanted to reach out and push his glasses back onto the bridge of his nose.

'Can I help yer?' he asked, leaning through the small window as he hitched up his belt, underneath a protruding belly.

Taking a step closer, Mia could see beads of perspiration on his upper lip, even though she could barely feel the tips of her fingers.

'Hi, I'm Mia. The new constable.' She gave a hundred-watt smile and waited for him to smile back and welcome her to the team.

Instead, his eyes flicked to the side, where an open door led to the bowels of the building, and then back to her. 'Oh yeah? But you're not rostered on today. Full team's already in.'

'I know. Thought I'd come and introduce myself.'

This time he smiled. 'Don't be too keen, you'll show us all up. I'm Marty Hooper. Front desk is my game.' He stuck a pudgy hand through the window and shook hers.

'Hey, Marty. Good to meet you.'

'I'll buzz you through.'

Mia waited until the heavy security door clicked open and then went in. The phone at Marty's elbow rang and he snatched it up.

'Broad River Police Station, Senior Constable Hooper speaking.' Tucking the phone in between his shoulder and ear, he pointed towards the open door and nodded for Mia to go through. She hesitated, wanting him to come and introduce her to everyone else.

'Barking dogs, you say?' he asked the person on the other end of the phone. 'For how long? Uh-huh. I see.' He dropped the phone down and put his hand over the speaker. 'They're all through there getting their morning coffees.' He gave her a nod and another smile, indicating it was safe for her to go through.

'Right.' A few purposeful steps towards the opening and she was hit by a blast of hot air from the heater and a tall, blond-haired man in the doorway. He side-stepped and she did the same. They tried again but ended up standing in front of each other.

Her first thought was: *Geez, how embarrassing.*

The second was: *Wow, you are freaking hot.*

The third was: *Oh my god, this is my new sergeant.*

'Sorry.' Mia smiled and stuck out her hand at the frowning man. 'Constable Worth, Sarge.'

'Yes?'

'I'm, ah, just checking in today. Starting the day after tomorrow.'

'Right.' He stood there as if he was waiting for her to say more.

Mia took a step to the left, leaving the doorway open. 'Sorry to get in your way.'

The sergeant looked irritated. He strode past leaving her standing alone.

A door slammed and the window rattled.

'Ignore him,' Marty said in a low voice from the front desk. 'He's had a bad morning. The hierarchy are on his case. Not enough speeding fines. The rest of them are in there. Go on, you'll be okay.' But there was a hesitancy in his voice that made her anxiety fizz.

Mia headed towards the laughter and voices, her heart hammering inside her chest.

When she entered the room, four heads swivelled to look at her. While they were looking at her, she assessed them.

Four men—two constables, one senior constable and one plain clothes, who must be a detective. And no one was talking now.

'Hi, I'm Mia Worth,' she said. 'The new connie.'

The men looked from her to each other. More silence.

Finally the oldest-looking one took the lead. 'Well, good to know yer. Senior Constable Greg Toombes.' He put down his coffee cup and held out his hand. 'When do you start?'

Mia shook his hand, making sure her grip was tight and firm, and told him she started in two days.

'You must be on the same shift as Richie here.' Greg indicated a bloke sitting at the table in full uniform. His legs were stuck out from the table and he was leaning back in his chair, regarding her carefully.

'Mia.' He nodded and glanced away. She wasn't sure if the expression of annoyance on his face was for her or if he always looked like that.

'Looking forward to working with you.' Mia smiled and nodded. She looked at the others, waiting for an introduction, but Richie just gave a cough.

A trickle of annoyance ran through her.

After a short silence the other two coppers spoke at the same time.

'Drew Edwards.'

'Detective Noah Field.'

'Coffee?' asked Greg.

'Sure. Just thought I'd pop in and get the lay of the land before I start. Anything going on?'

'Quiet as church on Monday,' Drew said. 'When'd you graduate?'

'Few weeks back. I grew up in Barker, so I sort of know the area, but I haven't been back in a long while.'

'Milk and sugar are there,' Greg said, handing her a cup.

Mia heaped a spoonful of sugar and poured some milk into the cup. The first sip was strong and bitter, like it had been poured from the pot of a detective who'd pulled an all-nighter trying to solve a murder. She had to fight not to screw up her face.

'A local then. You'll have your work cut out for you.' Noah stood up and grabbed his cap from the table, putting it on his head. 'I'd better go and file that last report. Nice to meet you, Mia. Guess we'll be seeing you around.' He left before she could say anything.

'Settled in?' Greg asked.

'As much as I can. Didn't have a lot to unpack. Travel pretty light.'

'That's good to know.' This came from Richie.

'Why do you say that?'

Richie gave a careless shrug. 'Can't see you lasting out here.' He stood up and looked her up and down. 'This is men's country. Big burly farmers and strapping young lads who play footy. You're such a small thing. Not sure how you'll go in the broad town of Broad River.'

Mia swallowed at his words, and no one said anything. They all just avoided her eyes. What she wanted to say was 'That's not even funny, you dick.'

Richie gave her a smile which was more a grimace. 'Better get going. Got some people to check on. Coming, Drew?'

Drew, who hadn't had a chance to say a word, put down his cup and gave a nod towards Mia. 'See you soon.'

With the chairs suddenly vacant, Mia sat down and looked at Greg. 'Something I said?' she asked.

'Ignore them. They'll get used to you. Don't like change, that's all.'

'I'm sure they haven't done their whole policing career here,' Mia said, putting her cup firmly on the table. 'They must've come across policewomen before.'

'Can't answer that, but I can say there's never been a lady copper here in Broad River. So, congratulations on being the first.' He gave her a nod.

'Not sure if that's going to be a blessing or a curse,' Mia said, her heart still beating a bit faster than it should, thanks to Richie's words.

'You're going to have to get used to it. This is a conservative community who are probably going to take a while to accept that there is now a policewoman here. There will be loads of people who do a double-take or who won't give you the respect a police officer deserves until you've shown you can do the job. Especially some of the old dyed-in-the-wool blokes.' He sighed. 'It's not so much you're a woman but people around here judge on ability rather than anything else.'

'I can handle it.'

'Hope so. Look, don't worry about Richie. He comes across all hard-arsed and macho—does it to all the new connies—but he's not like that really. You'll have to prove yourself. Not the way it should be but,' he shrugged, 'it's the way it is.'

'And none of you blokes feel the need to stop him?'

Greg ignored that. 'So, you grew up in Barker?'

Mia took the hint. There wasn't to be any more discussion about what had just happened. That was how misogyny crept into workplaces. Just feign ignorance or pretend no one had seen anything. She'd let it go for now, but only because Greg didn't seem too bad.

'Yeah. Left a long time ago. When I was still in primary school. I remember coming across here to play netball, but it's only a distant memory. We ended up in Adelaide and then when I was in year eight, Nana wanted to move back here so I went to boarding school before joining the force.'

'Do you remember many people? Might make it harder, if you do?'

Privately, Mia agreed, but she wouldn't let him know that. 'Nah, not really. I think the only thing might be if they remember my name. Don't think there'll be any issues like that.' She picked up her mug again. 'How long have you been here for?'

'Oh, I guess five years. Probably should move on, but my kids go to the school here and they're happy. Pretty cruisy lifestyle, really. It can be hard being a copper in a small town, though. Everyone expects favours from you. Sometimes it's easier not to make any friends.' He gave a lopsided smile. 'But then kids come along and suddenly you're taking them to birthday parties and it just all happens.'

'I'm expecting there will be a few curly moments.' She got up and tipped the rest of the coffee into the sink and washed it away. 'Do I have a desk?'

'Yeah, I'll show you around.' He got up and Mia was taken by his height.

'Far out,' she said. 'Did you all have to put your feet in fertiliser or something when you got here? I feel like I've walked into the Valley of the Giants!'

Greg gave a loud laugh. 'Fee, fi, fo, fum,' he said with a grin. 'Maybe it's the good clean country air, but I'll see if I can find a bucket of horse shit for you to put your feet into. We might be able to add an extra few inches to you yet.'

'Well, at my five foot nothing, I'd take any extra height you can give me,' she said.

'Through here is the squad room. We've each got a desk. Yours is here, next to Richie. You'll be working with him mostly. And this,' he pointed to the whiteboards lining the wall, 'is where we put up our weekly plan. So, you can see today that squad car one, that's Richie and Drew, are out on the RM Williams Way conducting speed and vehicle checks.

'Marty and the sarge are here in the office, and I'm about to head out towards Tantara township to check on a few people. There's a couple out there who have a disabled son who sometimes need a hand, and a widow who lives alone. I usually do all the community policing. Want to come for a spin?'

'I would, but I have a couple of other things I need to do before I start,' she said, running her hands over her desk and looking at the computer. She should set up her email address and get sorted.

'Just a bit of local knowledge: if you want fresh fruit and veggies, the grocer gets their stock in on a Tuesday and the supermarket gets restocked on a Thursday.'

'Cheers, I hadn't actually given that any thought.' She wanted to ask if there was a netball team she could join, but they'd probably already started the season. And would they welcome her? Mia gave a half shrug to herself. Wouldn't matter either way. If they didn't, she'd just keep trying until they accepted her. Her high school teachers had always written on her reports that she was 'tenacious'.

'I'll be off then. Leave you to it.'

Mia held up her hand and nodded towards the sarge's office. 'Good bloke?'

'Great bloke. But stay out of his way when he's shitty. Like today. Like a bear with a sore head after the weekend loss. And apparently we didn't catch enough speeding drivers over the last month. I actually think that's a good thing. Maybe the word is getting out there.'

'Won't help the bottom line of the department though, will it? Anyway, thanks for the heads-up.' She didn't ask about the weekend loss. That was none of her business.

When Greg left, Mia sat at her new desk and ran her fingers over the keyboard. One of the policewomen she'd spoken to before she'd joined the academy had told her to expect the kind of reaction she'd got from Richie. You usually copped it from the blokes who weren't good at their job and knew it, so they had to belittle others.

Apprehension settled in her stomach as she looked at Richie's desk. There was nothing to indicate he had a family or wife. Just a bare, tidy desk with a football trophy on the corner. She leaned forward to read what it said. *Best and Fairest.*

Ha, she thought. *We'll see.*

CHAPTER 5

'This is a disaster,' Rhys said as he stared at the dying crop, arms crossed and shoulders hunched against the bitter winds that blew across the flat land. 'I'll lose my organic rating. It'll stuff everything I've worked for. Everything!' He clenched his fists together as he spoke, and Dave stepped forward and put his hand on the younger man's shoulder. Rhys could clearly see dollar signs going up in smoke.

'I'll try to get to the bottom of this,' he said. 'How long have you had your organic status for?'

'Only a couple of years. I've just started to pick up markets for lamb and grain. And now . . .' He looked around, despairing. 'Everything I've worked for. Gone. And for what good?'

Dave gazed across the paddock. The plants were a horrible yellowing colour, while the paddock next door was a vivid green. Some parts of the land were bare, and it was obvious to Dave that the grain hadn't germinated and come up. Well, the seed would have germinated but the little plant had died as quickly as it had sprouted.

Rhys Martindale's farm was through the ranges and out on the flatlands where there was supposed to be a higher rainfall than Barker. Some of the old-timers said that the ranges blocked the rain, or the fronts weren't strong enough to get up and over the hills to make it to where Dave lived.

Even though parts of the land were green from the extra millimetres, it still had the same desolate feel as the land surrounding Barker. He pulled his jacket tighter, wishing he had a beanie like Rhys.

'How do you know it's been sprayed? Are you sure it's not just been too dry for too long? Been a while since we had a downpour.' Dave already knew the answer—he'd spent enough time on his family's farm growing up to know the difference between the effect of a chemical and the land being too dry—but he had to ask.

Without answering, Rhys grabbed a shovel from the back of his ute and shoved it into the ground, digging deeply. He grabbed a handful of dirt for Dave to feel. 'There's moisture there,' he said.

Dave saw the dirt clumped together, held by the dampness. He looked around trying to spot vehicle tracks. Tractors were heavy and, even on hard ground, they'd leave an outline, no matter how faint. There were none where he stood now.

'Have you upset anyone lately?' Dave asked. He walked further into the crop, and squatted down. None of the plants were going to survive. They were weak, yellow and shrivelled.

An old sprayer might have left a few strips of green, but it looked like the one that did this may have had a GPS in the cab. Tight lines and no blocked jets.

Pulling a plant up, he looked at the roots. They were unhealthy, stunted. An agronomist would call them 'pruned'. Dave decided to put a few in an evidence bag and take them back to the station, along with a shovelful of soil. Maybe the lab could run some tests. Determine what type of chemical it was. Or perhaps he'd call into the farm merchandise store and see if the resident agronomist was in. See if they could throw some light on what was going on here.

'Not something I try to do,' Rhys finally answered his question, 'you know, pissing people off.' He ran his fingers through his hair. 'Going organic isn't something that happens overnight. It takes four years from the time you last spray any chemical until you're able to sell grain as organic and there's a real process to get through. Audits, reviews.' He spread his hands out. 'The records you have to keep!'

'Who's got the farm next door?'

'John Manson. And he's not organic. That's why I leave a gap between his fence and mine in case some of his chemical drifts across. He's pretty considerate though. Never sprays when the wind is blowing in the wrong direction. We talk a lot.'

Dave hadn't realised John owned land out this way. His home farm was on the opposite side of the range. Still, it wasn't unusual for a farmer to have properties in different sections of a shire. Sometimes you just couldn't buy the farm next door. 'And all of the others around here know you're organic?'

Rhys nodded. 'They're all respectful of my decision.'

'You're sure you haven't upset anyone? Only needs to be something small. Did you pull the best man off the footy field on Saturday? Or not even play him?'

Rhys was shaking his head. 'No, I didn't coach on Saturday. Like I said, I took Carrie to Adelaide so we could have a week away. I promised her we'd do that for our wedding anniversary after we finished seeding.' He walked towards the road and stood with his arms crossed, the wind tousling his hair. 'Ha! Look at this.' Rhys bent down and pointed to a cigarette butt on the ground. 'This will belong to whoever did this. Neither Carrie nor I smoke.'

Dave moved the twenty metres or so to where Rhys was standing and checked the ground. The tracks were only slight outlines on the soil surface and very hard to notice unless he was looking for them. At one spot, there was a kicked-up patch of dirt, which Dave assumed was from a couple of boot prints when they'd got out of the tractor to open the gate. 'These tracks, are they from when you seeded?' He pointed to the imprints and glanced around again. 'When did you last have rain?'

'Few weeks ago. Not much, about five mils. Enough to cover my old tracks. These are fresh,' Rhys said and then reiterated his previous point. 'We don't smoke.'

'Stay here and I'll get some wet evidence paper bags,' Dave said.

'Right you are.' Rhys blew on his fingers to warm them up. 'Mongrel day for this too. I can't think—'

Dave assumed he kept on talking, but the wind took the words away as he walked towards his vehicle, keeping his eyes on the ground as he searched for more evidence. It didn't take long to fetch the small forensic kit he always had with him.

Slamming his car door shut, he sauntered out onto the road, his eyes downcast looking for more tractor tracks. There were some turning into the paddock, but they seemed to stop at the gate, not go any further. He could see where the gateway had been used as a turning circle for a tractor recently. Unsure if it was the same one, he took a few photos and moved on.

The gate was twisted and bent, the rust flaking, but no one had hit it on the way in or tried to open it. It was just old and buggered. Nothing looked out of place. No wire freshly cut. With the temperature below ten degrees, his fingers were burning with the cold, making a fiddly job more difficult.

His gloved hands picked up the cigarette butt, after photographing it in-situ, and then added the evidence number into the file. He took close-up photos of some of the plants then pulled up another couple and placed them in a new bag. 'Can I grab your shovel? And if you could hold this open.' Dave handed Rhys a wet evidence paper bag and dug into the earth.

'I'll get a video of all of this and take it back to the station. Send it off for testing. Trouble is, with these butts, we're only going to know who it is if they're in our database already. Or if we find out who did it, then we can get a DNA sample from them and match it to this butt, hopefully. The plants and soil . . .' He shrugged. 'I'll get an agronomist onto it.'

Rhys was gazing across his dying crop. 'Jesus, Dave.' He turned and his face was creased with worry. 'This is real serious. I'd only just put the crop in and, with compost and fuel prices where they are, I can't afford to seed again. I've got no insurance for this sort of thing.' He squinted into the distance then spoke again. 'God knows what they've sprayed it with. Might be a chemical that stays in the soil for ages and kills anything that comes up. I'll have to get a sample and take it to the department of ag and see if they can test it. I don't want to try to sow anything else in here until I know.'

'And I'll do my best to find out what it is too. Mate, how do you prepare your land for seeding when you're an organic farmer?' Dave asked. 'Most farmers would spray with a herbicide to get rid of the weeds. What do you do, plough? '

'Yeah, cultivate. It's just another fancy word for ploughing but cultivate sounds nice. Oh, I know it's frowned on by the conventional farmers, who say that if it doesn't rain and the wind gets up, that the top soil will blow away, but I have to kill the weeds so they're not in competition with the barley. This way I don't have to muck around with chemicals, and slowly kill myself and the land.' He stared at Dave. 'I. Don't. Like. Chemicals.' His voice was short and clipped.

Dave nodded. He wasn't fond of chemicals either, but he'd never tried to farm without them. Again, he marvelled at the difference from where he grew up to here. The vastness of the land never ceased to amaze him. The large flats of land, covered in . . . well, nothingness. The occasional tree or scrubby bush. Cattle and sheep stretched out over the land grazing, but this area didn't have tall gum trees leading down into a creek bed or the rugged, stony hills of Barker. It was flat country and, without anything in its path, the wind swept across it, unrelenting.

'Pity there's no CCTV out here,' Dave said.

'Reckon I might put some cameras up,' Rhys said, kicking the dirt with the toe of his boot. 'Seems we gotta look out for ourselves out here.'

'Well, we do our best, Rhys, but there're some fairly large distances to cover out this way. And often on the weekends we're tied up in town keeping the peace after the pub shuts, or making sure no one has taken to the roads when they shouldn't have.'

'I know all of that, Dave. Wasn't having a crack at you, just making an observation. Seems to me that these types of things are happening with more frequency, you know? I heard the other day that there was a generator, a mobile fuel tanker of diesel and some AdBlue stolen from a farm down south. I mean, who does that? Sure, fuel prices are high, but really. That sort of act is just low. About as despicable as this.'

'Yeah, we know that's going on, but unless we're on the spot it's pretty hard to do anything until someone finds it and lets us know or there's security camera footage where we can see faces, numberplates and the like.'

Rhys pulled his beanie down tighter over his ears. 'Well, this paddock is buggered now and there's nothing I can do about it. All I can hope is that when I go to the certification mob, they'll let me drop this paddock and keep my accreditation on the rest of the farm.' He looked up at the clear blue sky. 'I don't know if that's possible.'

'I need to get back and start working on this, but I just want to go over a couple of things with you. Let's get out of this wind.' Dave indicated towards his vehicle.

'Want a cuppa? I can call Carrie and get her to put the kettle on.'

'No, not now, mate, this won't take long,' Dave said, getting his statement form out. 'I'll write this up and get you to sign it, but thanks anyway.'

The car doors slammed as they both got in. Dave started the engine and turned the heating on full bore. 'God, it's cold out there.'

'If there wasn't any wind it'd be quite a pleasant day.' Rhys twisted in his seat as Dave rubbed his hands together. 'What do you want to know?'

Putting the paper onto a clipboard, Dave slipped his glasses on and wrote his detective and station ID numbers and the date on the top, then looked across at Rhys. The young farmer smelled of diesel, sheep and grass, and for the first time, Dave noticed his jumper was ripped and there was blood around a jagged edge. 'Get caught going over a barbed wire fence?' he asked, nodding towards the tear.

Rhys looked down at it as if he hadn't known it was there. 'Bloody stuff,' he said. He rubbed his hand over the blood. 'Didn't feel anything. Right, where to on this?'

'When did you realise the crop was dying?'

'This morning. About eight a.m. Hayley was going to a friend's house and I met her mother halfway, you know the distances out here and all, so we shared the drive. Anyway, thought since I was out this way, I'd come down to check everything out. Got ewes on the other side of the road that are near lambing. Always need to keep an eye on them.'

'And this is the first you knew of the problem? No one had called in to mention the crop was dying? Seems to me that some of your neighbours would have noticed when they were driving along the road.'

'Yeah, could've done, but we're farmers, Dave, not nosy neighbours. We might ring someone if they've got a sheep with flies, or something life threatening, you know, but we don't go round passing judgement on others farming methods.'

'And you said you'd been away . . .' Dave let the question hang. He had to make sure Rhys's story was consistent.

'Yeah, like I said, I promised Carrie I'd take her to the big smoke for the week. Left Monday and came home yesterday. Sunday. Mum and Dad looked after Hayley for us.'

Dave kept repeating questions he'd already asked until he came back to the idea of someone wanting revenge.

'You don't remember having cross or angry words with anyone?' he asked Rhys. 'Think hard about this. It could be the slightest thing.'

'Nah, I don't reckon. I've been a bit under the weather and knackered from finishing seeding, so I haven't been out much lately.'

'What about Carrie?'

'She works at the post office over in Melrose every second week, but she hasn't mentioned anything.'

'I might give her a call and check—or rather, have her call me.'

Rhys fixed Dave with a worried frown. 'Do you really think someone could have done this because we pissed them off?'

'Gotta look at all angles. Even you.'

Rhys snorted. 'Of course,' he said without any humour in his voice.

Dave handed over the clipboard and watched Rhys sign.

'Don't worry, Rhys. I know that's easier said than done, but Jack and I will get to the bottom of this. If there's anything I can do for the certification company let me know.'

'Thanks, mate. Appreciate you coming out.'

They shook hands, and Rhys got out of the car, hurrying back towards his ute, his body hunched against the wind.

Dave reversed out and drove back towards Barker, thinking through the possibilities. Who would want to ruin a man's work and set him up for financial failure?

He'd pull the footy club list off the Barker Footy Club Facebook page when he got back and check who Rhys had been coaching this year. But this felt like something more than a petty grudge. Whoever had killed Rhys's crop was out to destroy him too. In Dave's experience this felt personal.

He gave a bit of a sigh as he realised he'd need Kim to help him navigate Facebook. Or maybe Jack could.

Yeah, Jack might need to be in charge of this investigation. Give him something new to think about. Dave tapped his fingers on the steering wheel and nodded to himself.

With that decision made, he flicked on the ABC and listened to the morning program, all the while keeping an eye out for any crazy drivers who might try to run him off the road again.

An old Slim Dusty song was playing as he pulled into the station. He noticed Mrs Darby's car was gone from the kerb near the pub. The street was quiet. He smiled, that's the way he liked Barker.

'I'm back, Joan,' Dave called out as he came in the back entry. He heard her answer but couldn't make out her words. 'What's that?' he asked, walking into his office and then through to hers.

'That firearm you wanted to take possession of has been brought in by Mr Manson,' Joan said. 'I've locked it in the safe. Here's the paperwork.' She held out a couple of pieces of paper and Dave took them, holding them away from his body to make sure all the signatures were in the right places. He felt for his glasses on his head.

'And how was our Mr Manson today?' he asked.

'About as annoyed as he was when he was talking to Jack.'

'Excellent. Another happy customer,' Dave said with a grimace. 'I'll put these on Jack's desk. Thanks, Joan.'

Tucking the pages under his arm, he took his keys off his belt and opened the gun safe in his office to check the gun against the details that had been given. He made sure the chamber was empty. 'Did he bring in any bullets?' Dave called.

'Just the gun.'

Sighing heavily through his nose, Dave knew that meant a visit out to see John Manson to collect any bullets he had. John wouldn't be happy to see them.

Dave put the forms on Jack's desk and started to turn away, when the corner of a document caught his eye. He dropped his glasses onto his nose and checked he was seeing correctly.

Nudging the notepad out of the way, Dave read the rest of the application form.

Detective Training School. DTS.

Applicant's name: Senior Constable Jack Higgins.

Officer in charge: Detective David Burrows.

Detective recommending: Detective David Burrows.

'What the actual fuck?' Dave wondered softly.

CHAPTER 6

The loud knocking on Mia's door sent her flying out of bed, still in her pyjamas. She tried to get her bearings as she stumbled to the door and yanked it open.

Through sleep-filled eyes, she saw a short, older man with grey hair and wire-rimmed glasses standing there. His suit was well worn and it looked like he may have dropped some Weet-Bix on his bow tie.

She took all of this in before she asked who he was.

'Sorry to wake you, Mia. You are Mia, aren't you?'

'Ah, yeah. And you are . . .' Aware she probably had crusty bits of sleep in the corners of her eyes and bad breath, she took a step back and turned slightly, rubbing her face.

'Dr Thompson. I care for your grandmother at the nursing home.'

Mia's eyes widened and she took in a sharp breath. 'Is she okay?' Her hands reached out to him as if to ward off any bad news that was coming her way.

'Oh yes.' Pushing his glasses back on his nose, he frowned. 'Well, I assume she is. I haven't been there this morning, or received a call-out, so I would surmise that there is nothing amiss.'

'Then, why . . .' Mia shook her head, trying to clear the sleep bubble around her. 'Why are you here?'

'To talk. May I come in? I apologise for waking you.'

'Ah, of course. Sure.' She wrapped her arms around her chest as he walked in. 'Kitchen is through there.' Mia pointed and made for the bedroom. 'I'll be right there.'

Slamming the door to her bedroom shut, she took a couple of deep breaths and glanced at her watch: 7 a.m. In country areas, most people started their day when the sun rose.

She threw off her PJs and rummaged around on the floor for her bra. Finding a pair of jeans and a jumper in her suitcase, she searched for a shirt, finally finding one in the bottom drawer. A couple more deep breaths and a comb through her unruly hair then she went out to greet her visitor.

'Sorry,' Mia said, when she found him in the kitchen, sitting up straight, his hands folded, at the table. 'I wasn't expecting you.' Then she looked over at Dr Thompson. 'Was I?'

Giving a quiet laugh, he said, 'No, my dear. I was passing and thought I would drop in. The nurses at the home said you wanted to speak with me.'

'Right. Um, coffee?' The kettle should be on the bench and she hoped she had milk and sugar.

'That would be nice, thank you. Black.'

'I feel I need to apologise. I'm not usually so scatty, I just didn't . . .' What she really wanted to say was, why the hell are you here?

'It's my mistake. I assumed you'd be up at the crack of dawn like your grandmother.' He fixed her with a stare that made her want to giggle. His eyebrows were the offspring of John Howard's and they wiggled when he talked.

There were two cups in the cupboard. One with a crack and chip, the other, on inspection, was intact. Mia spooned coffee from a tin into the good cup and found a tea bag for herself, before leaning against the bench. 'I would have been up, but I only finished unpacking yesterday and I was beat. And yes, I did want to talk to you.' It was her turn to use her brows and she raised them at him. 'I didn't know doctors still made house calls.'

'Many people are too sick to come to the surgery and it's my job to make them as comfortable as possible, so I am more than content to go to them.'

Dr Thompson was proud of the way he cared for Broad River's community, Mia realised. His grey hair, glasses and deeply lined face made him seem old, but his energy and clear, intelligent eyes gave him a youthful feel. He could be anywhere from fifty to eighty.

The whistling of the kettle brought her back from her thoughts and she poured the water into the cups.

'Did you want anything to eat? I think I've got—' casting around the kitchen, she saw a loaf of bread '—toast and Vegemite, or jam.' She placed the coffee in front of Dr Thompson.

'I've had my morning porridge,' he said, 'that sets me up for the day. Now, what would you like to ask me about your grandmother? I guess you're concerned about her failing memory?'

The chair's feet scuffed the lino floor as Mia pulled out the only other chair and sank down. She took a sip of sweet tea and said, 'I don't understand dementia, Dr Thompson. I know there are seven stages, but I don't know where she's at and how much time I have with her.' Mia quickly took another mouthful of tea. Maybe the swallowing action would dislodge the lump in her throat.

'The fear and anxiety that goes with dementia is understandable,' Dr Thompson said, 'but your grandmother is in good physical health. Frail, of course, due to her age, but still in good physical health. Her mind, however, is at stage three of dementia, which is called mild cognitive impairment.'

'Stage three?' Hot tea sloshed over the side of Mia's cup and landed on her hand. Gritting her teeth, she put the cup down. 'What does that mean?'

'I'm sure you've already noticed some of the symptoms. Forgetting the names of friends and family members, losing or misplacing important items—her glasses, medication . . .'

'A key?'

'Yes, anything like that. And difficulty with retaining information. If you asked her a question about an article she read, she wouldn't be able to tell you about it.'

Mia nodded. 'Yeah, she forgot where she'd put a key yesterday and she was having trouble eating her dinner.'

'That would be quite common at stage three. The nursing home is certainly a safe place for her.'

'I can see that, even though she doesn't like it. I wish I could look after her, but . . . there's work.'

'We all do. Sometimes, as much as we want to care for our family, it just isn't practical. Living in Broad River makes it more difficult because we don't have the services that bigger towns and cities have—Silver Chain and the like—to keep people in their own homes.' He took a sip of his coffee and glanced discreetly at the large silver watch on his wrist.

Quickly she asked another question. 'How long will it take before she deteriorates further?'

'I can't answer that. Every patient is different. But I have noticed your grandmother is beginning to teeter more towards stage four than three. There has been a decline in her cognitive function over the past two months.'

'Is there any way of testing or—'

'There is certainly an assessment which can be completed, but it sometimes agitates the patient more than helps them.' Dr Thompson paused for a moment as if assessing his next words. 'Mia, I understand this is going to be difficult for you, especially without any family support, but I prefer to let my patients live in a bubble of warmth and kindness. Putting them through unnecessary testing causes stress to them and their loved ones.' He sat upright and looked her straight in the eye as he spoke. 'In most cases dementia is incurable and irreversible. Playing cards and doing crosswords—activities that will use her mind and keep it active—might slow the decline but, in time, Clara won't remember your name, or who you are.' He softened his voice. 'As family, we often want answers that doctors can't give. All I can promise you is that I will be open and frank, but without putting Clara under any duress. Does that sit well with you?'

Mia realised there were tears rolling down her cheeks. Dr Thompson was talking about the woman who'd raised her after her mother died. Her nan who had come to school sports days and swimming carnivals, and paid for her to go to boarding school. Nana had cheered her on from the sidelines in everything she did, and now there would come a time this amazing woman wouldn't be able to recognise her own granddaughter.

'Okay,' Mia finally managed.

Dr Thompson leaned over and patted her hands. 'I'll be with you every step of the way, so there's no need to be frightened. Clara is in very good hands at the nursing home. They treat their clients with dignity and respect, so you can be sure she will continue to be well cared for there.'

Mia nodded. This old doctor had shown her more kindness than Mia had seen from a stranger in years. Throughout her time as a cadet, graduating to be a copper, she saw the bad side of most people. The yelling, abuse and anger. 'I'm so glad you called in to tell me this,' she said in a low voice. 'Thank you for taking the time and for caring.'

Dr Thompson smiled as he stood up and pulled down the cuffs on his shirt. He was a strange gentleman. Prim and proper. 'That is what I do. Now, Mia, I also understand you are the new constable so I am sure our paths will cross often.'

'Yes, I am.' She stood, unsure whether to shake his hand. His concern had made him seem like an elderly uncle or grandfather rather than the doctor and she wanted to kiss him on the cheek.

'Well, the best of British luck to you, my dear. You will certainly give them all a shake-up at the station. It will be interesting to watch.'

'What do you mean?'

But the doctor had already passed her and was heading down the hall. 'I'd best get on with the rest of my rounds. I'll be in touch.'

'Thanks,' was all Mia could manage.

Dr Thompson closed the door gently behind him and Mia finally brushed her tears away.

Alone in the house, her fingers ached to dial Chris, but he was at work. Instead, she took her cup of tea outside and breathed in the frigid air.

The lingering hint of frost was on the lower parts of the lawn and dewdrops hung from the tips of the trees' leaves. On the ground, the beetles were busy turning the soil near the empty patch of dirt in the back corner.

Mia walked around the small area of lawn, feeling it crunch under her feet. Frosts were known for drying everything and she wondered if she needed to put the sprinkler on, even though it was winter. The grass did look brown in a few places.

She picked her way along the garden bed. The knee-high planter boxes built of old railway sleepers contained some hardy-looking plants she didn't know the name of. When she plunged her fingers into the dirt, it was dry.

Perching on the sleeper wall, she closed her eyes and listened. The galahs screeching over at the creek, a couple of magpies warbling in the distance and the whoosh of a passing car were the only things that broke the silence.

For years and years her nan would have listened to similar sounds, sitting outside the shop on the splintery wooden bench on the street in nearby Barker.

A burst of curiosity shot through her. The shop was calling.

CHAPTER 7

'And where are you going, dear?' Clara asked, pushing the receiver closer to her ear. She hated the phone these days. More often than not she forgot who she was talking to, and it was much harder to keep track of the conversation when the person wasn't in front of her.

'I'm driving across the plains on the way to Barker, Nana,' Mia said. 'You'd love it—the colours on the hills are purple and pink all mixed in with the green grass and there are flowers spread across the sides of the road.'

'They won't be flowers, dear,' Clara said. Surely Mia should know better than that! 'They're weeds. Salvation Jane are blue and the pale red ones will be hops. If you're lucky you might see some fringe lilies, but you'd have to get out of the car to spot them. Walk across the hills and fossick around on the edge of the creeks where the ground is still moist.'

Clara brushed her hands over the arm of her chair as she thought about how Theo Marshall would occasionally bring her a bunch of the beautiful purple flower. Their name came from the edge of the flower, which was just like a fringe from a 1920s dress. They'd always been her favourite.

'I'll go for a walk when I get home and see if I can see any.' Mia paused. 'Nana, I wanted to check. When you gave me the key you said you still owned the shop. Is that right?'

'What shop?'

There was a pause and Clara looked around, waiting to hear the voice again.

'The shop in Barker, Nana. Simpson's Haberdashery.'

'Oh yes, of course!' Clara felt the flood of embarrassment hit her cheeks. 'Sorry, dear, I lost track for a moment.' She paused as the door opened and someone came in holding a cup. The woman put it down and smiled as she offered Clara two biscuits in a clear cellophane wrapper. She screwed up her nose and shook her head. 'Aren't there any homemade ones?' Clara asked.

'What?' A voice from a long way away answered her, but the mouth of the person standing in front of her didn't move in the way it should for the word 'what'. She was saying something else.

'Here's your morning tea, Clara. The biscuits are nice. I'll leave them here for you.'

'Nana?'

Clara looked around. She heard her name but couldn't see Mia anywhere. 'Where are you, dear?' she asked. 'I can't see you.' She reached out to put a small teaspoon of sugar in her tea and realised there was something in her hand.

'Nana, I'm on the phone.'

There was Mia's voice again.

'If you're on the phone, why are you talking to me then?' She looked at the woman standing next to her. 'Have you seen Mia? I can hear her but can't see where she is.'

The woman had a name tag on her breast. It said Casey. Was this the same one who'd been here the night before?

Leaning forward, Casey touched the thing in Clara's hand. 'Mia's talking to you, Clara.' Gently, she put the phone back to Clara's ear.

'I'm here, Nana.'

Bewildered, Clara looked at Casey and then at the receiver in her hand. 'I'm getting a bit confused, Mia. It might be better if I talk to you another time.' Clara gave the phone helplessly to Casey. 'Do you know what to do with this now?' she asked.

⌐◞

Mia stared at her mobile. Call ended.

Casey must have hung up for Nana. A hand squeezed hard at her heart and she felt her nose prickle. She sniffed and ran her hand over her face, then looked out the window again.

She'd wanted to describe the country to Nana. The large stony hills that towered above the car as she drove through the winding creeks. The large gum trees that three people wouldn't get their arms around. *How old are they?* she wondered. The galahs, sweeping and swooping through the trees and bathing in the puddles, from the shower of rain the night before. Their feathers ruffled. The rusty iron gates leaning to one side and the barbed wire had snapped from the large strainer posts making it hard to keep stock in, or the kangaroos and emus out.

A house came into view as she rounded a corner. A large stone building with a wide verandah. It was in the middle of nowhere; nothing, except for the railway line running alongside it and a tank high up on a stand so the long-gone steam trains could access water. Even from the road, the stand looked splintery and bowed, as if it couldn't bear the weight of the tank above.

Bumping over the railway line in a couple of places, Mia lifted her foot to slow at the one house rail siding not far out of Barker. She laughed at the sign that said *Minbarra, slow down*. It made her think it was the township that needed to slow down rather than the cars driving through.

Nothing had changed in Minbarra. It was still as lonely and derelict as it had been when she was a child. A hill to one side of the road and on the other the house. A shiny, small four-wheel drive sat under the lean-to. She could see a flash from red flowers in pots on the verandah as she drove by.

Maybe Nana would like to come for a drive on the weekend. That could be a way to get her mind clear again. Out of that small, sterile room and into the wide land she loved. To watch the sunset—the hills light up with deep blues as the shadows slipped over the land then the gold and pinks as the last few rays kissed the hills before the sun slid below the earth's horizon. Perhaps Nana would like to sit on the wooden bench outside the shop, or even behind the counter again. Running her dusting cloth across the top like she used to.

The squeeze on her heart loosened as she put a plan together. Some time soon, she would take her grandmother out. If the roadhouse was still open, they could have lunch watching the cars come and go, and perhaps Nana would even see some people she knew. If she remembered them.

Sitting in a room looking at four walls would do nothing to halt the dementia that was eating at her grandmother's brain.

Rounding another corner, Mia saw the sign that said *Barker*. She took a breath. She hadn't been here since she was a kid and yet it felt so familiar.

The trees lining the median strip hadn't changed and neither had the roadhouse. The paint may have been a little more faded, but the blue, white and red Ampol sign still rose into the sky, next to the prices for petrol and diesel. Further in, the post office and police station were opposite each other. Mia parked in the main street. The town seemed to be thriving. There was a pub on the corner, then the stock and station agent, a deli, IGA and newsagency. She noticed a cafe that looked new. Her stomach rumbled. Maybe she'd grab a sausage roll or pie.

The engine ticked as she turned it off and the silence engulfed her as she stared at the shop in front of her.

Simpson's Haberdashery was painted above the door, faded, but not peeling. Curtains hung in the windows, blocking her view of what might be inside, and it looked like some of the young kids had drawn in the dirt covering the windows. Crude drawings of penises and breasts, along with *Wash me* and *Jazzy loves Craig.*

When she looked at the rest of the street, it was tidy and clean. Freshly painted walls, gleaming signs and windows, and the grass in the median strip had been mowed only days ago.

The key felt heavy in her hand. Was the shop really still her nan's as she claimed? It looked like it might not have been touched since they'd left Barker all those years ago. Her fingers itched to ring George Walker, but she didn't have his number.

If the key opened the door—well, she wasn't breaking and entering, was she?

Slowly, Mia got out of the car, her eyes not leaving the entrance. She glanced around, wondering if anyone had noticed her, then she looked back at the shop. What would she find? Anticipation trickled through her and she slammed the car door and moved towards the lock.

The sound of laughter rose into the air and footsteps pounded the cement pavement, startling Mia from her dreamlike state. She turned in the direction of the noise and saw a group of young kids running towards her. Mia took a step closer to the wall, so they wouldn't knock her down, but they turned sharply and disappeared inside a smoothly sliding door.

She became aware of the smell of coffee and chips and her stomach rumbled again. Putting the key in her pocket and her handbag over her shoulder, she followed the kids into the cafe.

Breathing in the warmth of baking, Mia stood at the counter, behind the kids who were all ordering milkshakes and soft-serve ice creams.

'Now, Casper, do you think your mum would like it if you didn't take a milkshake home to your sister?' the lady behind the counter asked one of the kids.

'I'm not taking her one, Mrs Grattan. She's boring.'

'But maybe—'

'I haven't got enough money.'

'Are you sure?' The woman grinned down at Casper, then she shot another little boy a look. 'What about you, Angus, does your mum know you're here?'

Mia didn't hear the answer, because she was thinking how nice it was to be back in a town that cared for its occupants. The city hadn't been like that. Neither had the police academy.

'Can I help you there, love?' The woman had turned her attention from the kids to Mia.

'Hello, could I grab a coffee and a toasted ham, cheese and tomato sandwich please?' she asked, digging in her handbag for her purse.

'Sure. You passing through?' the woman grabbed a premade sandwich and put it into the sandwich press then turned to the coffee machine.

'Something like that. Here to check out Simpson's old shop.' She put her handbag on the counter. 'Do you know anything about it?'

The woman looked over her shoulder. 'Simpson's old place? Now why would you be asking about that? No one's been in there for years.'

'My grandmother is Clara Worth. Her family used to run the store and lived here a million years ago.'

This time the woman turned fully and stared, openly curious, at Mia's face. 'Surely not that long ago, love. You'd have a little bit of grey hair if nothing else.' She gave another grin and searched Mia's face before saying to herself quietly, 'Well, there you go. Bill! Bill, get out here! Clara Worth's granddaughter is in the house.'

Unsure whether being Clara's grandchild was a good thing to these people, Mia stood awkwardly and waited for Bill to appear. When no one came through the swinging doors from the kitchen, Mia introduced herself.

The woman put the coffee on the counter. 'I'm Annabelle. Never knew your grandmother. We've only lived in Barker for the last ten years, but we've always wondered about that shop. In fact, we made some enquiries about it a few years back, through the council, but we didn't get anywhere. Only that Clara still owned the building, but no one seemed to know how to get in contact with her. We'd love to lease it from you. This place, well, you can see . . .' She indicated the size of the room. It was small and crammed with local paintings and produce for sale.

Mia was sure they could fit in another few tables if they got rid of the clutter.

'We've got such plans for expansion and there's no other shops available on the main street, except that one,' Annabelle said

Well, that answered that question. Mia picked up one of the many cups on display, all painted with a country scene, and looked around. Bookshelves leaned against the walls, groaning under the weight of tins, plates and other things for sale.

'It's lovely in here,' she said. 'Cosy. Why would you want to move?'

'Too small and there would be more chance of letting this place out than that huge shop of your gran's. Why hasn't she done anything with it?'

Finally, the doors from the kitchen swung open and a man wearing a blue apron came through. He had a shock of white hair, a beard and glasses.

Mia had to stop herself from giggling. He looked like Santa.

'Hello there, Clara's granddaughter,' he said, holding out his hand with a friendly grin on his face. 'I'm Bill Grattan. Nice to meet you.'

Mia returned the greeting and looked pointedly over to where her sandwich was being toasted.

'You make sure you let us know if you're going to lease that shop out,' Bill said, wiping his hands on his apron. 'We'd really like to take it off your hands.'

'I don't really know what Nana's going to—'

'Such an eyesore as it is,' Annabelle said, tutting as she put an egg flip under the sandwich and dragged it onto a piece of baking paper. 'Makes the street look a bit drab, you know.'

Mia knew how important a main street was in a country town. If it wasn't clean and tidy, tourists would drive on to the next town.

'We'd do it up really nice, so we would,' Bill said. 'What do you think, love?'

Mia shifted uncomfortably. 'Look, I understand . . .'

The door swung open and the bell at the top jingled.

A large grin split Bill's face. 'Dave Burrows! How goes it, sir?'

Mia turned and saw a man dressed in a police uniform. He was tall, with grey hair and blue eyes. His face was friendly but Mia could tell, just by looking at him, that his demeanour could change in an instant.

Dave Burrows? The name sounded familiar.

Dave waved from the door. 'Could I grab my usual, Bill? And one for Jack too.'

'Surely, surely.' Bill nodded.

Annabelle handed over the sandwich and coffee to Mia. 'There you go, love. You know where we are, if you need us.' She gave another smile and went back to the coffee machine. 'Maybe when you get it cleaned up we could come and have a look?'

'Thanks,' Mia said, adding *I think* in her mind as she went to leave. She wondered if she should introduce herself to Dave but he was busy talking to another couple sitting near the door.

When Mia opened the door a blast of cold air burst into the cafe. The door flew back, knocking into the wall, then swung back to hit her on the arm.

'You right?' Dave appeared at her side. 'Bloody wind, it's awful this time of year.'

'Yeah, I'm good, thanks.' Mia caught her breath and made sure everything was still upright. 'Look, didn't even spill the coffee,' she said with a grin.

'Excellent.' He gave her another friendly smile and held the door while she went through.

'You're the local copper here?' she asked.

'Sure am. One of two. Dave Burrows. Senior Constable Jack Higgins is my partner.' He looked at her as if he was trying to work out what she might want. 'Are you new in town?' he asked.

Shaking her head, Mia gave a slight laugh. 'Not really, but sort of. I used to live here when I was a child. Haven't been back for a long time. But I'm also the new connie over in Broad River.'

'Are you now? Well, that's a great piece of news. Stir those buggers up. How long have you been there for?'

'I start tomorrow.'

'First posting?'

Mia nodded.

'You'll be great. Let me know if you need anything.' He took his card out of his wallet and handed it to her. 'What was your name again?'

Grinning, she recognised Dave's line; she hadn't given her name, but it was enough of a prompt to get it out of someone who you were questioning. 'Mia. Mia Worth.'

'As I said, let me know if you need anything.' He shook her hand and left her standing on the street.

Suddenly, the key in her pocket was burning a hole and she needed to get to the shop and look inside.

The coffee and toastie gave her the vigour she needed, and a few moments later she slipped the key into the lock.

It turned with a loud click.

CHAPTER 8

A loud squeaking made Mia jump. What was it? Rat? Mouse?

Her heart was still hammering from when she'd heard the click and the key had turned. Everything her nan had told her seemed to be true. Mia wasn't sure if she was sad that she'd even considered her words may not be fact or happy that she was standing here, just inside the door of Simpson's Haberdashery.

The noise, she realised, was the floorboard where her foot was now resting. She jiggled up and down, hearing the squeak again, before raising her eyes.

The air was murky with dust and smelled stale and musty, as if water had leaked in. As her eyes adjusted, she could make out shelves with sheets draped over them. There were poster advertisements on the walls and toy aeroplanes, hats and cattle whips hanging from the ceiling.

Mia drew in a breath. It looked like Nana hadn't even destocked. She'd just covered everything and walked out. It didn't make any sense.

Pushing the door shut behind her, Mia took a few steps further inside before giving a small cry. Cobwebs! Swiping at her face and hair, she tried to remove the sticky web, but it wrapped around her hands.

'Get off, get off!' she cried, agitated, her hands flapping about her head, then onto her jeans trying to wipe the feathery feeling away.

It took a couple of moments to feel normal again, then she stretched her hands out in front of her, taking big swipes at nothing, hoping to shift all of the stringy lines before they came near her face again.

Not that she was afraid of spiders. She just didn't like the webs across her face and neck in case she pulled down a poisonous monster and its eight legs landed on her!

Further into the shop, she came to a stop at the first shelf, gingerly lifting the sheet up. Toys. Matchbox cars and dolls with tea sets. Teddy bears and games of checkers and draughts. Spinning tops and blocks and a pair of roller skates.

A few more steps in and another shelf.

Men's shirts in cardboard boxes. Jumpers. Some type of work boots spread out in pairs across the bottom shelf.

Mia turned slowly, her eyes searching in all directions. The counter. It still had the old scales on it that Nan used to let her play with. A container of lollipops and a vase with dead flowers. A pen and notebook. Dust.

On the back wall, very high up, were two narrow rectangular windows, letting a small amount of light in. Dust-draped cobwebs hung across them, and somehow, there was a blowfly, buzzing and bashing itself against the filthy window.

Mia found a light switch next to the side door. The large, old-fashioned switch made a loud click but nothing happened.

'Bugger.' She hadn't really expected the power would still be connected after such a long time but it was worth a try. A torch would have been handy. She made a note in her phone to ring the solicitor then turned on the phone's small flashlight and held it up.

'Why,' Mia asked, as she looked at the objects more closely, 'is everything exactly as it was?'

Anxiety tugged at her stomach. Something didn't feel good in here. Abandoned, deserted. Uninhabited.

Taking a breath and shaking off her nervousness, she continued her investigations. Simpson's Haberdashery was mostly as she remembered it, the kitchenware was right at the back, there were cushions and macramé hangers that were thick with dust now, a couple were even faded from where the sun had found a way in through the sliver of windows.

The dressing-room curtains were hanging unmoving, as if waiting for someone to push them back. Mia did.

A school uniform dangled from a hook on the wall. Waiting for a small child to try it on. Mia paused and looked at the uniform a bit longer. The material seemed to droop with loneliness, as if it had given up on ever seeing the fun of a school yard.

Further on, there were balls of wool in baskets and knitting needles hanging from display racks. Running her finger along the curved needles, she looked across at the counter and remembered Nana sitting there knitting brown socks for anyone who wanted a pair. It seemed to be how she kept her hands busy when there was no one in the shop.

Mia sank down on the stool behind the counter trying to process what she'd found.

Nana had always told her that they'd moved because her father had died. He was buried in the Barker cemetery and, once all his affairs were tidied up, her mother, Clara and Mia had packed up and left Barker, moving to Adelaide and Clara had only moved to Broad River when Mia was settled in boarding school.

Mia traced the number nine in the dirt on the counter. That was how old she'd been when her mother had been killed in a car accident.

Nine.

A little girl who couldn't understand why her mummy wasn't coming home again. Mia understood what death was by that age, but not why it had to happen.

Nan came into her mind and she closed her eyes, remembering.

'Mia, darling, I've got some very sad news.'

Mia had been setting the kitchen table for dinner. Three places as always. Nana sat at the head and Mia and Nicole either side.

'What's wrong, Nana?'

'Come here. Come and sit on my knee.' Nana's touch had been soft and dry as she'd run her aged hands over Mia's cheeks. 'Your mum, love. It's your mum. She's gone.'

'Where?'

Nana swallowed and seemed to grit her teeth together, before answering. 'She's died, darling girl. I'm sorry. There was a car crash on the way home from her work today.'

Mia hadn't cried then. Months had passed before the tears had started, then they hadn't stopped. For a long time.

They were running down her cheeks now, though. Sitting on the same stool as her nan used to, looking at the same things.

The notebook had her nan's writing on the top page. She dragged it closer to her, sniffing and wiping her eyes so she could read.

Order more blue wool for Mrs Fender. Six ply.

Buy milk, bread and butter.

Karen—then a party line number.

Mia wondered who Karen was. She flipped the page.

The daily takings and reconciliation seemed to be on that one, and the next page didn't have anything more than a few notes about getting a window fixed and checking the cellar.

Cellar?

Her training officer's voice came to her. 'Methodical, Worth. That's what makes a good copper. Methodical.'

She wasn't being methodical. She was all over the place. Emotional. Instead of looking for the cellar, she lifted up the curtain at the back of the counter and looked underneath.

Cleaning gear, sticky tape, scissors, measuring tape. Bullets in a cardboard box.

No gun.

Was she remembering correctly? Maybe there had never been a gun. Why the bullets then?

Her phone buzzed and she jumped.

The screen showed a photo of her with Josie, her closest, weirdest friend from boarding school, both with glasses of wine and wide smiles. Josie's hair was wildly pink and her sparkling nose ring always caught the light in photos.

'Hey, Jos, how are you going?' Mia pulled the cardboard box towards her and opened the flap.

'I'm just excellent!' She could almost feel her friend's laughter and excitement. 'You?'

'Yep, all good here. What's your good news? You sound happy.'

'You're not going to believe this, Mia.' Josie paused for effect.

'You'll have to tell me.'

'I got a job in Port Augusta! That's like, only about two hours' drive from you! We'll be able to have Friday nights together.'

'Really? Oh my god, Josie, that's fantastic. So close! What's the job?'

'Managing the computer store there. Nothing too inspiring, but it's a job and they're a bit tricky to come by at the moment. I'm packing up my house now and moving next week. There's accommodation that comes with the job, thank the lucky stars!'

'That's really brilliant news.' Mia picked up the bullets and inspected them closely. Maybe she should take them.

'What's wrong? You sound weird.'

'Nothing.' She tried to sound normal.

'Mia,' Josie sounded like she was giving a child one last chance, 'tell me!'

'Honestly, Josie, it's nothing. I'm in Barker checking out Nana's old shop. I can remember sitting here as a kid playing with the toys and scales. Bit of a trip down memory lane, that's all.'

'Oh, sounds mysterious.'

Mia laughed. 'No, nothing like that.' She looked at the bullets again and realised she'd just lied. It was everything like that: perplexing and eerie. 'When do you start the new job?' She tried to sound normal.

'Two weeks' time,' Josie said.

'Want me to come over and help you unpack if I'm not on shift?'

'I was hoping you'd say that. You know how much I hate packing and unpacking.'

'If you hadn't moved so much . . .'

'I know, I know.' They were silent for a moment. 'How's your nan?'

Mia sighed and got up from the stool, walking over towards the swathes of material. She ran her hands down a piece of windcheater fabric. 'Up and down. The doc came and saw me this morning, he said the dementia is progressing.'

'That's not good, Mia.'

'But expected.'

They were quiet and then Mia heard a ding. Leaving the counter, she followed the noise and found a wind chime in the window. Long silver tubes with a bird perched on the top. Josie was talking as she reached out to touch it.

'So how come you're in her old shop? Didn't she sell it?'

'Well, to be perfectly honest, I don't know if that's what I was ever told. Only what I assumed.' Mia quickly explained to her friend the story of the key. 'I'm a bit confused about what went down when we moved to Adelaide because the weird thing is the place looks like she just up and left in a hurry. Like overnight or something. Everything is just as I remember it, right down to a note about what she needed to order next.'

'Mia, you know I love you, right?'

Mia harrumphed. 'What I do know is when you say stuff like that, I'm not going to like what comes out of your mouth next.'

'Your police brain is getting to you. There's nothing strange about that. Maybe she couldn't sell the gear that was in there and she had to go because she was on a deadline for something; maybe something as silly as getting you to school at the beginning of a new term.'

'Don't be so sensible.' Mia realised the truth in Josie's words, but couldn't shake the feeling they weren't right.

Picking up another sheet and looking under it, Mia found the women's section. Jeans, shirts and jumpers.

'There are dead flowers in a vase.'

'Wow, they'd be crispy.'

Mia couldn't help but laugh. 'You're right there.' When she looked back to the counter her stomach did a flip. Why did she think there should be a gun?

'Well, I'd better fly,' Josie said. 'I'm heading to Bunnings to buy some packing boxes.'

'Haven't you got any left over from when you moved back from Melbourne?' Then rolled her eyes as she heard Josie scoff, 'As if!' Josie looked *and* lived like a gypsy, and sometimes Mia was jealous of her friend's freedom. Josie never worried about finding a job or not being able to pay her bills, she just did what she liked. Something like a free spirit.

Other times Mia couldn't think of anything worse than moving as much as Josie did.

'Ring me and let me know your movements.'

'Will do. Love you!'

Mia found herself repeating the words to empty air. They were so different, her and Josie. Maybe that's why they were such good friends.

Turning back to the counter, she glanced at her watch, then around the shop. Could there be a hidey hole some-where, like the false bottom in the jewellery box?

CHAPTER 9

Dave knocked on the door of Mrs Darby's house and waited a moment.

'Hello? Mrs Darby, it's Detective Dave Burrows.'

'We're in the lounge,' Jack's familiar voice called back.

Dave entered and looked for a doorway leading from the hallway into a lounge. The first one he looked into was a room with a single bed with a rose-studded bedspread and a rocking chair in the corner. A pair of pants was folded neatly on the seat.

Jack appeared. 'In here,' he said, pointing to the third door down.

Dave held up the takeaway coffee. 'Need a quick break?'

Looking relieved, Jack held out his hand. 'Not going so well,' he said in a low voice.

'Didn't think it would. Son here? Reckon I saw his car out front.'

Jack nodded and took a sip of the coffee. 'I'll whip outside for a minute. Cheers for this.'

Dave nodded and went into the lounge. Mrs Darby was sitting in a lounge chair, a deep purple bruise was coming out along the side of her face. The day after was always worse. Her son, Mark, was sitting next to her, apprehension spread across his face.

'That looks nasty, Mrs Darby,' Dave said as he sat down. 'Feeling okay otherwise? G'day, Mark.'

'Oh yes, such a silly thing to happen. I was only telling your constable a moment ago, it was just a little mistake. I know which pedal to push.'

'I'm sure you do. Trouble is that you could have hurt a lot of people. Imagine if it had been a Friday night and there'd been a few people at the pub.'

'Well,' Mrs Darby shifted in her chair, 'I wouldn't have been there on a Friday night. There are better things to do than drink beer all night, young man.'

Dave stifled a grin at the young man comment. If only! This morning he'd noticed the hair on his chest had a few greys in it.

'Even so, this is the second accident you've had recently.'

Jack came back into the room and sat next to Dave, some forms in his hand.

Mark leaned forward. 'Look, you're not really thinking about asking Mum to give up her licence, are you? She's only seventy-eight and very fit and healthy for her age. The last time she went to the doctor, he said she was fine in every which way.'

Jack nodded. 'We understand what you're saying,' he looked at Mrs Darby, 'and we want you to remain independent, but we also have to think of the safety of the rest of the people in town.'

Mrs Darby's chin started to wobble. 'Don't take my licence from me,' she whispered. 'How will I get to bowls in Broad River? Or the CWA meetings?'

Dave looked down at his hands, wishing these conversations were easier.

'And god knows I have to work!' Mark said. 'I can't be running her everywhere. Have you seen what type of social schedule my mother keeps?'

His attempt at humour fell flat.

'We're not taking your licence from you today, Mrs Darby, but what I have here is a certificate of fitness. You should have received one in the mail after your last birthday. The licensing department sends them out.' He paused and looked over at Dave, ignoring the look of relief that crossed both Mrs Darby's and her son's faces. 'This means you need to go to the doctor and get assessed to make sure that, medically, you are fit to drive.'

'So the doctor takes it away not the coppers?' Mark asked.

Dave frowned at the sharpness in his voice.

'We could take your mother's licence away today if we wanted to,' Jack said, putting the form on the table and tapping it.

A tear rolled down Mrs Darby's cheek and Dave threw Jack a calm-it-down look. He was surprised to see his partner's cheek twitching, which usually meant he was furious.

'We could do that,' Jack continued, 'but this is a big adjustment, so we'd like a medical opinion first. If the doctor says you're cognitively and physically capable to drive, then we'll conduct a driving test. If the doctor says the opposite, we'll ask you to surrender your licence. Now, Mrs Darby, I know—'

The elderly woman had stood up from her chair. She shook a bony finger at Jack, interrupting him. 'Now you listen here, my lad,' she said. 'I accidentally touched the accelerator instead of the brake. An easy mistake. A medical assessment from a doctor is not necessary and I won't consent to it.'

'Then we won't have any choice but to ask you to surrender your driver's licence today.' Jack looked at her steadily. 'It's your choice.'

The clock ticked, breaking the quiet of people accepting what had been said.

'You'll get old one day, young man.' Mrs Darby shook her finger at Jack again, but the fire had gone out of her.

'Maybe this is the best way, Mum. It's been a while since you were at the doctor's, anyway.'

'I don't like it.'

'We don't expect you to,' Jack said softly. 'And we're not only concerned for other people around Barker, but you as well. None of us wants to see you hurt.'

Again, silence filled the air until a clock chimed midday. Dave stood up. 'We'll wait until you get the form back to us,' he said. 'But in the meantime, Mrs Darby, please don't drive unless it's really necessary. We understand you have commitments, but we are strongly advising you to limit your time behind the wheel.'

Neither mother nor son said anything, they just looked at each other.

'Thanks for your time,' Jack said, and both he and Dave nodded at Mrs Darby and Mark as they left the room.

Outside, Dave clapped Jack on the back. 'You were bloody excellent in there,' he said. 'Sensitive to needs, tough when you had to be and got the end result we needed. Well done. I'm impressed.'

'Don't know about that. I hope she makes a doctor's appointment real soon.'

'Make a note to follow her up in a week if you haven't heard anything. My guess is that you won't have.'

Jack scoffed. 'I know I won't have.'

'Beer tonight?' Dave asked.

'Ah . . .'

'Actually, you don't have a choice. I've got something I need to talk to you about. See you at the pub after knock-off.'

'Two beers, thanks, Hopper.' Dave nodded towards the restaurant to Jack. 'Out there with you,' he said, handing over a fifty-dollar note when Hopper put the two large glasses down on the bar.

Jack frowned. 'What are you being all high and mighty for?'

'Because you and I have something to talk about.' Holding the beers in both hands, he turned around.

The door to the restaurant flung open and he saw a blur of dark hair, pants and jumper, and then felt the beer spill all over his hands and trousers and a warm body knock into him.

'Oh my god, I'm so sorry,' a female voice said. 'I'll buy . . . Oh no, it's you!'

Dave looked at the half-empty glasses in his hands, then down at the face of Jayde Tonkin.

'I'll buy you another beer,' she blurted out, her hands on her face. 'Far out, I'm so sorry.'

'Good to know you're still true to form,' Dave finally said, putting the glasses down.

'What?'

'You're still sticking to the middle of the road and going too fast!' He turned to Jack. 'Jayde almost ran me off the road.'

Jack let out a burst of laughter and Dave grinned too. 'God help your husband if you're always so speedy,' he said. 'I'd be permanently stuffed. But, in all seriousness, you are going to have to be more careful.'

Jayde didn't seem sure whether to laugh or be even more mortified.

'It's okay.' Dave put her out of her misery. 'Hopper, can we have another couple of beers, thanks?'

'I'll pay.'

'Yep, you can, by slowing down and watching where you're going. How'd you get on with your mum? Everything okay?' He used the tea towel Hopper had put on the bar to wipe his hands and trousers.

'What?' Jayde looked confused.

'Your mother. Was she okay?'

'Oh, she'd fallen over and hurt her leg. Didn't need a doctor, but I've dressed it and she's fine. I'll go and check on her again. Poor old Mum's had a bit of a fright, that's all.'

'We're more than happy to call in, if you can't get over,' Dave said. 'I head out that way once a week.'

Two beers appeared at Dave's elbow. 'Cheers, Hopper,' he said.

The barman touched his finger to his forehead. 'All good, boss.'

'Drive home carefully, hey?' Dave said to Jayde and tipped his head towards the restaurant to Jack.

'Sorry again,' Jayde said.

In the restaurant, Dave put the beers down on the table and grabbed a couple of coasters. Kicking out a chair with his foot, he sat down.

'What's this about?' Jack asked, joining him.

Dave held up his beer. 'Cheers, mate.'

Jack didn't answer but raised his glass.

'Right. What's going on?' Dave started twisting the coaster around. 'You applied for DTS?'

Jack put down his glass and stared straight at Dave. 'No.'

'The paperwork is on your desk.'

'Yeah, but I didn't send it in.'

'Why not?'

'Because . . .'

Dave raised his eyebrows and stared at his friend.

'I don't know,' Jack said.

'But you want to?'

'Yeah!' The word burst from him like a river starting to overflow. 'Yeah, I do. Look at all the criminals you've put away, all the crimes you've solved. I see what you've done with your career and I want a bit of that. I want to investigate offences and solve them. Put bastards like Steve Douglas behind bars.

'You've achieved so much and I've done bugger all. I need more than what I can get here.' Jack shut his mouth quickly, breathing heavily, still looking at Dave.

Dave took a sip of beer. He made sure his face didn't show his true feelings; he hated the thought of Jack leaving. 'So why didn't you put the paperwork in?'

Jack's sigh was heavy. 'You. Zara. Lots of reasons. I can't imagine Zara will want to leave Barker. Her mum's here, and she's been through heaps, with her dad and Will dying. I think she's just starting to feel settled. What if asking her to move to Adelaide undoes her?'

'Don't think you're giving her enough credit there, Jack,' Dave said. 'Zara is gutsy and she loves you. But let's put that part aside for a moment. Why else?'

'I'd be leaving you in the lurch.'

'The department would send me someone else. No biggie.' Dave caught the look of hurt across Jack's face. 'Sometimes you have to walk away from things to improve yourself. Trust me, I know. Doesn't mean you aren't good here or you won't be missed. Of course you will be. But if this is what you want, then leaving is the only option, and I sure as hell won't stand in your way. Mate, I know I've got a bit of the grey stuff and a few wrinkles,' he ran his hand over his hair, 'but I still remember how driven I was and what I wanted to achieve when I started out. You've heard me talk about how I had to work my way up before I was the detective in charge of the stock squad and what I had to go through to get there.'

The look on Jack's face indicated he was gathering his thoughts. He lifted his glass. 'Doesn't matter now anyway, the application date has passed.'

'Don't worry about that,' Dave said. 'Do you want to do the course? Obviously, you do. Now is the time to go and make your own career.' He gave a mirthless laugh. 'The state of South Australia is bigger than Barker. Hell, everywhere is bigger than Barker! There's still a lot out there for you.'

'You didn't hear me. The date . . .'

Dave leaned forward and put his elbows on the table. 'Do you want to be a detective? It's a yes or no answer.'

'Yes.'

'Right. I'll fix it so you can put your paperwork in. If they're full, you might have to wait until the next intake, but you might be lucky.'

'It starts in a couple of weeks!' Jack stared at him.

'Well, then, you'd better go and talk to Zara. Get your shit together. Leave the rest to me.'

'I don't . . .'

'You say nothing.' Dave held up his hand in a stop gesture. 'Now go on, get out of here. Talk to Zara. Tell her what you'd like to do.'

'She might not want to come.'

'You've got to have confidence in your relationship. Don't forget her head office is in Adelaide and she spends more time on the road between here and there than is good for her.'

A smile started to spread across Jack's face, then it faded. 'But you.'

'I'm at the end of my career. Wrong side of fifty and all that. You're only starting out. This is your time, not mine.'

'But I'll have to leave. They'll post me somewhere else once I pass the course.'

'That's right.' Dave looked at him steadily.

The grin again. Then Jack drained the last of his beer. 'They're right when they call you a legend,' he said, getting up.

Dave waved him away. 'You can cut that crap out right now. Tell Zara I said hello.'

CHAPTER 10

The gun sat in the wooden box on Mia's passenger seat and she kept glancing at it as she drove. There would be no explanation that would get her out of trouble if she was pulled over by her colleagues.

Still, when she'd knocked on the police station door in Barker, it had been locked up for the night and she hadn't wanted to ring the after-hours number. Having a gun that wasn't licensed to her wasn't an emergency. She would take it into Broad River tomorrow.

Her spotlights picked up the white lines of the road and she kept a keen eye out for any roos. On the way over, there had been a fair bit of roadkill. Not just roos, but emus too. Their feathers flapping in the wind when the cars drove by as if the bird still had life.

She'd found the gun box underneath a roll of windcheater fabric, near the entrance to the cellar. She'd been trying to open the cellar trapdoor. Tugging hard at the stiff lock, it had given away and she'd landed on her bum. Her hip had caught the corner of the box. Talk about a lucky find.

She'd have a beautiful large bruise tomorrow morning.

Unlike the cellar door, the box had opened easily. She'd smelled the gun oil immediately and shoved the papers and diaries to the side in search of what she knew was there. The metallic silver pistol had been at the bottom, wrapped in an oily rag.

In the distance, she could see the lights of Broad River. Another corner, a straight stretch and she'd be home.

In the background, the voices of late-night radio—Philip Clark and regulars from The Mighty Challenge. When she first left school, she'd worked in a fuel station and kept ABC Radio on for company. She knew most of the presenters and their schedules by heart. Night-time radio was always better than day-time radio.

The Nightlife Community wasn't helping her mood tonight though. The store . . . it bothered her. Why hadn't the stock been sold and the store packed up and empty? The expectation had been an empty room, save the cobwebs and decades of dust. That wasn't what she'd found.

Staring through the windscreen, Mia, not for the first time, wished her mother was still alive. Perhaps she would have been able to answer some of the questions that were pinging around her head. After all, all three of them had left Barker at the same time, for Adelaide.

Nana wouldn't be able to remember the answers, Mia suspected. Still, she'd give it a go.

And the gun bothered her even more. Why was it right near the cellar door, the windcheater material thrown haphazardly over the top, as if Nana was trying to hide it? Surely there were better places? Anyone could have pulled back the material and found it, just as she had.

She rubbed the side of her thigh and winced at the pain in her leg. 'Bugger it,' she said softly.

It was far too late to call in to the nursing home and see her nan now, and she wouldn't be able to get there first thing in the morning either. Her shift started at 7 a.m.

No, the questions would have to wait.

'The category we're in are big tourist attractions,' Philip Clark said through the radio speakers. 'Question five. In which town is the Big Galah?'

'Kimba,' Mia muttered, hardly realising she was talking.

She didn't hear the caller answer, but heard Philip say, 'Correct. Question six. In which South Australian town is the Giant Gum Tree?'

This time Mia's mind clicked in as the caller asked him to repeat the question.

She laughed. 'That's easy. Orroroo!' Easy when you live nearby and have seen it a few times.

Flicking on the indicator, Mia turned the steering wheel and rounded onto the main street, heading towards the back lanes. Her lights shone against the windows of her house as she pulled into the driveway, just as the third caller got the name of the town right, although they mispronounced it. Ooroo.

'That's not right! *Oor ro roo.*' She sounded out the syllables.

The night air was cool and filled with the smell of wood smoke. She took a few deep breaths, loving the aroma.

Her car beeped loudly across the darkness as she locked it and headed up the steps to the front door. Mia carried the box, and even though she knew no one was around to see it, she still looked over her shoulder to check no one was watching.

The front door lock clicked and she pushed on the door. It didn't move.

Frowning, Mia pushed again, but it stayed stubbornly locked. She shook the handle.

Nothing.

Turning the key back the other way, she heard it click again and this time it opened.

Standing in the doorway, she inspected the lock. Had she forgotten in her haste this morning to use her keys?

'Surely, I didn't?' she muttered to herself, then took a step inside. She switched the light on in her bedroom. Everything looked the same as when she'd left it that morning. Bed haphazardly pulled up, yesterday's clothes thrown across the end.

In the kitchen nothing had changed either.

She must've forgotten to lock the door when she left. Still, that probably wasn't unreasonable considering how she'd woken up.

The visit from the doc seemed like a week ago, not this morning.

Shutting the front door, Mia made sure it was secured this time. Then double-checked it. Not that she thought there'd be a problem in Broad River. The little town only had about three thousand people living in it, and the farming community lifted the council area to about four thousand. The mixture of elderly and young people was about fifty-fifty, while the place could nearly double in size on a Saturday when there was a footy match.

Her stomach rumbled. The toasted sandwich and coffee had been a long time ago now. She lifted the lid of the car fridge and looked inside, already knowing there was nothing worth eating in there.

The freezer section revealed a frozen meal, which she put in the microwave. Leaning against the bench, she closed her eyes and slumped slightly. Tiredness filtered through every part of her body. She was dirty, dusty and confused.

Tomorrow wasn't exciting her too much either. Her friend, anxiety, had been sitting quietly, but consistently, on her shoulder since her visit to the police station the day before. Richie's attitude hadn't been surprising, only irritating. Of course Mia had come across men who didn't think women were able to be police officers before, and she was more than adept in dealing with them. But no one, man or woman, should have to demonstrate they were capable when they started work. It should be assumed until shown otherwise.

There wasn't any doubting Richie's attitude towards her and she wasn't looking forward to adding it to the list of things to deal with on her first day in a new station.

With the gun taunting her from the bench, where she'd gently laid it, her unease was alive and well. What questions could it answer or stories could it tell? Mia wondered.

There was another four minutes before her dinner would be ready so she picked the pistol up and took it into her bedroom. Wrapping it in a towel and zipping it into the front pouch of an empty suitcase didn't do anything to ease her jitters. A hard shove sent it to the back of the wardrobe. Not ideal, but it would have to do for now.

On the way back to the kitchen, she paused to look at the photo next to her bed. It was from when she was eight, on her first day back at school after the summer holidays, with her nan and mum beside her. They were still tanned from the time they'd spent at the beach and Mia's dark hair was almost blonde at the ends from the sun. Only twelve months before her mother died.

A familiar pinch of pain wound its way around her heart as she picked up the photo.

Eight-year-old Mia only came up to Nana's armpits. Her hair was up in a short ponytail and her school skirt hung below her knees. The shirt looked about a size too big. Mia had always been short for her age, while her mum was tall and willowy, but they both had the same black hair and blue eyes.

There weren't any photos of her father, and even though she'd asked about him, she'd never been given much information. Her nan said Mia got her nose from him, but there had never been any stories like: *Oh, when you smile like that, Mia, you look just like your father.* Or: *Oh, you remind me of your dad, when you do that, Mia.*

Mia had been pleased to hear she had her dad's nose. She was very aware she didn't resemble her mum, except for her colouring. The peaches and cream complexion of her mum's hadn't been gifted to her. Instead, Mia's cheeks and forehead had been covered with acne as a teenager. There were still a few small scars above her eyebrows and in the dimple on her chin where the pussed-up pimples had taunted from. She'd squeezed hard and long, until the blood had come out as well as the bad stuff. Her nan had always told her off: *Squeezing them doesn't do any good. Dab on a bit of metho.* Maybe she was right about squeezing, but there was a lot of satisfaction when the whitehead popped. And metho stung like hell.

The microwave dinged. Mia put the photo down, questions about her father still whirring in her mind. He'd been a mystical figure all her life and she badly wanted to know more about him.

She glanced at the box full of papers, which she'd thrust into the corner of her bedroom, knowing there could be answers inside the wooden slats, but also knowing she was too tired and tomorrow was too close to open that Pandora's box now.

Flicking on the TV, she grabbed her dinner and watched the ending of *Muster Dogs* on the ABC, not tasting the lamb roast she was eating. Her phone in one hand, she scrolled through Facebook, then Twitter and finally Snapchat. Chris had sent her a couple of photos; one of his new desk and the other with his partner. An older woman, with Rogers written on her name tag.

Seems pretty good, this one, he'd said, with a couple of thumbs-up icons.

Mia quickly replied, using her thumb to touch the letters. *I reckon I've got a rogue. Wasn't too pleased to see I had a vagina.*

More fool him, Chris replied. *Hasn't seen you in action.*

Mia had been known for her strength and agility in the academy, but no one ever guessed she had a first-degree black belt in Taekwondo until she brought out the moves. Her mother had enrolled her in lessons when they'd first moved to Adelaide, knowing she had to walk home from school by herself. The confidence they'd given her had made her feel taller and stronger than the wispy five foot nothing she was.

Mia found a strong woman icon and sent it back, then typed, *You okay today?*

Yep, quieter. No more baptism by fire.

Quiet is good.

You?

Found a gun in Nana's shop.

Silence. Mia half smiled to herself. The phone might ring in about three, two . . .

The phone vibrated in her hand.

'What the hell?' Chris asked.

'Your guess is as good as mine.'

'What sort?'

'Handgun. I remember it being around as a kid, but I didn't think it would still be there. It's been two decades! Thank god no one else got their hands on it before I did!'

'What did you do with it?'

'It's in hiding. Not sure how I'm going to handle this yet.'

'You know you need to hand it in straightaway. Not a good idea for a copper to have an unregistered gun in their possession.'

'I don't know if it's unregistered. It's just not on my licence.'

'Don't split hairs. You know exactly what I mean.' His voice was edgy.

'I thought I might show it to Nana, see if it jogs her memory.'

In the silence, Mia thought she heard a tapping at the window. Taking the phone away from her ear, she listened. Then she heard Chris's voice again and focused.

'Or you could just take a photo,' Chris said. 'What if someone walks into her room and there's a gun in the hand of an elderly lady with dementia? I don't think anyone would be too impressed with that.'

'A photo might not do the job.' Although she knew Chris was right, she thought the feel of the gun—its heaviness and smell—might help Nana's memory, maybe something would jump back from the past.

'I'm serious, Mia. They could yank your badge for this.'

'I know, I know.' Mia put down her plate and leaned her head back against the couch. 'The station at Barker was shut when I left and I didn't think it was urgent enough to call the after-hours—' Her voice broke off.

Tap, tap, tap. Mia took the phone away from her ear again and listened. Nothing. A branch on the roof?

'Mia?'

'Sorry, I'm listening.'

'Just take a photo of the firearm on your phone and show her. See what that does. I really don't think you should take the real thing in.'

'Hmm.'

'You're going to, aren't you?'

This time a gust of wind blew a door shut further back in the house and Mia jumped. There were so many new noises to get used to in a new house! Then she remembered the unlocked front door, and she glanced over her shoulder uneasily. Maybe she should check it really was the wind.

With the phone to her ear, she rattled the windows and door, making sure they were closed tightly and locked. The noises were just the house talking to her, she told herself. This time she could ignore them and settle back in her chair.

'I don't know,' she said. 'I keep thinking it might make more of an impact that way, but,' she emphasised the word as Chris began to talk over her, 'I understand what you're saying. I'll think about it a bit more. Anyway, I have a box of diaries and letters to go through too.'

'When are you going to look at those?'

'When I've got a bit of head space. Who knows what I'm going to find in there. Hopefully things about my dad. Photos or something. I still don't get why there was nothing of him when I was growing up, no photos or anything. Certainly never any conversations about him.'

'Maybe photos were too painful to keep.'

Mia closed her eyes. Her body was so heavy; she needed sleep. 'Surely Nana wouldn't have got rid of them all? Wouldn't she want a memory of her son for later? When the grief wasn't so raw.'

'I don't know the answers. I'm just throwing a few ideas out.'

'It's just weird. Not having one thing left of him. Maybe they're all in the box.'

'I can't believe you didn't have at least a tiny peek.'

'Not even a minute one. I've had a big enough day as it is.'

'You sure have.' Chris's voice was soft. 'And you could be right about the box. And if not that box, maybe there will be another place where all the keepsake things could be. Special things, photos, letters. You know, all that shit. You should have seen the stuff we threw out when I helped Mum clean out Gran's place after she died. I reckon she had every freaking card I ever gave her!' He paused and Mia heard him take a sip of something. 'I'm sure you don't know everything about your nan.'

The special smile Nana used to give Mr Marshall came to Mia. Nana always got a bit giggly when he came around. Sometimes he'd perch on the edge of the counter and talk to Nan while she knitted; other times, they'd go outside to bring something in from his car.

Sometimes he'd bring Mia a book from the library and sit and read it to her. His voice had been deep and gravelly, and Mia had always thought he was a giant.

'I'm sure you're right,' she said. 'And I'm also positive that I don't need to know everything. But I would like to know a bit more about my dad.'

'As horrible as this sounds, time is of the essence then. Your nan's memory is only going to get worse, and if you don't start asking questions soon, you might never get the answers.'

CHAPTER 11

Jack let himself into the house he shared with Zara, nervousness shooting through him. He'd never thought about leaving Barker until the last major investigation he was involved with, although the idea of becoming a detective had been around a while. As much as the revelations that the school principal had molested his younger sister and murdered his cousin—and everything else that investigation had revealed—had scarred him, it had invigorated him too.

He'd heard all of Dave's old war stories, from when he was undercover chasing cattle thieves in Queensland or protecting a young Aboriginal man from a spiteful and vengeful white family. Dave had told him about the bodies he'd found, along with a pallet full of drugs in the north of Western Australia, and the crimes he hadn't managed to solve.

'Every copper has some of them,' Dave had told him. 'At least one case, or several. They might not really haunt

you, but they'll certainly tap you on the shoulder sometimes. And let's not forget, Jack, I worked with a team. I
didn't bring any of these mongrels down single-handedly.'

Dave was just being modest.

And Jack was envious. The number of cases Dave had
solved was astronomical, and he wanted a piece of that.
Dave had cautioned him numerous times that being a
detective wasn't all it was cracked up to be. There were
long, tedious hours wading through evidence and witness
statements. You had to follow up with witnesses and take
phone calls from people who thought the crime could
have been committed by their ex-boyfriend's stepbrother.
'Because, ya know, mate, I saw him with a girl who looked
like that once and he just looked like he could do something awful to her.'

And the crime scenes were never pretty. Jack had also
never forgotten the adrenalin that had rushed through him
when he'd gone undercover to try to infiltrate an animal
welfare group. Two weeks of living on his wits, four years
ago had been the start of his yearning to be more. Every
other case he'd worked had only brought him another notch
closer to wanting to be a detective.

Nothing could shift the bubble of excitement from Jack's
stomach when he thought about arriving at a scene and
being the one responsible for bringing closure to a family
who were in the depths of grief, or bringing a person to
court for stealing someone's livelihood.

He also knew of the guilt that still weighed heavily
on Dave's shoulders when he talked of the loss of his

mother-in-law and family. Well, talked was an exaggeration. Dave said very little on the subject, but Jack knew the incident with Bulldust had changed every facet of his life. The remorse never left his friend. Neither did the regret of missing out on seeing his two daughters grow up, after his ex-wife had barred him from seeing them.

Dave always brushed over the marriage break-up. 'I'm glad it ended,' he'd say. 'Otherwise, I wouldn't be with Kim.'

Even so, Jack saw his friend's sorrow when his girls were brought up. They were close now, but Dave had missed many years of their lives.

'That you, Jack?' Zara called from the office.

He took off his jacket and breathed in deeply. 'Sure is.'

She appeared at the door with a smile. 'Hey, you,' she said softly, coming towards him for a kiss.

'Hey, you back.' Jack slipped his arms around her waist and pulled her close. 'Good day?'

There was silence for a moment, then Zara answered. 'Busy. Two stories written and submitted, talked to Lachie and—'

'And what did your slave driver of an editor want you to do for him? Write another fifty stories by tomorrow?'

Zara laughed. They both knew the *Farming Journal*'s editor was so laid-back he could be horizontal.

'Nope, just another three stories for later. They need editing, but they're not going in this week's paper, so I'm all yours tonight. Want to go to the pub for dinner?' She looked at him sheepishly. 'I was too busy to organise anything.'

Jack held her hand as they walked down the hallway. 'Now, why am I not surprised?' he asked.

'I got caught up in an interview. But on the good side, I lit the fire. The lounge room is warm.'

'How'd I get so lucky?' Jack replied with a grin, opening the fridge and pulling out a beer.

'Don't be silly.'

'Wine?'

'Sure, why not? So, dinner at the pub? I need to see if Hopper has got any goss for me.'

'Not sure,' Jack answered, getting out a wine glass. 'I've just come from there with Dave. It's fairly busy.'

'Oh. Maybe takeaway from the roadhouse then?'

'Yeah, or I could cook?' He opened the fridge to see what ingredients they had.

'Jack, I didn't do the shopping either. Sorry.'

Jack wanted to be annoyed, but he hadn't had time to do the shopping either and Zara was looking at him with a regretful expression on her face along with a half smile. They were opposites: he was a creature of habit, while Zara was the epitome of chaos. She worked hard, like Jack did, but he was methodical, and probably, he acknowledged, a bit of a plodder. That's what made him a good copper and would make him a brilliant detective. Dave had told him that once, a while back. Jack had stored the compliment away.

Zara, on the other hand, had no trouble breaking the rules to get the answers or stories she was looking for. She was passionate about the articles she wrote and getting the information the agricultural industry needed. They were chalk and cheese. Yin and yang.

How would she react to what he had to say? The nervous fizzing in his stomach made him feel slightly sick and he had to hide behind the mask that his training at the academy had taught him to present.

He handed her the glass of wine and then led her into the lounge.

Laughing, Zara followed behind. 'What are you doing, Jack?' Her hair was falling around her face and her eyes were bright with mischief.

He sat, pulling her down, holding one of her hands. 'Sit here. I want to talk to you about something.'

'Oh.' The word came out softly as Zara's eyes widened. 'Do you now?' She looked at him expectantly and leaned behind her to put down her drink. 'This sounds interesting.'

'This is going to come out of the blue,' Jack said, nervously. His hands were sweaty, but he didn't want to let go of Zara in case she ran away when he told her. 'I'd—' he stopped and looked at her '—I'd like to apply to become a detective.'

Zara was still for a moment, and Jack could see her comprehending what he'd just said. Then he saw a flash of disappointment before she rearranged her face into a grin. 'You'd make a great detective,' she said. 'I bet Dave thinks so too.'

'Yeah, that's what we were talking about tonight.'

Jack searched her face. The penny hadn't dropped yet.

'When do you start? And how do you—' Zara stopped.

He could see the realisation crash into her. Too many emotions crossed her face for Jack to name.

She leaned back and picked up her glass. 'You'd better tell me how this all works.'

He spoke quickly, hoping that might take some of the edge off his words. 'It would mean moving to Adelaide,' he said. 'Now, I know this might not suit you. You've got your mum and your work here. But I can't do the course from Barker. The DTS has to be done at the academy.' He wiped his hands on his pants, then took a sip of his beer. 'And there's a bit more to it. If I pass, I won't be stationed back here. I'll have to cut my teeth somewhere else.'

'DTS? What's that? Detective Training . . . What? School?'

Jack nodded.

'Will you ever be stationed back here?'

'Not for a long time. Barker doesn't need two detectives. Only a sergeant and senior connie really. Dave was lucky to get stationed here with his qualifications.'

He could see Zara wanted to make a sarcastic remark. Probably something like 'Haven't you seen what's happened around here lately?' because more than once they'd joked about the area becoming like *Midsomer Murders*, but she kept her mouth shut and her body very still as she processed what Jack had told her.

'It doesn't matter if you don't want to shift with me, Zara,' Jack rushed on quickly, wondering why he'd let Dave talk him into this. 'You can stay here, and we'll make us work in other ways.'

But of course, it mattered! He wanted to come home to Zara every night and tell her about his day. Hear about hers. Snuggle into bed with her, smelling her freshly washed hair. Hear her laugh . . .

'Jack, you're not listening!' Zara pulled his hand towards her mouth and kissed his palm.

'Sorry.' He focused on her face, seeing a large smile and a look he recognised as patience.

'You were freaking out in your head again, weren't you?'

'I, ah . . .'

She shushed him.

'You're right, it's pretty out of the blue. There's a fair bit to take in, so sorry if I don't seem over the moon with the idea. But I am.' Smiling, Zara put her hand to his cheek and looked at him intently. 'You'll have to explain what happens from here, because I know nothing about the DTS.'

'I'm not sure yet either. I didn't put the paperwork in on time, but Dave says he can fix it and get me in. Might not be this round. Could be the next one. I guess it's all up in the air until I know which intake I can get into.'

Zara nodded. 'Okay, so like in the next twelve months or sooner?'

Jack looked at her. 'Maybe in a month?'

That stilled Zara again, then she nodded. 'Okay.' She crossed her arms over her chest. 'What about Dave?'

Jack shrugged. 'I don't want to leave Barker, or Dave, but at the same time, I do. It's the weirdest feeling.' He wondered how to explain it to her. 'He seemed fine with it tonight. Told me I had to get out and do what I had to.'

'So,' she spoke slowly, 'let me get this right. You want to leave Barker, where you've lived for, what?' she raised her hands. 'Seven years? And go to . . . Adelaide? What's brought this on? I thought we were happy here.'

'We are,' Jack said, desperately trying to work out how to tell her he needed more than that now. 'I don't know . . .'

'Come on, Jack, of course you do. There must be a reason. I know you, and you would've been thinking about this for ages. I can't believe you haven't talked to me. And obviously you hadn't spoken to Dave before tonight either.'

Jack saw the hurt on her face and cursed himself. 'Yeah, you're right. I wasn't sure how to bring it up with you. You left Adelaide to come up here and take care of your brother before he died. You left your job and—'

'Whoa, hold on. I didn't leave my job. I changed my office address. I still go to Adelaide to see Lachie and all the crew in head office. I can just as easily change it back again.'

'Sorry, I meant you've made your life here too. Your mum is on the farm and I didn't want you to have to choose to come with me. You've got your career and—' he broke off and looked her in the eye '—so do I.'

'And we should be able to make them work together.' Zara spoke firmly.

Jack regarded her carefully. 'What does that mean?'

'As a journalist, my work is flexible, just so long as I have internet. So I can go wherever you go, Jack,' Zara said quietly. 'Sure, I'll miss Mum, and strangely, considering I didn't really want to move back here at the time, I'll miss

Barker too.' She shrugged. 'I've had a lot of fun here in the last couple of years, but there's been some really crappy times too, don't forget.'

'Yeah.' The worst time Jack could remember was standing near Zara as the footy club blokes lowered her brother's coffin into the grave. They hadn't been together then, but Jack had noticed Zara and he'd wanted to be able to take away the pain she was feeling.

'But none of that matters if I'm going to be with you.'

'Seriously?' Jack couldn't quite believe what he was hearing.

'Yeah.' Grabbing her wine, Zara smiled at him over her glass. 'What happens at DTS then?'

CHAPTER 12

The one word note on her desk was clear.

Worthless.

Sometimes Mia hated her surname. Worth. It wasn't the first time that joke had been pulled, but it set the tone for her first day.

No prizes in guessing who had written it.

'Dickhead,' she muttered, screwing up the paper and tossing it towards the bin.

'Did they leave you a love letter?' Marty Hooper said from the doorway. 'Don't worry about it, if they did. Those blokes always like to play a few practical jokes on anyone new.' His large frame leaned against the wall, and he wore a smile almost as large as the stomach straining against the buttons on his shirt. 'Welcome, officially, to Broad River cop shop.' He spread out his arms. 'A quiet little country town that can change at any moment.'

'Thanks, Marty, that sounds like a bad crime TV show!'
Mia smiled back. 'Looking forward to the challenge.'

'The guys will be back shortly. They go down to the
bakery every morning and get a coffee. You'll have to let
them know your poison so they can get you one.'

Mia didn't think that was going to be an option. With
Richie's attitude, it was more likely she'd be given a coffee
after someone had spat in it, or worse. Although maybe
Greg would be kinder.

'Worth, welcome to Broad River.'

A low, gravelly voice filtered through the doorway from
behind Marty, who straightened and nodded, before leaving
Mia's sight.

'Sarge,' she said, taking a few steps towards the door.

Sergeant Zach Tyler walked in. His tall frame seemed
to fill the room and his icy blue eyes locked on hers. Mia
squirmed under his scrutiny. She was yet to see the 'good
bloke' Greg had mentioned.

Drawing herself up to her full five foot height, she tried
to smile confidently.

'Settled in?' he asked, standing in front of her, hands
in his pockets.

'Yeah, not too much to organise. Ready to get out and
about.'

'Richie will be back shortly and you two can head out
on patrol up RM Williams Way. It's school holidays and
there are a lot of caravaners around.'

'Great. Be good to see a bit more of the area. Ah, Sarge, can you tell me a bit about the town? Is it busy? Any drugs, graffiti? Anyone I have to look out for?'

'Oh, look, Friday and Saturday nights are the same in any country town,' the sarge said dismissively. 'Heap of people get on the gas in the pub. Some try to drive home; some have more brains. We usually do a bit of a drive-by early in the evenings. See if there are any troublemakers' cars there, then make sure we're around when the pub shuts. Sometimes there're fights, sometimes not. Not really any trouble with high-school kids regarding drugs, as far as I'm aware. Broad River is a quiet place, with a few normal outbursts during the year.'

'Hey, boss, what about the Starling lad?' Marty called from the front desk.

Zach leaned against the closest desk and crossed his arms. 'Yeah, well he could become a problem. Bloke just left school and hasn't been able to find himself a job in the six months since. Caught him lifting a few things recently. I think he's bored rather than bad. There's a difference.' He stared at her, those hard eyes assessing her again. 'I hope you know that difference, Worth.'

'Yes, Sarge, I do. Does he have any mates?'

Pursing his lips, Zach nodded. 'Yeah, there's a group of about six, they all play footy together. All the others have jobs. Farm employees, a fitter and turner—his mates are busy during the week. You know the saying, idle hands, idle minds. I don't like seeing that anywhere.'

117

'Do we have any police-run youth groups?' Mia scratched around on her desk, looking for the pen she'd brought with her.

Zach scoffed. 'Out here? Where do you reckon I'd pull that money out of the budget?' He tossed his head a bit. 'You interested in running something, Worth?'

'I like young people, Sarge.' Mia nodded. 'Don't like seeing them turn from bored into bad—' She broke off as the banging of the screen door echoed through the station.

An expression that Mia couldn't read passed over Zach's face. Maybe he didn't like it when his own words were thrown back at him.

'Here are the troops,' Zach said. 'Have any trouble, let me know. You're with Richie.'

Drew, Richie and Greg came in with coffees, their cheeks glowing red from the cold wind.

'Sorry, Worth,' Richie said as he pulled the chair under his desk out with his foot and plonked himself down. 'Didn't know what you wanted, so couldn't get you anything.' He held his takeaway cup up in a cheers gesture.

'Thanks for thinking of me, Richie.' Mia smiled, hoping it looked a lot more friendly than she felt. 'You'll know the way I take my coffee by the time we've finished our patrol today.'

Drew gave a whistle and clapped Richie on the shoulder. 'Better look out, man.'

Greg just threw both men a bored look, stopping short of telling them to cut it out.

Mia ignored them all, while she clipped on her belt and checked the contents.

'You boys still in high school?' Zach asked, appearing again from his office. He wore a frown. 'Give her a chance until she proves otherwise. Come on, let's get on with it.'

Mia opened her mouth but quickly shut it again. What the actual hell? *Until she proves otherwise.* Like they all expected her to stuff up. Anger surged through her chest, and once again, she drew herself up, determined not to let any of them get the better of her today. Or any day. Misogynistic pricks.

'We off then?' she asked, hardening her eyes at Richie.

He smirked at her as he lay sprawled in his chair.

She fought the urge to put her foot firmly in the back of the chair and send him hurtling towards the wall. Instead, she smiled and walked through the office, heading for the front door and the patrol car parked against the kerb.

The seconds seemed like forever until she heard a heavy sigh behind her.

'Just like my missus. Bossy as fuck. Catch you later, fellas. I'll be looking for a beer tonight.'

Laughter rose behind Mia, but she didn't turn.

Outside, she stood by the car, waiting for Richie to unlock it. He smirked again as he pulled open the door and climbed into the driver's seat. Without using the keys.

Mia sagged a little. Of course, they would rarely lock the cars out here. She got in and pulled her seatbelt on as Richie accelerated away, with a small screech. Mia saw a young boy riding his bike along the footpath. He was grinning at the car with a look of awe on his face.

Great role model, she thought.

The blinker ticked as they turned a corner and drove towards the edge of Broad River: through the dip where the ducks crossed the road, over the train line and out past the pub and machinery dealers, until they hit the wide-open agricultural land.

The paddocks beside the road were flat with large gum trees dotted here and there. Most of the fences had broken wires and bent fenceposts. Didn't matter that the fences were buggered though. It was crop as far as Mia could see. Not how she remembered it from her childhood when the paddocks were packed with merino ewes.

In the distance, stone farmhouses pressed against the range of hills that ran north–south. The buildings and machinery looked tired. Dilapidated.

Their patrol car seemed like the newest thing in the district. Other than the large, lazily swinging wind turbines atop the line of hills, catching the wind. *Whoomp, whoomp, whoomp.* Generating power to light and cool the homes across South Australia.

'Aren't they huge eyesores?' Mia commented, nodding towards the windmills.

Richie didn't answer.

'They been up there long?'

'Nope.'

'Pretty controversial, weren't they? Seem to remember reading something in the paper about them.'

A one-shoulder shrug.

Anger began to burn in Mia again. She changed the subject. 'How long have you been in Broad River?'

'Few years.' Richie kept his eyes on the road and drove carefully at one hundred kilometres an hour. He checked the radar for every car that went by and seemed content not to have any conversation with Mia.

She looked out of the window, racking her brains for more questions. He was her partner and it was important they got along. What could she say that would prove her 'worth'? Even as she had the thought, she knew no words would change his mind.

Why did she have to anyway?

Greg's words came back to her: 'He does it to all of the new connies, until they prove themselves.' So not a gender thing? She wasn't so sure.

'You're married then?' she asked him. 'Heard you mention your wife. Got kids?'

Richie turned to stare at her for a second then looked back at the road.

Mia tapped her fingers on her legs now. The countryside was flying by and she recognised places and landscapes. The abandoned stone pub with the sagging verandah on the side of the road. It had been tens of years since anyone had propped the bar up there.

They drove past the airstrip on the outskirts of town and a well-maintained community hall with two tennis courts next to it. Weeping pepper trees covered in red pods.

'One wife, two kids, both at the primary school. Boy and girl,' Richie finally said, in short, sharp words.

Then he leaned over and turned on the radio. Music pulsed through the speakers, too loud to continue a conversation.

Stuff this, Mia thought. She reached over and turned the radio off, then swivelled in her seat to look at Richie. Even with his sunglasses on, she could tell he was glaring at her.

His jaw was twitching and his knuckles on the steering wheel were white. Signs he was trying to keep his temper from erupting.

'Sorry, Richie, have we got off on the wrong foot? Is there something I've done wrong?'

Richie made to turn the radio on, but she put her hand in front of the button.

'Would you mind answering my question?'

'Don't have an answer for you.' He turned away, leaning his elbow on the window, staring moodily in front.

'Look, this is my first day. Is there a problem?'

'What do you think.' Statement not a question.

'Well, let's talk.' Mia pushed her sunglasses up on her head and looked over. Richie's face had changed from an arrogant smirk to dislike.

'No need. We didn't ask for a connie, for *you*, to come here.'

'There was a vacancy . . .'

Richie pulled up in a cloud of dust beside the road.

Feeling uneasy, Mia kept her hands in her lap and waited.

Richie put the car into park and yanked on the handbrake. He leaned close enough for Mia to smell the stale coffee on his breath. It took everything in her willpower not to pull back. Instead, she kept looking him in the eye.

'Yeah.' Richie's voice was low and menacing. 'There was a vacancy. But not for a new connie or a woman. I like working with coppers who've got experience. No fuck-ups that way.'

The engine changed tone as the air conditioner kicked in.

A million responses raced through Mia's mind.

Why does that matter?

What's your problem with women?

Your dick so small you gotta take it out on others?

She said none of them.

Instead, she unclipped her seatbelt and got out of the car, slamming the door hard. She dragged in angry breaths, before turning, her pointer finger aimed towards him.

Richie was out of the car too. Leaning his elbows on the roof, watching her, amused.

'You bastard! You arrogant . . .' She broke off as she took a step closer to him. 'What's your problem with women coppers?'

Richie threw his hands up in the air. 'No need to get emotional.' He got back in the car and slammed the door, revving the engine a couple of times.

Taking a few breaths to calm herself, Mia closed her eyes. God! She'd played right into his hands.

Back inside, Mia reached to put on her seatbelt and turned to apologise. Richie was being a prick, but she shouldn't have responded like that.

'Well,' Mia said finally looking straight ahead, 'I guess this is going to be a long shift.'

CHAPTER 13

Mia flung her jacket onto the lounge.

'Bastards,' she hissed as she went to the bedroom and undressed. 'Mongrels.' Flinging clothes from the chest of drawers, she found her workout tights and shirt and pulled them on, still seething.

The trip with Richie hadn't improved. He'd pulled over a couple of cars to check licence plates, including a businessman who was late for a meeting in Adelaide. Richie hadn't done anything except sit in the driver's seat and play on his phone, while Mia had called in the licence numbers and written a speeding ticket.

Out on the street, she did a few stretches to warm up and then walked briskly along the footpath. A couple of blocks later she broke into a jog, keeping her pace steady as music blasted through her headphones.

The beat was heavy, and she ran in time to the drums.

Doof, doof, doof. Her breath settled into the same tempo as her feet and everything else seemed to disappear. Her disappointment, her humiliation and Richie's smug smile. All gone in the haze of cement footpaths and her measured gait. One step in front of the other.

The rhythm of running soon calmed her. Her running app told her she'd completed eight kilometres at an average pace of seven minutes per kilometre. Faster than her normal time, but that wasn't surprising considering how angry she'd been when she'd first walked out the gate.

She slowed to a cool-down walk, her hands on her hips and breathing heavily. A car went by and Mia wondered how long it would take her to recognise all the cars that regularly frequented Broad River, and how long it would take for people to realise she was the new copper.

She was now only a block away from the nursing home, she checked the time.

Dinner would have come and gone by now and Casey was probably taking the nightly cups of tea and Milo around to the residents. Mia decided to head towards her nan.

The outside lights were on, even though the dimness of the evening was only just setting in.

'Hello, Mia. Come to see Clara?'

Mia spun at the male voice behind her and smiled when she saw it was Dr Thompson.

'I'm a bit late.'

'Wouldn't worry, they'll let you in. Family should always be able to visit at any time.' He smiled and Mia noticed his bow tie was slightly crooked.

'Have you had a busy day?' she asked.

The doctor kept up a cracking pace as he moved towards the door, but the way he lifted his glasses and rubbed his eyes told Mia he was tired.

'I went to Barker to run the childhood vaccination clinic today.'

'I didn't realise you covered that area.'

'They have a hospital and nurses, but the doctor who was there left and hasn't been replaced. I go over there once a week to run a clinic. Speak with the nurses every day and do a teleconference if things are more severe. I am hoping another doctor will start in due course.' He held the door open for her.

'Lots of kilometres for you then.'

'That comes with rural living. Of course, the drive is a good way to unwind. Now, I must check in on a couple of patients, but I'll see you again soon, Mia.' He nodded to her, spoke quickly with the receptionist and headed down a corridor before tapping gently on a door.

Mia heard him say a warm hello before the door clicked behind him, then she headed down the opposite passageway.

'Who's there?' Clara asked when Mia entered, her nan's voice sounding as if she had been asleep.

'Just me, Nana. Mia.' She thought she'd better add her name, in case Clara became confused.

'Hello, dear.' Clara was leaning forward, brushing the crumbs from her dressing-gown. 'Have a good day?'

At those words, Mia's heart felt like it was going to explode from hurt. She wished she could tell Nana everything. About the patrol with Richie and the horrible note that had been left on her desk, but she was frightened of upsetting her.

Instead, she sat down and took Clara's hand and held it to her cheek. She breathed in the familiar scent of Vaseline Intensive Care lotion and the vague smell of soap.

'Are you all right, love?' her nan asked softly.

'I'm fine. Long day. How was yours? Did you go for your walk?'

Fitness had always been important to her nan and, even now, failing memory and all, she walked every day.

'Oh yes.' She paused. 'We went out into the garden and walked around. It was lovely to see the roses.'

'They've got heaps of flowers here, haven't they?'

'But not an ounce of smell! I don't know why the gardeners plant the ones without a fragrance. The blooms are beautiful, but they don't seem like a rose when there's no—' she waved her hands around '—thingy.'

'Smell.'

A word known two sentences previously and forgotten so quickly. The thief kept stealing.

'Yes.'

The only noise in the room was the low hum of the TV and the ABC news.

Nana refocused. 'Were you at the police station today?'

Mia nodded. 'We did a patrol out towards Barker.'

'That's nice. What did the countryside look like?'

'Seems like livestock aren't the flavour of the month. All I saw was crops.'

'Young people don't like to work anymore.' Her nan's tone was sharp. 'Cropping is easy. Sit on a tractor in the air conditioning.'

Mia raised her eyebrows in surprise. The last time she could remember hearing her nan use that tone was when she had snuck out of her boarding school and caught a tram to Glenelg to watch a movie with a boy. It had been a school night and exam time, so all leave had been revoked. Mia hadn't cared. The boy had been worth the grounding she'd got later.

She wondered what Brad was doing now. They'd gone out a few times, but once school had finished their brief relationship had fizzled into nothingness.

'I went to Barker yesterday.' The words were out of her mouth before she realised she'd said them.

'Did you?'

'I took the key you gave me. To the shop.'

'Oh yes, the key,' Nana said. A pause. 'To what?'

'The shop,' Mia repeated. 'Simpson's Haberdashery.'

'Ah . . .' A peaceful look settled on Clara's face. 'My store.'

'It looked the same as I remember it.'

'So it should! I left it like that.'

Mia picked up Clara's hand again and rubbed her thumb back and forth on the top. 'There's heaps of clothes and fabric. Crockery . . .'

'I had to keep it stocked well. Didn't want to run out of anything. In 1922 when my dear mum, god rest her soul, was in charge, there was a large flood. Nine inches over a week. I'll never forget it. Water stretched out across the flood plains as far as you could see. Made the ranges look like islands. All the roads were cut off. Couldn't get supplies in and out for weeks. That's why I always kept as much as I could.

'Mum's shelves were empty by the time the first load of freight could get through and there were people who were hungry. I was too.'

Mia had read somewhere that the past was the easiest place for people with dementia to live. It had been a long time since Nana had said such a coherent sentence without stopping to search for words, or because she'd forgotten her train of thought.

'You were hungry?' Mia asked.

'Oh yes. The tinned food ran out about two weeks in, but we managed. We always did back then.' Clara smiled, lost in memories. 'Do you know, dear, Mrs Burns came in wanting five tins of Spam. There was only her and her husband living together at the time, and we wondered what on earth they wanted that many tins for! Turned out they were feeding the meat to their cats.'

Mia laughed. She was trying to work out what questions to ask her nan that wouldn't upset her.

'And Mr Ford, he always insisted on collecting his stores at exactly two o'clock on the dot. Once everything was loaded, he would make it to the pub twenty-five miles down the road by four. Then he'd drink two beers and set off home again.' There was a silence. 'I could tell you the whole town's preferences for food and clothes; what wedding presents were bought before the bride and groom opened them. We always knew everything that was going on in town.'

'Everything?'

'Ninety per cent of things, I'm sure.' Clara seemed very certain. 'I was the first after the police to know that Old Joe, the shepherd from the plains, had perished out in the bush. You know why? Because I had to organise for his body to be buried. No family.'

'Why did he die?'

'Ah, poor old Joe. Nice fella, but goodness me, his dog, Ripper, meant everything to him. Dingo killed that animal and Joe couldn't accept he was gone. He kept searching and searching. He died looking for him. I believe—' Clara leaned forward as if to share a dark secret '—that Joe died from a broken heart, not lack of water. That dog was his only companion. Only family . . .' Her voice trailed away.

Mia opened her mouth.

'I've been out on the flats late at night,' Clara continued, 'when it's pitch black. No moon, only the stars for light and I've seen the lantern light.'

Goosebumps crept across Mia's arms. 'As in . . .'

'Yes, Nicole, Joe is still trawling the countryside looking for Ripper, long after his death.'

Mia's heart was beating a tad too fast for her liking. She didn't believe in ghosts, but the way Nana told the story had Mia hanging on every word. And she'd just called her by her mother's name again.

Clara straightened up and her face cleared from the dark memory. 'Mr Lewis donated half an acre of his land to the Uniting Church. I think I was almost the first to hear about that, because he couldn't keep his mouth shut. Always thought he was cut from a different cloth, that man.' She tutted.

'Then Mrs Took, I knew she was cavorting with Mr Knight before the rest of the town did. See, her husband, Mr Took, liked Turkish Delight chocolates. One day she started buying a different chocolate: Rocky Road. Now there were only four people in Barker who bought that chocolate and three of them were women. Didn't take long to work out what was going on there. Sure enough, Mrs Took left her husband and took up with Mr Knight about three months later.'

Mia felt a giggle erupt from her chest. 'Nana you were a regular old gossip!'

'Oh no, dear. I never said a word to anyone about what I knew. That was what made me a good shopkeeper. People would come and sit at the counter and talk to me, assured what they said would go no further.'

'You must have loved being there.'

'Oh, Nicole, you know I do.'

'Nana, it's me, Mia,' she said, still stroking her grand-mother's hand.

'Of course!' There was impatience in Clara's voice now. 'That's what I said.'

Knowing it was futile to argue, Mia nodded, her sadness welling again.

'Was the store very dusty, dear?' her nan continued. 'I'll have to make sure everything is spotless. The dust storms make it hard to keep the place clean . . . That fine red dust filters into everything. The duster is down in the cellar. I must bring it up when I go down there next.'

Mia decided to answer in the present day. 'Yeah, it was pretty dusty, Nan, and there were lots of spider webs, but I can get them all cleaned up easily enough.' Mia took a breath. 'There was a gun, Nan—'

'No, there isn't.' Clara interrupted. 'Absolutely not.'

'Actually, there was. I brought it home with me, but I think I'll have to give it to the police because—'

'What?' Clara half rose and looked around. 'No, it can't go to the police! And the gun has gone, Nicole. I told you. We made sure, Theo and I . . .' Her hands ran up and down her thighs quickly.

'I'm Mia, Nana.' She knew she had to move away from the topic of the firearm, otherwise Clara would be too agitated to sleep.

'Of course, you are,' Clara said, but Mia had the feeling her nan didn't know what she was agreeing to. Her face closed over again. 'We mustn't talk of it. We made a promise.'

'Okay, okay,' Mia soothed. 'It's okay.' Her mind was racing. What had Nana been involved with?

'You can't give it to the police.'

'I won't. I'll keep it safe.'

'That's a good girl. You always were a good girl, Nicole.'

'Nan,' Mia spoke gently, 'why didn't you sell all the stock when you left? Why didn't you sell the building?'

Clara looked at her and Mia could see by her eyes that she was back in the present day. She knew exactly who she was talking to and about what.

'Surely that's obvious. I always intended to go back.'

CHAPTER 14

'DTS, Detective McLeod speaking.'

'Dave Burrows here, Macca. How're you getting on?'

'Dave? Mate! Great to hear from you. It's been a few years.'

'Sure has. Still lining up new dees?'

'Best job in the world, mate, teaching the next generation of detectives. What about you? You still out bush somewhere?'

They continued to catch up, while Dave pushed Jack's paperwork around his desk. The heavy stone sitting in his stomach hadn't gone away since his conversation with Jack last night.

His friend's text late yesterday evening had been excited. *Zara's on board.*

When Dave had told Kim the news, her look of shock expressed how he was feeling inside.

'Mate, I'm guessing you're not ringing for a yarn,' Macca said after they'd exhausted their small talk.

'Spot on.' Dave picked up a pen and started tapping it up and down on the desk. 'I've got a young bloke who's been working with me out here in Barker for about seven years. Great bloke. Got a real good head on his shoulders and would make an excellent, methodical dee.'

'Oh yeah?'

'He filled out all the forms but got nervous about asking me to support his application.'

'Why?'

'Just worried about leaving me in the lurch, 'cause there's only two of us at the station.' Dave purposely didn't say anything about Zara. Macca wouldn't want a trainee detective who might be tied to apron strings. Dave knew that wouldn't happen to Jack and Zara, but Macca didn't.

'What do you want from me?'

'Wondering if the DTC was full for the next intake?'

There was a pause and Dave could hear Macca flicking through papers on his desk.

'Well, as it happens, I've had a bloke from down south pull out, so I've got a spot. Can you get the forms through to me ASAP?'

'Just got to put my ditty on them.' Dave kept his voice energetic, but his stomach had dropped.

'Good. Get 'em through and I'll send him the confirmation email this afternoon.'

'Jack'll be grateful. Thanks, Macca.'

136

'You want him to move on?' It was as if Macca had read Dave's mind.

'Mixed feelings,' Dave answered honestly. 'I don't want to see him leave, but he has too much potential to sit here at the arse end of the earth. He needs to start making his own career.'

'Sorry about taking him off your hands then. But I'll look out for him.'

'Cheers, mate. I know you will.'

'Get that paperwork through and get him organised. I'll see him in a couple of weeks.'

'Thanks, again.'

'Welcome.'

Dave slowly put down the phone, already feeling the loneliness of being the only copper in town.

Jack was like his right hand. Always there.

And now his desk was going to sit empty.

Had Spencer felt like that when Dave had gone undercover or taken the job in the stock squad? Dave had never given his old partner a thought when he'd made those decisions because he had a goal he was aiming for. The stock squad. And because Spencer had come to him with those opportunities. He wouldn't have left Dave wallowing in Barrabine for years. No, Spencer looked for openings for Dave when he thought he was ready for them. That's what good mentors did.

And that was why Jack had to do the dees' training.

Picking up his mobile phone, Dave's fingers hovered over the screen. As soon as he told Jack it was all systems go, he'd have lost him. Right now, he was still his partner.

'Get a grip, Burrows,' he muttered to himself. With a quick movement, he unlocked the screen and hit speed dial.

'It's Dave,' he said unnecessarily when Jack answered the phone. He didn't know why he always introduced himself when he knew his name would come up on the other person's phone.

There was an intake of breath and Jack said, 'How'd you get on?'

'You're in. Confirmation will be in your inbox this afternoon. I'll make the necessary calls to the powers that be. Don't worry about coming in this morning. Do what you need to, packing or whatever. Just swing by late this arvo and check your emails, all right?'

'Are you sure?'

'Mate, you've got less than fourteen days and a shitload of things to do, so I'd get on with it if I was you.' Dave knew he was sounding gruff and instantly regretted it.

'No worries, I'll see you this afternoon. And, Dave, thanks. This is really important to me.'

'I know. See you later.' Dave hung up and opened the messaging app.

They're on the move, he sent to Kim.

He pushed his chair back from the desk, and leaned forward, his elbows resting on his knees, face on his palm.

The phone dinged. Ignoring it, he took a few more deep breaths and then stood up. This was Jack's choice and it was a good one.

Kim's text showed a sad face with a tear.

The door between the front desk and their offices was shut. Joan didn't know anything about this yet. She'd be as upset as he was.

Dave opened the door and saw Joan bent over the filing cabinet, a pile of paper on top.

'No rest for the wicked,' he said, grabbing a chair and rolling it towards her. He turned it around and sat facing the back, watching her work.

'I must have been extremely bad in a previous life,' Joan said, glancing up, her silver-rimmed glasses perched on the end of her nose. They matched her grey hair. 'You two keep piling up this paperwork. I thought we were supposed to be going digital.'

Dave laughed. 'I think there's always going to be paper-work in a cop shop.'

Joan straightened and closed the drawer, doing her best to ignore the screech as she did. 'Got any oil?'

'That's horrible! I'll bring some lithium grease in tomorrow.'

'I'm sure you and Jack will have piled up more reports for me to file by then.'

'Well,' Dave leaned back and breathed in deeply through his nose, 'you'll only have to keep up with me from now on.'

Joan stopped plumping up her short hair and stared at Dave. 'What do you mean?'

'Jack and Zara are leaving for Adelaide in a week or so. Jack's going to do the detective course down there.'

Joan didn't seem to have words for this bombshell.

'I know. Pretty out of the blue, huh?' Dave added.

'You're telling me! You two have worked together for ages. Why does he want to leave?'

'He wants more,' Dave said simply. 'And I'm not going to stand in the way of that. Plus, he'll make a great detective.'

'That he will.' Joan sank down into her chair. 'It's really sad, but . . .'

'Yep, exactly.' Dave got up and patted Joan's shoulder before going back into his office.

Pulling up his email account, he slowly typed out a message to Steve, their boss, and told him of the changes, before hitting send. Then he grabbed his jacket and hat and went to find the patrol car.

He needed the wide open road.

⁓

Kim tapped on Zara's door and waited, pulling her fingers up into the sleeve of her jumper. Her chest hurt a little at the thought of her neighbours moving, but she understood the reasons. What Kim needed to know was whether Zara was comfortable leaving her mum.

Jack opened the door and his face split into a smile when he saw her.

'Packing is hungry work,' he said, eyeing the cake she was holding.

'You're always hungry, Jack,' Kim said. 'You could be lying horizontal on the couch doing nothing and you'd still want something to eat.'

'Anyone would think he was a teenager,' Zara said, peering over Jack's shoulder. 'Can never fill him up. Hello, Kim.'

'Need any help?'

Jack held the door further open so Kim could come in. She kissed Zara on the cheek then made her way to the kitchen, noting the packing boxes already in the lounge room as she went.

'You're moving fast.'

'We need to get to Adelaide as soon as possible so we can get unpacked and set up before I start,' Jack said, shifting the newspaper off the bench.

Zara had put the kettle on, and was getting the cups from the cupboard, when Jack's mobile rang.

'Better get this,' he said. 'Real estate agent.'

'Gosh, what a whirlwind time!' Kim said, sitting at the bench.

'We took a punt that Jack would be able to get into the first intake,' Zara said. 'But yeah, it's all happening very quickly.'

'Too quickly?' Kim cocked her head to the side and watched her friend. She looked tired but energised.

'I don't think there can be any other way,' Zara said, putting tea bags into the cups and picking up the kettle.

'If we drag this out, we probably won't go. And this will be great for Jack's career.' When she put the cup of tea down in front of Kim, Zara put her hand over Kim's. 'But I'm going to miss you.'

'And I you,' Kim said, feeling tears prick her eyes. She cleared her throat. 'Now tell me, your mum. What's—'

'Mum is great. Did she tell you her news?'

Kim shook her head.

'Well, I think she's going to make some big life decisions too. Must have been about a month ago that she came for dinner and told us that she and James are both considering retiring. Can you believe that? I never thought I'd hear that word come out of her mouth. So . . .' she dragged the word out, 'that might mean they're going to sell Rowberry Glen.'

'Lynda is going to sell the family farm?' The words almost stayed stuck in Kim's mouth she was so astonished.

'I know, I never thought it would be an option either.'

'How do you feel about it?' Kim picked up her cup of tea and watched her friend carefully. A lot of big changes in a short space of time had brought Zara undone in the past. The upheaval of losing her brother and father so close together had seen Zara pushing her friends away and drinking too much. Spending her time working obsessively.

'Do you know, I was devastated when Mum first mentioned it to me.' She looked down and picked at an invisible crumb on the bench. 'Devastated. I couldn't understand how she could even contemplate it. That place has been in our family since the early nineteen hundreds.'

'Yeah, it's a hard call.'

'But in reality, Kim, I'm not going to farm it. I could, but Jack isn't into farming and I love my job as a rural reporter.' Zara shrugged. 'I thought about buying the farm from Mum and leasing it out, just so the family name was still attached, but the figures don't work. The lease money wouldn't cover the interest on the loan I'd have to take out, so . . .' Her voice trailed off and she shrugged, with a sad smile. 'Anyway, I've had time to get used to the idea now. Just needed a bit of that . . . Time.'

A little ping of sadness sat in Kim's chest as she thought about another family farm being sold. Hopefully another family could afford to buy Rowberry Glen.

They could hear Jack talking in the lounge. Something about picking the keys up to their new house.

'Mum said something,' Zara continued. 'Can't remember exactly how it went but it was like, "Farms can't always stay in families. If the next generation haven't grown up on that land, it won't mean as much to them as it does to those who have cared for and loved it."'

The words were true, no matter how heartbreaking.

'Oh Zara,' Kim said.

'No, it's okay, really it is.'

'What are Lynda and James going to do?'

Zara gave a little laugh. 'When I was out there last time, I saw some caravan brochures on the kitchen table, so I'm guessing they might be joining the grey nomads.'

Kim half smiled, thinking back to the terrible day when Zara's father was killed in a car accident, then the day Will died. *Funny how life has a way of making things work out when they've been so shitty*, she thought.

Jack came into the room, beaming. 'Everything is coming together nicely. We can get the keys for the house as soon as we hit Adelaide.' He put his arm around Zara. 'I'm really looking forward to this. Got ourselves a nice little place in the hills.'

This time, Kim smiled properly.

CHAPTER 15

'Why are you looking so tired?' Clara leaned forward and put her fingers on Mia's face. 'You've got black-rimmed eyes.'

'I didn't sleep too well last night. There must be a tree outside tapping on the window. I got up and looked a few times during the night, but I couldn't work out where the noise was coming from. Still getting used to all the sounds of the new house.'

'Maybe you need to get someone to come and trim everything. Get any branches away from the roof.'

'I could.' She brushed a fly away and leaned towards one of the apricot-coloured roses in the garden. 'Beautiful.'

'That's a Just Joey,' Clara said.

Mia glanced over at her nan, who was sitting on the wooden garden bench. She was wearing a navy-blue skirt and a thin woollen jumper. Her sunglasses looked too big for her face and her powdery make-up didn't cover the lines the way Mia was sure Clara hoped they did.

How can she remember something like that, and not my name? When Mia had left the previous evening, Clara had called her Nicole over and over. This morning, she'd been a mixture of Nicole and Mia, but a Just Joey rose? Nana had the name at the tip of her tongue.

Her face was warm with anger, but the lack of memory wasn't her nan's fault.

The sun took the chill from the wind and lifted Clara's skirt a little. Her bony hands smoothed the hem down and she looked out across the garden. 'I always wanted a nice lawn,' she said. 'Look at this buffalo grass. Thick and spongy. Just the way a good lawn should be. You could roll bowls down here.'

'Yeah, I guess you could.' Mia was itching to ask her nan about the gun, which she had in a bag next to her.

Her nan took a deep breath, her pleasure at being outside clear. 'Smell that? There's rain coming.'

The sky was blue and clear. Not even one fluffy cloud on the horizon.

'How can you tell?'

'Can't you smell the moisture?'

Mia sniffed, again looking at the sky. She couldn't work out what her nan was talking about. All she could smell was clean, fresh air. And the exhaust fumes of the clapped-out car that had just driven by with a noisy muffler.

'Nana.' She leaned forward and took Clara's hand, waiting until she refocused on her. 'Nana, I need you to look at something for me.'

'What's that, dear?'

She only had half an hour before she was due to start her afternoon shift. Was it enough time? Maybe. She couldn't be late for work. Richie would have a field day with how women can't be relied on, or always run late. She could almost hear his taunts about how long it took her to do her make-up.

Late last night, Mia made the decision to hand the gun in at the police station today. As much as she wanted to keep it hidden she knew it would only unsettle her. There were too many questions and risks surrounding it—as Chris had alluded to in their phone call.

She'd fought with herself about giving it over, but Chris's text at midnight, when he'd knocked off, had tipped her over the edge.

I hope you've handed the firearm in.

Simple words, but they made her realise what she needed to do.

'I wonder if you could tell me about this.' There were only a few moments between when Mia's hand disappeared into the bag and when the pistol was held out in her hand, within her grandmother's sight.

Nana stared, mystified, then recoiled violently. 'Where did you get that? How come you have it?' Her hands flew to her mouth, then lowered to clutch at her upper arms. 'It should've gone.' She tried to push the gun away, and accidentally knocked it from Mia's hand. It landed on the lawn with a hollow thud.

Half rising from her chair, Mia snatched it up and put the pistol out of sight. 'Sorry, Nana, I didn't realise—'

Her nan clawed her hands towards the bag. 'No, Nicole, it can't be here. You must put it back. Wherever did you find it?' She glanced over her shoulder as if someone was going to come and take her away.

Mia berated herself. Her nan was agitated now. Wild eyes and shaking hands. This wasn't something she should have rushed.

She spoke gently. 'It's okay, Nana. The firearm can't hurt you or anyone else. I've made it safe. There're no bullets in it. Can you take a few breaths for me, and when you're a little calmer, I'll tell you how I found it?' She breathed in deeply and let her breath out in a whoosh, indicating for her nan to do the same.

A willy wagtail flew down and perched on the lawn near them, wagging his long, feathery tail. With a little beak and a strong voice, he sang briefly, then danced his way over to the flowers where he perched on a branch, waiting for an unsuspecting insect.

Her nan's eyes were darting from one side to the other, as if she was expecting someone to come around the corner, while her arms were still wrapped around her upper body in a hug.

'You okay?' Mia asked softly.

'I don't know why you've got it.' Clara's voice had dropped to a whisper.

'Nana, I found it in a box under some material when I went to Barker a couple of days ago. It was near the cellar door. I wondered why you had it there.'

'No.' Clara took a few more shaky breaths and her face relaxed. 'Show me again.'

Her nan had let her arms fall and now sat up straight, squaring her shoulders. Eyes holding her granddaughter's.

'Are you sure?'

Nana nodded. 'I need to see it.' Her words hung heavily between them.

Mia put the bag on her nan's lap and let her reach in.

After a moment's hesitation, Clara pushed back the edges of the bag and looked inside.

Gently, she ran her fingers over the steel. Her face seemed to droop, and the lines there were etched deeper than they had been only moments before. Clara brought the gun to her chest, clutching it close to her heart. 'Ohhh . . .' The word was drawn out with such pain and anguish, Mia couldn't fathom what heartache Nan would have experienced.

She drew in a sharp breath, frightened of what she was going to hear. Nana's reaction had been so strong, so emotional, there must have been some horrible crime committed with this firearm. A murder? A hold-up . . .

'This was your grandfather's.' Nan's voice was shaky and quiet.

Mia didn't understand the words for a moment. 'My grandfather's?'

'Yes.' Clara covered the gun back up again and handed the bag back to Mia. She ran her hands over her eyes, her face suddenly impassive. 'He was a star in the pistol club. A champion. Won many competitions. His name is on the honour boards.'

'But . . .' Mia was struggling to match this story to the reaction she'd just seen. She'd been trained to watch people's body language. Often it told her more than the words that were coming out of someone's mouth. Lies could be easily detected if you were watching people close enough. Although she couldn't imagine why Nana would.

Her nan nodded. 'I kept it. A keepsake. This was his most treasured possession, so I made the pistol mine when he died. And it made me feel safe. Not that there were ever any problems. I knew it was there, though.' Her voice lowered as she spoke.

'Is it registered?'

'I've got no idea, dear.' Clara flicked her wrist as if she didn't care. 'But I don't think the police station is the right place for an heirloom, do you?'

Mia gaped at her lucidity. Then she held her grandmother's gaze. Was she trying to send her a message? If she was, Mia wasn't any good at reading it.

'I have to hand it in, Nan. I could lose my badge for having an unregistered firearm in my possession.'

Her nan seemed to shrink. 'Can you get it back?'

Unsure if Nan was asking about her badge or the gun, she went with the latter. 'I'll need to get a licence. It'll have to stay in the police station safe until then. You understand, don't you?'

Her grandmother stared out across the garden, seemingly not listening. 'He was a crack shot, your grandfather,' she said quietly. 'Could hit the bullseye on the target almost with his eyes shut.'

Mia had never heard many stories about her grandfather either. Only that he had died young. Heart attack while he was unloading supplies from the train.

'Did Dad shoot too?'

The question was out before Mia could stop it and Nan pulled back a bit.

'Oh no. No, he wasn't much good.'

'At shooting?'

'At anything really.'

'What have you got there?' Marty asked, when Mia placed the gun gently on the top of the counter.

'What does it look like?'

Marty inspected it, giving a loud, long whistle. It was enough for Richie to kick back his chair in the office and slide across the floor to look out into the front area. Mia ignored him.

'Whoa, that's a Colt single-action army revolver. Where'd you get that?' Marty's voice was reverent as he leaned forward and touched the barrel.

'It was my grandfather's. Like it?'

'Yeah, it's a nice piece.' Picking the firearm up, Marty examined it closely. 'Real nice.'

'I want to apply for a licence.'

Richie sauntered out; his thumbs stuck through his belt loops. He stood back but leaned over from the waist and looked down.

'What do *you* want a licence for?' he asked.

Mia looked at him as if he were simple. 'So I can keep it.'

'What would you want with that?' Richie scoffed.

'Let's just say there's sentimental value. I'm sure you'll understand that, Richie. You know how emotional women can be and all.' She turned her back on him. 'Can you give me a hand to get a licence?' she asked Marty.

He nodded. 'I'll organise the forms.' His eyes glanced from Richie back to Mia.

'I'll give you fifty for it,' Richie spoke up.

Mia caught Marty's look of astonishment before he gathered it up. 'It's certainly a nice piece,' Marty said. 'Well looked after. I'll pop it in the safe and get the forms for you.'

'Thanks, Marty.' She eyed Richie, not trusting the offer. 'I told you, it's sentimental.'

Richie shrugged and walked back to the office. 'Your loss.'

Mia looked at Marty.

He leaned forward and whispered, 'Google Colt single-action army revolver. These babies are worth a bit more than fifty bucks. He's being a dick.'

'Gee, I'm surprised.' Mia grinned, happy she had an ally. 'Thanks, Marty.'

'You got it. I'll leave the paperwork on your desk.'

'Have we had any call-outs?'

'No, but you'll have to do a drive by the pub shortly. Footy training tonight and all the boys usually end up there. Reckon the boss will be back in the next ten minutes and he'll give you a bit of a rundown.'

Mia nodded and looked towards the office. Richie was back in his chair, looking down at his phone. She wanted to stay out here in the front office with Marty so she called out to his retreating back. 'How long have you been here, Marty?'

'I think I was born here.'

'That long?'

'Maybe longer.'

The click of the gun cabinet locking was Mia's signal to move behind the counter. 'How come you've got the office job? Don't like being on the beat?'

'Nah, I'm non-operational. Hurt my knee in a car chase about ten years ago. Banged it up good and proper. I didn't want to leave the force so they made me desk-bound, which I'm happy with.' A grin crossed his friendly face. 'Kids were in school and we didn't want to shift. I know it's too quiet for some,' his gaze slid across to Richie, 'but I like the simple life. Great place to raise the kids, know your neighbours, all that sort of—'

The phone rang.

Mia noticed Marty walked with a slight limp as he went to answer it.

'Hello, Gina. Got a problem?' Marty asked after a moment's pause. 'Uh-huh. Okay, I'll send a couple of officers around right away.' Giving Mia a wink, he hung up. 'Here's your first case. Gina Humphries has spotted a couple of teenagers in her back yard. One wearing a green hoodie and jeans; the other a black jacket, cap and trackies. Good for that?'

Mia nodded. 'Reckon we can handle it. Coming, Richie?'

'Why would someone report a couple of kids in their back yard out here?' Richie exclaimed. 'She's a bloody nuisance that woman. Not the first time she's rung for nothing.'

'I'm seeing a trend here,' Mia muttered. She let the front door slam behind her and made it to the patrol car before he did. She thought briefly about getting in the driver's seat, but decided she didn't need to excite the enemy any more than he was. She glanced up and down the street—a couple of cars parked on an otherwise empty road.

The screen door banged and Richie headed towards her. He looked furious, so she opened the door and got in the passenger seat.

'Waste of time,' Richie muttered as he started the car. 'What crime could they be committing in her back yard? Stealing some lemons?'

'Or a lawnmower or motorbike,' Mia said.

Richie scoffed. 'Gina Humphries wouldn't have any of those.' He yanked at the seatbelt and clicked it in, pulling away from the kerb with what Mia realised was his customary squeal of tyres. 'See, this is where you new connies don't know much. You don't know the locals or the lay of the land.'

'I guess if you were willing to share the local knowledge you have, none of the new connies would have any problems,' Mia said in a singsong voice.

Richie cast her a deadpan stare and continued to drive in silence.

Mia mused whether this posting was actually going to be feasible. With so much antagonism from Richie, she didn't see how their partnership could work. Trusting and having each other's back were vital.

Her eyes searched the streets as Richie drove. The footy oval was empty, as were the tennis courts.

'Should we try the deli?' she asked.

'Why?'

'Teenagers need to eat. It's cold. Hot chips maybe?'

'No.'

'Right.' Mia wanted to screw her face up in anger. This had to stop. She'd go to Zach when she got back and ask him to talk to Richie. No, that would make things worse. Did she just put up with it? *Shit.*

Silence stretched out between them again.

They turned onto the main street and saw two boys, one wearing a green hoodie and the other a black jumper, walking along the footpath.

'Fuck the deli,' Richie said scornfully as he pulled over. He wound down the window as the teenagers looked across at them, their faces half hidden. 'Boys,' Richie said.

'Shit,' the one wearing the green hoodie said, and took off at a run.

The other one didn't say anything, just started to lift his sleeve.

CHAPTER 16

Mia was out of the car, chasing the green hoodie, before she'd had time to think.

She sighted the boy as he ducked around the council building and ran down a narrow path, high wire fencing on either side. Mia dragged in air as she followed, the belt around her waist moving up and down heavily. Should she get out her taser gun? Not yet.

In the distance, she heard yelling and she slowed slightly, looking over her shoulder. The main street was hidden around a corner. Putting her head down, Mia put on an extra spurt and gained a couple of feet on the boy.

'Stop!' Mia yelled in between breaths. 'Police!' Her voice wasn't as strong as she'd hoped it would be. She was puffed despite being in peak condition.

Pumping her arms harder, she made some ground until she could hear green hoodie's jagged breaths. Reaching out she tried to grab his jumper, but he ducked down another laneway and ran until he came out onto a street with wide footpaths.

Her legs began to tire. This little bugger was much younger and fitter than she was and he wasn't carrying an extra four kilos of tasers, handcuffs and a Glock. She had to keep going, though. Chris's voice popped into her mind: 'Show Ric the dick that you've got this!' And Josie's: 'Run, baby, run!'

'Hey!' she yelled again. 'Stop, police!'

The boy hurtled forward and stumbled, his arms waving about as he tried to regain his balance. Mia realised what was about to happen and managed to put her hands out, giving his back a slight shove.

He fell forward and skidded along the pavement, with a yell, Mia close behind.

'Get off me!' he shouted, his voice echoing off the buildings on either side of the street.

'Mate, you've just caused yourself a whole lot of hurt by running from the police like that,' Mia said, puffing but reaching for her handcuffs. 'That wasn't cool. Why'd you run from us?'

'Get off me!' he yelled again. 'I haven't done anything.'

'Really? You bolt like that every time a police car stops next to you?' Once he was secure, Mia got up and bent over at the waist, her hands on her knees, trying to catch her breath. She heard a car pull up alongside them.

'You took your sweet time,' she said.

'Constable Worth,' the gruff voice of Senior Sergeant Zach Tyler said as he opened the door, 'you and I are going to take a little walk, while Constable Hooper here takes Ben back to the police station.' He bent down and helped the boy in the green hoodie up. 'What do you think you're doing, Ben?' he asked.

One shoulder shrug.

'Your parents are going to be mighty annoyed with you.'

No answer.

Zach let out a sigh. 'You'd better talk to Senior Constable Hooper here and tell him exactly what you were doing, otherwise there's going to be trouble. All right?' He turned his attention to Mia who was staring at him.

What's going on? she wondered.

'Take the cuffs off him, Constable Worth. This is Broad River not Kings Cross,' he snapped.

Anxiety was running through Mia. She was getting the impression she'd done something wrong. But what? She risked a glance at Marty who had clambered out of the driver's seat and was waiting to take Ben's arm. He just gave her a small smile. Not the broad one he usually favoured.

When the handcuffs were released, Ben rubbed his wrists, still looking at the ground.

'Sorry, Zach,' he said softly.

'What were you doing in Mrs Humphries' back yard?' Zach asked.

'Just mucking around.'

'Didn't take anything?'

'Nah.'

'Sure about that?'

The boy hesitated.

'Seems to me that you were up to more than just mischief-making.'

Zach crossed his arms and continued to stare at the boy, while Mia stood silently alongside him. Her boss had hardly spoken to her and yet she already felt like a kid being reprimanded at school.

'Charlie wanted to scare her. Just scare her, not take anything.' He paused. 'Or break anything. Mrs Humphries rang Charlie's mum yesterday and told her that she'd seen him smoking down at the park. He got in trouble.'

'I see. And you tagged along for the ride.'

This time, Ben looked up furiously. 'That's what mates do. You've always told me that.'

Mia blinked. Her gaze slid across to Marty, who hadn't reacted.

'I didn't mean following them blindly when you know they're about to do something wrong.' Zach looked over to Marty. 'Take him home. Tell his parents what he's done and that I'll be over later.'

'Good-oh, boss,' Marty said. 'Come along, young trouble-maker.' He gently pushed the boy towards the car.

Zach didn't look at Mia until Marty had driven away. 'Walk with me,' he finally commanded. He spun on his heel and started back towards the station. Mia had to jog to keep up.

'What is the first thing you're taught at the academy, Worth?'

Mia's mind tumbled as she thought of about five different things. Then she landed on the answer. 'To have your partner's back, Sarge.'

'So why did you think it was a good idea to chase after Ben and leave Constable Milne behind with Charlie?'

'To make sure we got them both.'

'How is that having your partner's back?'

Mia was silent.

'You made the choice to leave your partner.'

'Yes, Sarge.' Mia nodded.

'Richie and you could have had a stern chat with Charlie at the station, or even there on the street, while you worked out what had happened. That would have been enough to scare him into telling you who his playmate was. Charlie knows where Ben lives, so you *both*—' he emphasised the word '—could have followed him up later. He wasn't going anywhere.'

'I'm sorry, Sarge. I thought we needed to apprehend the other suspect.'

'Suspect?' Zach spun to face her. 'Jesus, Worth, this is Broad River. A little country town where nothing happens. I've already explained that to you.'

'Sarge, he took off as we pulled up. That kind of behaviour usually indicates they've done something wrong.'

'Don't make excuses. You can see how small this town is. We would have tracked him down and gone to see his parents. Next time, stay in your seat and take your lead from Constable Milne, who has much more experience working Broad River than you do. I don't want a repeat of this.'

'Sarge,' she said, nodding. 'I'm sorry.'

'You're a lightweight, Worth. God knows why they've sent you out here. Keep on like you are and you'll just stir up trouble, and I don't like trouble in my town. Understand?'

'Yes, Sarge.'

He sped up, leaving her to walk on her own.

She stared after him. 'Shit,' she muttered, rubbing her hands over her face. 'Shit, shit, shit.'

⌒

Mia unlocked her front door, just as the sun was beginning to sink over the horizon, sending long shadows and golden light across the land.

Wood smoke rose into the air and the smell of dinner cooking from houses nearby made her stomach rumble.

Her phone dinged. Chris.

How'd you get on with Ric the Dick?

She didn't answer, just threw the phone on the bed and stripped off her uniform before heading to the shower.

What a balls-up.

Holding her hand under the water she waited for the warmth to come through the pipes, brooding on what Marty had told her.

The sarge was the footy coach for the under sixteens. He knew all these boys and treated them like they were his own. Mia hadn't mucked up as badly as she thought she had, Marty had said. 'It's just that this is a country town

161

and we handle things a bit differently here. What you did was textbook perfect . . . for the city.'

The water wasn't getting hot.

'Yep, and that about sums up today,' she said, and grabbed a towel, wrapping it around her tightly. She padded through the house and out the back door to where the gas bottles were. 'Surely the real estate agent checked these were full before I moved in,' she muttered.

Two gas bottles were hooked up and she wriggled one from side to side. Empty.

The other moved just as easily.

'You're kidding me?' she burst out. Just in case she was wrong, Mia flicked the tab over to the spare bottle and turned the green handle on.

Back in the bathroom, she waited. The water coursing through her showerhead continued to be frigid.

'This is enough to drive a woman to drink!' She turned off the tap and rewrapped the towel around her cold body, then stomped out to the lounge room where she turned on the bar heater and flopped on the couch.

Reaching for the remote, she watched a news report about some music awards. Coloured pictures of pop stars flicked across her screen. P!nk dressed in a glittery sheath, Taylor Swift in an off-the-shoulder sequined dress, with her trademark bright red lipstick. Taylor was holding some kind of trophy at shoulder height and thanking people.

Mia wondered what type of barriers they'd hit from people in the music industry. She was sure their rise to fame hadn't been without people trying to tear them down. Perhaps that's where Taylor's song about haters had stemmed from.

The next headline was about a politician apologising for sexist remarks he had made about a staffer. The woman who had made the complaint was facing the TV cameras speaking candidly.

'It's everywhere. Misogynistic bullshit. What makes blokes think they can behave like that?' Mia pointed the remote at the TV and turned it off, disgusted.

Dropping her head back on the couch, she closed her eyes and breathed deeply. She needed to calm down if she wanted to go to sleep any time soon.

Suddenly her eyes flicked open. Her gaze slid across to the TV. A prickle ran across her skin and she slowly sat up.

The top of the TV was empty.

A few days ago, she'd lovingly placed a large photo of her graduating academy class there.

She got up, tucking the towel around her tightly, wishing she'd put on a pair of trackies and a jumper so she didn't feel quite so vulnerable. She peered behind the TV—nothing but a dead earwig.

'What the . . .' she said aloud, confused. She spun slowly around, looking for the photo.

Surely she hadn't moved it. Had she?

The room was sparsely furnished so the picture should be easy to spot.

There! On the windowsill. Mia looked at it carefully, then back at the TV. She hadn't lived here long enough to need to dust, but there was a faint outline of where the photo had been sitting.

Slowly, she gazed around the whole room again. Nothing else was out of place.

And there it was again, the soft tapping of the trees on the roof and a little shudder moved down her spine.

She ran into the kitchen, looking around. Her plate from this morning was still on the sink and the chair just slightly pulled out, the way she had left it.

In the bedroom, Mia checked under the bed, making sure there was no one hiding, then in the cupboard. There was nothing amiss. Her bedroom was untouched.

Still, a little trickle of fear ran through her. Had someone entered her house while she'd been at work?

Inspecting the front door, there wasn't anything to suggest the older lock had been tampered with, but would she really know? The door handle was the type favoured back in the seventies—a pulldown handle with a large lock to fit a key almost as long as the palm of her hand.

From the dresser, she snatched a bobby pin, opened it up and then fished around inside the lock. Nothing happened. No click, nothing. She moved to the back door, trying the same thing.

Again, she couldn't unlock the door, but was that her inexperience or were they unpickable? Chris's words from a night out a while ago came back to her.

'Any door, car or normal type of lock is pickable.' He'd used his fingers to make quotation marks around the word normal. Later that night, he had shown her how to pick the lock of his car. They'd been in within about fifteen seconds.

Back in the lounge, she looked at the photo wondering if she *had* shifted it and forgotten. Maybe that's what it was.

Well, it had to be! When she wasn't here, the house was secure, having not made the mistake of forgetting to lock it again.

Mia picked up the photo and looked at the smiling faces of her colleagues. Their WhatsApp group had quietened since they'd all graduated and had started their new positions. She wondered how the other women were getting on. Maybe she should call some of them.

Placing the photo back where she could see it, the uneasy feeling in her stomach hadn't gone away.

CHAPTER 17

Dave leaned on the counter of the farm merchandise store, one of the dying plants between him and the local agronomist, Max Cooper.

'Well, to me this looks like a residual spray,' Max said, closely inspecting the yellowing on the leaves. 'See here the roots are stunted. Pruned, we'd call them. They haven't had a chance to develop normally.'

'In English, mate,' Dave said with a grin.

'The chemical has been applied to the soil before it's been seeded. There're a few chemicals that have a long-lasting effect. Something like Atrazine would kill the plants just as they were germinating and that's what this looks like.'

'Right so this would have to be deliberate?'

'Absolutely. One, because I know Rhys doesn't own a boom spray and that's the only way this chemical could have been applied evenly to make sure every part of the paddock was affected. Two, I also know how hard he's worked to get that organic certification. I've done soil tests for him to work out what type of compost would be best to act as a fertiliser, if lime or gypsum needs to be applied. You know, all that sort of thing.' Max scratched his head. 'This is pretty frightening, Dave. Have you got any idea how it's happened?'

'Early days, mate, early days.' Dave thought a moment. 'You mentioned a chemical called Atra-what?'

'Atrazine.'

'How long is the residual on that?'

'About a month.'

'And it will affect all types of grain?'

'It certainly will barley.' Max nodded towards the seedling.

Dave nodded and referred back to his notebook, even though he didn't need to. 'Yeah, that's what Rhys told me he'd seeded.' He tapped his fingers for a moment. 'How much chemical would it take to do this?'

'Depends on what rate it was applied. If you let me have that soil sample, I can get it tested for you.'

'I'll need to keep some of it for evidence, I brought you another bag of it.' Dave scratched his head with his pen. 'What records are kept about chemical sales?'

'Batch numbers, invoices to purchaser, invoices from chemical company, all that sort of thing.'

'Would it be hard to get a print-off of all the people who have bought Atrazine in the last, say, two months?'

'Not at all.' Max went to the computer and pressed a few buttons and the printer behind him started whirring. Eight sheets of information came through.

Dave looked over them, noting they were the trading names of farms rather than individual names. He recognised three and knew they belonged to Craig Johnston, Mark Waters and Cranky Joe Newman, but he wasn't sure of the others.

'Who are these five?'

'High Yields Cropping is Rick Walter; Agro Pro is Abel Keegan; Hilltop Farm, Rachael Murphy; and Ovine Acres is owned by Harley and Natalia Stokes. Jancarter Pastoral Pty Ltd is a corporate.'

Dave wrote down the names. He only knew two of them. Returning to the reports he pointed to a figure in a column. 'This is the amount they bought?'

Max leaned over. 'Yeah, that's right.'

'And a ballpark litre amount for spraying?'

'How big was the paddock?'

Dave pulled out the map Rhys had given him. 'This is the one here. Hectares are documented.' He indicated a figure.

Max tapped on the calculator then wrote down a number and handed it to Dave. 'You'd need at least four enviro drums of the stuff. That's four hundred and forty litres.'

Dave glanced down the page and saw no transaction that was just four drums. That would be too easy!

'Is there any other chemical that could have been used that has a residual?'

'Yeah.' Max listed off a couple of others.

'Can you print out who has bought them too, please?'

A few moments later, Dave held all the information in his hand. 'Righto, Max. Thanks for your help.' He pushed the plants and soil across the desk. 'I'll leave these with you, and wait to see what you find out. And if you could keep your ear to the ground, please?'

'Sure, no worries, Dave. I know where to find you.'

Dave gave a wave and headed back to the station, walking briskly, his head down against the wind.

Not five minutes later he was inside sitting at his desk when there was a knock at the door and Jack stuck his head in.

'Got a minute?'

Dave smiled and pushed his glasses onto his forehead. 'Sure do. Got your instructions from Macca?'

Jack nodded. 'Car is just about packed.'

'You know we can't let you go without a farewell party.'

'That's sort of what I wanted to talk to you about. The boys from the footy club are going to have a few beers down the pub tonight and a few of Zara's friends are going to turn up too. Nothing big because we've got to head off early in the morning.'

'Sounds like a plan. Wouldn't miss it for the world.' Dave hid the fact his stomach dropped when Jack said the words, *early in the morning*. It was happening far too quick for his liking. 'How're you feeling?'

Jack grinned. 'Shit-scared. Excited. That sort of thing.'

'That's how you're supposed to feel. I'd be worried if you weren't. It's a big move and comes with some pretty hefty responsibility if you get through the course.'

Jack picked up a pen and started to play with it. 'What's your best bit of advice?'

Dave thought. 'Remember the people you're working for. The bosses will tell you that you're employed by the force. And you are. But you're not *working* for them. There's a difference. The detective inspectors will bang on about budgets and not to work extra time and all that sort of stuff but you're working for the victims and their families. That should spur you on to do your best. Keep in constant contact with them. And I'm not only talking about murders. People are scared by the simple act of a break and entry, and they want answers. If you communicate well with them then they'll relax and trust you. Give them your time and don't fob them off.' Dave flicked his hands out. 'You know all of this, Jack. That's why you'll make a good detective.'

'I thought you might say something about being methodical.'

'I didn't need to because I know you're always methodical. A good investigation is to start at the beginning and slowly work your way through. Don't assume, and always ask more questions than you need.' Dave grinned. 'If I think of anything else, I'll let you know!'

'What are you working on?' Jack leaned forward.

Dave pushed over the information he'd gathered from Max. 'Just looking at the people who have bought chemicals that have a residual life. Max says the paddock must have been sprayed before seeding time.'

Jack flipped open the file and drew out the photos. He looked at them carefully while Dave stood up and stretched.

'You don't think it was sprayed by a tractor?'

'I didn't say that,' Dave said. 'The fact it was sprayed pre-seeding wipes out any tracks that would have been left. Rhys has been over the paddock in his tractor since. Max said he doesn't own a sprayer.'

'Contract sprayers?'

'Yeah, well that would be an option. But only if they were out-of-towners who weren't in the know; anyone local would surely question why they were being asked to spray an organic farm.'

Jack nodded, putting the photos down. 'No prints? The gate looks too rough to hold any.'

'None. You need something as smooth as glass to lift an impression from.'

Dave regarded Jack, an idea working over. 'You're pretty involved with the footy club. How's Rhys accepted there?'

'He's one of the good guys,' Jack said, glancing over the incident report Dave had started to write. 'Gets on well with everyone in the club. Helps out behind the bar after he's coached. He was the treasurer there for a couple of years before he became the coach.'

'No arguments after a few too many beers then?'

Jack shook his head slowly. 'Not that I can think of.'

'What about any of his playing list? None of those blokes mind being benched or yelled at?'

Jack smiled. 'The word is "encouraged". We don't yell.'

'That right?' Dave rolled his eyes.

'Jamie Parsons can get a bit snitchy if he doesn't play a full game, but he's getting better under Rhys's coaching. But, Dave, these blokes aren't going to spray his land.'

'My thoughts exactly, but it's still a line of investigation. I have to start somewhere. I wonder if Rhys grows better crops than someone else and they're jealous.' Dave stilled as his mind raced.

Jack shot up from his seat. 'There is something,' he said, glancing at his watch. 'Come on, we've got time to get out to John Manson's place and get back again before the beers tonight. I'll tell you on the way.'

Dave stood up, grabbing his jacket. 'You're not supposed to be working.'

Jack looked at him. 'Can't forget who I'm working for.' He walked quickly out the door towards the car park.

Dave watched him go and nodded, pride spreading out in his chest. That man was going to go far.

⌒

'Doesn't look like John Manson is that tidy,' Jack said, taking in the tangled wire fence on the side of the road. 'Reckon the stock have walked through that fence and kept walking, pulling it with them. There's the driveway.' He pointed to a mailbox made from a twenty-litre oil drum, bent and dented.

'I can just imagine a cow standing there, shaking her leg, trying to get rid of the wire and causing more damage.' Dave turned the vehicle where Jack pointed. They were silent as they drove in, past more mangled fences and a few empty diesel forty-fours strewn across the paddock. 'And the gear . . .' He indicated to the machinery dotted around the yard, while the shed stood deserted. 'All of this would be twenty or thirty years old. Much smaller and less modernised equipment than what's available now.'

'Short of a quid, do you think?' Jack asked.

'Could be. Looks like he's a bit of a muddler.'

Dave switched off the car and sat still for a moment, before energising himself. 'Only one way to find out.'

They opened their doors at the same moment John Manson appeared on the verandah. His overalls were fresh and cleaned and his white beard neatly trimmed. Dave observed him, then took a glance around the yard. The house and garden were tidy. Sturdy railings held up flowering bougainvilleas and heavy grapevines, while the small lawn was mowed and edged.

'What are you lot doing here?' John asked in a resigned tone. 'I took the bloody gun in like you asked. Can't you leave a fella be?'

'G'day, Mr Manson,' Jack said, rounding the car and taking the steps up to the verandah two at a time.

Dave leaned against the car, his arms folded, letting Jack take the lead.

'Thanks for bringing the firearm to the station. We've not come about that, but we will pick up the bullets while we're here.'

'What do you want if it's not about that, then?' John glanced from man to man and shoved his hands deep in the faded blue overall pockets.

The curiosity was only muted, Dave thought. Not really the look from a guilty man.

'Just wanted to ask a few questions about that block of Harcourt's you tried to buy earlier this year.'

The older man cocked an eyebrow, which almost hit his vivid white hair. 'What about it?'

'I heard that you were very keen to buy the property.'

'I was,' John agreed. 'I've been waiting for that land to come on the market for years and years. Always wanted to add it to my place.'

'Why was that?'

John gave a half grunt, half snort at Jack's ignorance. 'Think about it, young fella.' He pointed to the east. 'My boundary is on that creek, where those river red gums stick out. Right on the horizon there.'

Both Jack and Dave turned to look.

'Harcourt's land is right next to me.' He leaned against the wall. 'Long time ago, back when my father was still alive, we used to own that place. Ended up having to sell it in the eighties when interest rates were high. Didn't want to lose all the land we'd put together, so we sold enough to cover our debt and get the bank off our back. Being able to get that land back into our name would give me a great deal of satisfaction. Not to mention another three thousand acres. Could run about another three thousand sheep with that country. More sheep, more coin.'

One DSE to the acre, old language, Dave thought. The Dry Sheep Equivalent, the sheep numbers that farmers were able to run on their land, was always lower this far north.

Jack wrote a couple of notes down and looked back at John, who was now fishing around in his front pocket.

Laying out a tin of tobacco, he went about rolling his own cigarette.

Dave hated smoking but there was something addictive about watching experts at work. Rolling your own ciggies was a skill.

'I can understand why you would have been really pleased to get the land back,' Jack said. 'Family ties and all.'

'Good country over there. Because it's that little further south it gets just a smidge more rain.' The old man winked. 'Money in mud, not dust, lad.' He put the cigarette in his mouth and lit it, speaking around the rollie. 'What's your interest in all of this, if I've done all the right things with the gun?'

'Who bought Harcourt's in the end?' Jack asked.

John grunted. 'Not me. Rhys Martindale paid through the nose for it.'

A beat of silence.

'Were you angry?'

John regarded Jack for a moment, then took his cigarette out of his mouth, pointing it at the younger man.

'I know what this is about. We've all heard what happened to Rhys Martindale's crop and you reckon I did it because I missed out on some land?'

Jack held his gaze. 'We're following up with all the neighbours, Mr Manson, and you are just another line of enquiry.'

Dave wanted to slap Jack on the back. Good answer!

'Let me tell you, Higgins, I wouldn't waste my fuel. Yes, I wanted to buy that land but I wasn't so disappointed that I would spray out Martindale's crop. I might be old, but I'm not bitter.'

Jack smiled. 'I'm sorry you didn't get the land, Mr Manson.'

'That is what is called life.'

Dave pushed himself off the car and opened his door, ready to get in, when Jack started talking again.

'A couple of last things, just to tidy up,' Jack said, not moving.

Dave shut the door and folded his arms, digging his hands in underneath his armpits. The day was normal for Barker at this time of the year. A vivid blue sky, with an icy westerly. A droughty, cold day. Rain never came from the west. Even if it did rain, the soil temperature was low and the pasture germination would be very slow.

Dave tuned back in to what Jack was asking.

'And you say you were here by yourself?'

'You haven't told me when.'

Jack paused and Dave quickly intervened.

'You're right, John, we haven't got a time frame, but perhaps the question is rather, have you noticed anything suspicious over the last couple of months? People driving the road at odd hours, vehicles that you don't know, or even vehicles that you do know but in an area that is unusual?'

'Or even vehicles that you don't know but you've noticed keep coming back,' Jack added.

Even as they spoke, John was shaking his head. 'Nope, nothing like that.'

'You don't need time to think about it?'

'Lad, I've lived here for longer than you've been alive. I reckon I'd know if something was out of kilter, don't you?'

'Is there any truth in the rumour that you had an argument with Mr Martindale in the stock agent's office recently?'

Slowly, Mr Manson dropped the cigarette on the cement and stubbed it out with a dirty boot, his eyes never leaving Jack's.

'Yes, there is.'

Dave's interest picked up. Jack hadn't told him anything about an argument.

'Can you tell me what it was about?'

'Yes, I can. I was hoping Martindale would fix his boundary fence. Those crossbred rams of his got through his busted fence and in with my merino ewes.'

Crossbred rams? Dave wanted to put his hands over his ears—no one called White Suffolk Rams crossy rams anymore. They were Terminal breeders.

'Cause you some problems?'

'Some of my ewes got in lamb out of season. Those bloody rams are as horny as a teenage boy and act on their feelings.' It was the old man's first sign of anger and Dave eyed him carefully.

'Yeah, ewes pregnant out of season would cause you a lot of problems, I'm sure,' Jack said.

'It does. They drop when it's cold, the lambs are more likely to die. And there's little feed. Mums don't milk like they should. Lots of problems.'

Jack looked across at Dave, who held his gaze now. He gave a slight nod and the soon-to-be detective took a breath.

'What was Mr Martindale's answer to your request?'

'He wasn't going to fix it!' The old man looked indignant. 'You know, Higgins, good fences make good neighbours.'

'Yours are looking like they might need a bit of maintenance.'

'Surely they do, but only in the cropping paddocks. Where my girls are, well, I try and keep them locked up tight. Trouble is, these young bucks got out on the road and went sniffing. Then they pushed their way through my fence. In the middle of the farm!' Manson was indignant. 'I didn't want him to pay to fix my fence, mind,' he said. 'Only to fix his own so it didn't happen again.'

'And he wouldn't?'

'I drove by there yesterday and still nothing has been done.' John tapped his foot as if he was putting a full stop on the end of a short, sharp sentence.

Dave waited.

Smiling, Jack put his notebook back into his top pocket. 'Okay, if you could grab the bullets, Mr Manson. Thank you for your time. It's been most enlightening.'

CHAPTER 18

The pub was full of rowdy blokes, clinking glasses and giving a rousing cheer when Dave and Jack walked in.

'Ready, fellas?' the captain of the A grade called. He raised his hands like an orchestra conductor and everyone in the room started to sing—if you could call it that—'For he's a jolly good fellow'.

'Whoa, whoa, whoa,' Jack yelled above the noise, putting his hands over his ears. 'You can stop that any time soon.'

Laughter broke out and Dave pushed a beer into his hand and raised his own. 'Here's to you,' he said.

Before Jack could take a sip, someone grabbed his arm and turned him around, pushing him through the crowd.

Dave stood back and watched as his friend laughed and shook hands with the fellas. It was a strange feeling. Maybe this was what it felt like when your kids moved away from home or got married. His chest hurt a little. Not that he'd tell anyone that. Not even Kim. Although he wouldn't have to tell her; she'd already know.

He felt a soft hand slip around his waist and turned to see his wife standing alongside him. Zara and her friends were in the mix of the footy blokes. Her smile was wide as Jack put his arm around her and she looked up at him. The mixture of love and happiness that passed between them made Dave's heart squeeze a bit harder.

'Okay?' Kim asked.

Dave nodded. 'Course.'

His wife squeezed him. 'It's okay not to be.'

'What, and show everyone I'm not the tough copper everyone thinks I am? Don't be ridiculous, woman,' he said in a gruff tone, but a smile played around his mouth. Watching Jack exchange a few slaps on the shoulder with some others, Dave gave a sigh. 'He needs to go and do this. You should have heard him asking John Manson questions this afternoon. It's like he's already kicked himself up another notch.'

'He's been taught well,' Kim reminded him.

'Maybe, but he had to have the aptitude and drive to want to do this.' He paused. 'Not that I ever doubted he did.' Dave raised his glass to his mouth again, then realised Kim didn't have a drink. 'Do you want something?'

'I'll get a wine in a moment. Here comes the girl of the hour.'

Kim nodded towards the throng of people and Dave shifted slightly to see Zara, still smiling, pushing her way through the people towards them.

'Dave, you're here!' She gave him a hug and kiss.

He smiled down at her. 'I had to bring the other guest of honour.'

Zara laughed. 'I'm glad you did.'

'All ready to head off?' Dave asked.

'Yep, leaving at eight o'clock in the morning.' Zara jiggled on her toes, like an excited little girl. 'I can't wait to see the house we've got. I've only looked at the photos online, but it seems really sweet. And modern. Hopefully, there won't be any draughts the way there are in older houses!'

'And work? Will you be back in the head office of the *Farming Journal*?'

Another roar went up. Jack was standing in the middle of a circle of men, grinning like a Cheshire cat. Dave watched as Zara flicked a fond look towards him.

'Yep, as soon as I want to really,' Zara said. 'I'd like to get unpacked and settled before I head in, but I guess it depends on how quickly we get sorted.'

'I'm sure it won't take too long,' Kim said. She turned around as more people came into the pub's dining room. 'There's your mum and James, Zara. You'd better go and talk to them.'

'Be back shortly,' Zara said and danced across the floor, waving to her mum.

'Oh, to be young again,' Kim said wistfully. She leaned in closer and whispered in Dave's ear. 'I have to admit I'm a little jealous. When I was helping them pack boxes, I felt like I was suddenly at the other end of life. It was pretty awful, actually.'

Dave smiled down at her. 'I know. Me too. Talk about changing of the guard. Still, we're lucky we get to be old. Don't forget about Zara's brother. How old was he when he died?'

'Early twenties at best. And her dad.'

'And my mates.'

They were quiet, taking in the enormity of life and their gratitude at being alive.

'You know, I saw a cartoon picture on Facebook once,' Kim said. 'It was a young couple holding hands, walking towards the end of a jetty and they passed an older couple on the way back. That seems to be how life is. Young ones going where us oldies have already been.'

'Good analogy,' Dave agreed.

'Dave?'

He turned at the sound of his name and saw Hopper standing nearby. The publican beckoned him over. Dave followed, thinking it was strange he was out from behind the bar, but then he saw another three staff running back and forth.

'Been made obsolete, Hopper?' Dave asked, leaning up against the bar and putting his foot on the rail that ran across the bottom of the bench.

'Nah, wanted to talk to you. I heard about that bad business with Rhys Martindale.'

'Oh yeah?' Dave leaned forward, interested. He knew that Hopper had been one of Zara's best sources, but the man had never contacted him to pass on any information before. Dave had always assumed Hopper was happy to chat to journos but drew the line at coppers and he'd never pushed him.

'One of my girls, Sophie, she heard something. Dunno if it's any use to you.'

Dave glanced over at the bar staff and noticed a short girl with bouncy, curly brown hair and a large smile. 'That her?' he asked.

'Yeah.'

'Want to give her a break?'

Hopper nodded and pulled open the swing door, letting himself behind the bar. He nodded at Sophie and she put the beers she'd just pulled on the bar, fossicking through the coins on the bar mat, then slipped out the side, handing Hopper the money as she went.

'G'day, Sophie. I'm Dave. Got a problem?'

She motioned him around to the corridor that led to the toilets. 'Busy tonight,' she said, rubbing her forehead as if she had a headache. Her smile had faded the minute she'd stepped out from behind the bar. Rubbing the back of her neck, she tipped her head from side to side.

'Don't think this party will last long,' Dave said. 'Jack and Zara are leaving tomorrow and they've got an early start. When the guests of honour leave, it'll only be the hardcore who stay.'

'I hope you're right. I've got to get home and start on the office work.'

Dave looked at her carefully. 'What other job do you have?'

'Work in the office of Mum and Dad's employment agency, Farm Employ. They're based in Port Augusta, but—'

'Oh yeah, I've heard of you guys. You've placed a few employees into farms around here, haven't you?'

Sophie nodded. 'I'm a qualified accountant, but I was a bit over the city by the time I finished studying. Wanted a break.'

'Is that why you're working behind the bar? I don't think I've ever seen you in here before.'

'I go out with Craig Johnston, so I come across a couple of nights a week to see him. Just wanted something to do in the middle of the day while Craig was at work. I spoke to Hopper and he put me on the lunchtime shift, but he needed a few more hands tonight so he asked if I'd come in.'

'Right. And so how can I help?'

'Well, a while back, I saw a tractor on the side of the road parked up near the Martindale place. It was a John Deere tractor and the driver was out of the tractor, holding her mobile phone. Looked like she was trying to get range, so I stopped and asked her if she was okay. I thought she might have broken down or something.' Sophie closed her eyes tiredly.

Or perhaps she was remembering, Dave thought. He stayed quiet.

'Anyhow she hadn't had a breakdown, she needed directions to Rhys Martindale's place. Google Maps never seems to work out here.'

A yell went up from the bar, as the jukebox blasted the intro to 'Working Class Man' and the blokes from the footy club started to sing, arms around each other.

'And did she say why she was looking for Rhys's place?'

184

'No, just that she needed to find it.' Sophie paused. 'I'd never seen her around here and, when I think back, there wasn't any name on the side of the tractor or boom spray.'

'Most farm-owned machinery don't have names on them,' Dave said.

'But most contractors do.'

Dave nodded, feeling in his pocket for his ever-present notebook. 'Can you describe her?'

Sophie screwed up her face. 'Not really. It was some time ago now . . . But she was wearing a t-shirt. I remember thinking that was strange because most farm workers wear shirts. I'm sorry, I've been trying to remember since I heard about the crop dying, but there's not much that comes to me.'

'Keep trying and something might pop up when you're least expecting it. You said this was a while ago. Is there any way that you can narrow the time frame down? Do you remember what you were doing when you came over, maybe?'

'I'll check my diary when I get time to look at my phone. See if there's something in there that might jog my memory, but when I saw you come in tonight I really wanted to let you know.'

'Can you give me your contact details and we'll make a plan to catch up?'

Sophie pondered his words, shifting her stance and looking at the floor.

Dave waited.

'Look, I don't know if it's useful either, but the boys are pretty annoyed with Rhys as the footy coach. He's hard and sometimes a bit—' she shrugged, her eyes darting to the doorway as a figure entered and pushed past them, into the toilet '—mean. That sounds petty. Uncompromising? I don't know, they get the shits with him.'

'Anyone in particular?'

Sophie shook her head. 'I'm never at training.'

'Has Craig said anything to you?'

'Just that they don't like him much and he doesn't bring the footy team together.'

'Okay. Thanks for speaking up, Sophie. We'll catch up tomorrow.'

'You won't tell anyone I've spoken to you, will you? About the footy stuff.'

'Not unless I have to. Look, this offence is criminal damage—it's a jail-time crime. And if anyone in the footy club is responsible then I have to know. People in the community can't just go handing out their own punishment willy-nilly. That's for the law to do. So, good job, thank you.'

Sophie gave him a nervous smile and didn't say anything more. She just headed back to the bar as quickly as she could.

Dave stayed there thinking about Jack's questioning of John Manson earlier, and the interesting piece of information that John Manson and Rhys Martindale didn't seem to get along that well. Now he knew that the A grade footy team didn't seem to like their coach either.

But where did a woman driving a tractor fit in?

Kim pulled Zara into a hug, tears in her eyes. 'I can't tell you how much I'm going to miss having you across the road,' she said.

Dave was leaning on the car, waiting for his turn, his shoulders hunched away from the bitter chill of early morning.

'It's going to be so weird,' Zara said as she pulled back and brushed a few stray drops from her cheeks.

'But wonderful.' Kim took Zara's hands in hers and shook them gently. 'This is such a fabulous opportunity for you both. Who knows where you'll be in a couple of years from now.'

'Heading up the newsroom for the ABC, I'd reckon,' Dave said.

Zara laughed and let go of Kim's hand to take Dave's. 'So funny how you didn't like me when I first arrived and now you're one of my best friends,' she said.

'Who says I like you now? You're still a journo.' He grinned and gave her a hug.

'I know you can't break that strong man image,' Zara said.

'Too right.'

Kim came to stand alongside Dave. She held up a bag. 'I've cooked some things for you for a few nights. I'm sure you'll be buggered by the time you arrive and . . .' Her voice trailed off. She pushed the food into Zara's hands.

Zara seemed unable to say anything so she turned and placed the bag on the back seat.

Jack appeared on the steps and closed the door with a bang. He looked at them all, the excitement on his face clear.

'We're ready!' He bounded down the steps, coming to a standstill at the car.

'Right, well, we won't hold you up.' Dave held out his hand to Jack. 'Stay in touch. I want to know how you get on.'

'You'll have no choice. I'll be ringing. And I said we'd be back for the grand final and the show.'

Dave nodded, thinking that Jack still had some things to learn. If he was in the middle of a case, or investigating a murder, he wouldn't be turning up, no matter how much he wanted to.

Don't forget who you work for.

'We'll look forward to seeing you whenever you can get here,' Kim said. 'There'll always be a bed at our house.' She tried to smile again, but this time the tears flowed.

Zara gave a little whimper and the men looked at each other.

'Righto,' Dave said, opening the passenger door for Zara. 'Let's get you on the road.'

Kim and Zara hugged again, and then Kim gave Jack the full force of one of her hugs, grabbing his face to kiss him on the cheek.

Dave and Jack shook hands again, then gave each other a quick man hug, before Jack got into the car, clearing his throat as he did. When he put the car in gear and took off, he looked straight ahead, rather than at Dave or Kim.

His eyes were red.

'Stay safe,' Dave said softly to the tail-lights of the car.

He put his arm around Kim and they watched the vehicle disappear around the corner.

Neither of them said anything for some time, until Kim squeezed Dave's waist. 'Come on, I'll get you a cup of tea.'

'I should go into the office,' he said, even though it was the last thing he wanted to do right now. He didn't want to sit across from Jack's vacant desk and feel the emptiness of the cold station.

Jack had always been there. From the first case he worked, where he reconnected with Kim and investigated a car-jacking that had involved her niece, to now, seven years later. Jack was a staple. Solid. Always around.

Now he wasn't.

'Joan will ring you if something comes up,' Kim said, taking his hand and leading him across the road to their house.

CHAPTER 19

'Broad River Police Station,' Marty answered the phone in his official voice, while doodling on the pad beside him.

Mia was placing a coffee next to his elbow and he nodded at her before his eyebrows shot towards the sky.

'Sorry, could you slow down and tell me . . .'

He grabbed at his notepad and began scribbling words that didn't make any sense to Mia.

Tahlia . . .

Sunroom . . .

Looked in . . .

He motioned for her to get the sarge and then focused back on the call.

'Ma'am, I need you to stop, please.' He made a calming motion with his hand that the woman on the end of the phone couldn't see.

Mia turned and hurried to the sarge's office, putting her head around the corner. 'Excuse me, Sarge. Marty needs you.'

The sarge gave an annoyed sigh and threw his pen on the desk. It only took him four strides to get out through the door and near Marty.

While Mia got her thoughts together, she realised the atmosphere in the station had changed.

Greg Toombes had almost run through the door, in uniform. Mia started. He wasn't meant to be on duty.

Richie was pacing next to the front desk and indicating he needed more information from Marty, who was scribbling as fast as he could.

Mia saw the sarge pulling on his jacket and checking his waist.

She raced towards Richie and was at his shoulder as he tumbled out the front door.

'Mia!' Zach barked out her name. 'You stay here. Marty, you're with me.'

Marty half stood, then sat down, astonishment across his face as he looked at the sarge.

'Quick! On your feet, man. There's not a second to delay.'

Mia could hear the sirens, already disappearing into the distance. Richie had gone with Greg, and Zach was on the phone now.

What was wrong?

'Noah? We have a missing child. A four-year-old. The Chellows' farm is fifteen point eight kilometres from the highway off Lake Moore Road. Need you out there immediately.' He pulled the phone away from his ear.

'Sarge,' Mia said. 'I should be—'

Zach turned and pointed to her. 'I want you here, where you're most useful. You don't know the lay of the land out there. The phones are the best place. Marty, are you ready? For god's sake, let's go!'

Marty seemed as stunned as Mia. He was struggling to gather himself, get his heavy belt on and follow Zach. Trying to move as fast as he could with his limp, he glanced across at Mia and mouthed, 'Sorry.'

Zach was halfway out the door but he turned back, obviously remembering something. 'I want the closest stations to send their best people,' he told Mia. 'Phone them and get it organised.' Then he disappeared out into the street.

Anger burst through Mia's chest. She was supposed to be out there with Richie! Her! Not Marty. He could barely walk one hundred metres with his buggered-up knee. She was a young, fit constable—someone who had just proved she could sprint hundreds of metres—and she was the one being benched.

What the actual?

The radio spluttered to life and she listened as Zach proceeded to give further orders, then she realised she hadn't done anything he'd asked yet.

She found the number for the Barker Police Station and dialled, still fuming at the injustice.

'Barker Police Station, this is Joan,' a friendly older voice answered.

'Good afternoon, this is Constable Worth from Broad River Station, could I speak to Dave Burrows?'

'I'll have to get him to call you back,' Joan answered. 'He's out at the moment.'

'It's urgent.'

Joan must have picked up her tone because her answer was almost as short and curt as Mia's.

'Number?'

Mia recited it and hung up.

It was less than a minute before the phone rang, but that had been enough time for her seething to intensify. She'd picked up her phone to text Chris but was interrupted.

'Burrows here.' The tone was both official and warm.

Mia quickly remembered her meeting with Dave Burrows in Barker—the steely glint in his eyes.

'Thanks for calling back, Sarge. We've got a missing four-year-old girl. A Tahlia Chellow.' She told him the address. 'My sarge has asked for all officers to attend.'

She heard him let out a breath.

'Any more details?'

'Not that I have.'

There was a silence, the tick, tick, tick of the clock on the wall, almost in time with her blinking.

'Right, see you soon. Are you on the ground?'

'Keeping the home fires burning,' she answered.

Another exhale. The phone line sounded muffled. 'Affirmative. On the way.'

'Will pass it on.'

She hung up and the phone rang again, almost instantly. She heard a young male voice. 'Broad River Police Station? This is Campbell Duncan from the *Flinders Times*.

I understand there is a missing child in Broad River. Would you like to make a comment?'

Mia reared back and almost dropped the receiver. How did they know already? *Shit!* She hadn't been given any instructions on how to speak to the media.

Gathering her thoughts, she said, 'I cannot confirm that. However, police are responding to an incident west of the town of Broad River. When more information becomes available, we will make a statement.' She hung up without waiting to hear what else he had to ask, her heart beating fast.

Horrible questions would probably be asked: who is it, what happened, did the child run away? Could the child have been taken by her father/mother/brother/uncle? Is there a history of violence in the family?

Who could answer any of those questions without being on the ground?

Not her.

There was another phone call. Warily, Mia answered the phone, telling the caller they'd reached the Broad River Police Station.

'Oh, hello, love.' A warm and genuine voice this time. 'I'm Shirley from the CWA. Do you need me to organise a group of ladies to make sandwiches and to feed you all?'

Mia marvelled at how quickly word got around the town and, again, she felt out of her depth. Thanking Shirley, Mia told her she'd get back to her as soon as she knew.

Helpless, Mia made notes of the two phone calls. If she was on the ground, she would have more idea what to do than she did here. She'd be searching any little nook or cranny, asking questions of the parents, double-checking sheds and machinery for hiding places. Checking CCTV for motor vehicle movements. All the things she knew how to do!

But she didn't know how to answer Shirley's question. Frustrated, she checked her emails and made herself a coffee then stood at the window, thinking about the missing little girl.

Outside the clouds were a murky, dirty grey. They were sliding across the sky at the same rate that the wind was blowing. Soft but steady.

Earlier, she'd heard the startling noise of tiny stones being thrown on the roof but had then smelled the moisture and realised it was the sound of rain. When she'd gone for a run this morning, the air had been brisk and held the hint of ice.

Today was not a nice day for a child to be missing.

Her thoughts slid to her nan. In the past, on a day like today, Nana would have made hot chocolate or cocoa and poured the hot, smooth liquid into a thermos to take into the shop with her. Mia would have had a cup with her breakfast, her belly filled with the warmth of the drink and her nan's kiss on her head before she'd left for the shop.

The radio came to life again, static mainly, but she could hear a siren in the background. A voice she knew—Richie—instructed a team to 'head north in a grid-like pattern'.

Answers of 'Affirmative' or 'Roger' came through, and Mia realised that she wasn't so angry anymore.

Slumping in her chair, she took another sip of coffee, then adjusted the volume of the radio.

What if she phoned Zach? She could ask what to tell the media if they rang again, or the CWA ladies. Then she wondered if that was the right course of action. Maybe not.

The map! she thought.

On the back wall, there was a map of the council area. Finding the highway, then Lake Moore Road, Mia traced her finger along the thin line, until she thought she'd found the farm. She hadn't been given GPS co-ordinates, so she was only guessing. Her stomach dropped when she saw a large lake close to the house. Whether or not it had water in it, she didn't know, but for a young child it wasn't ideal.

The door swung open and the wind howled through the office, causing the plastic plant in the corner to sway like a real one and all the pamphlets and brochures to ruffle.

Mia turned and made her way to the window, plastering a smile on her face, ready to greet the general public.

'Hello, how can I—' She broke off and looked at the man who had just entered. Confusion crossed her face. 'You're not supposed to be here. You're supposed to be out on the search ground. And how did you get here so quickly?'

Dave smiled and crossed to the front desk window. 'I was in Broad River when you rang. So, what's the go?'

'Ah,' Mia turned around and pointed at the map, 'the property is here.' She moved across to tap her finger on the road she'd found moments before. 'Do you want to come around? I'll let you in.'

She punched the code into the door and it swung silently open, letting Dave enter behind the counter.

'Here,' she tapped the map again. 'Four-year-old girl, like I said before.' She paused and looked at the map again. 'There's a lake here.' Mia's words were heavy.

Dave stared at the map and rubbed his chin.

'The media called. I didn't know what to tell them.'

'They're quick, aren't they?' He shook his head in disgust. 'I have a love–hate relationship with them. They can be vultures and very helpful, almost within the same breath.'

'And the CWA ladies want to know if we need food.'

This time, Dave burst out laughing. 'Good on them. If there is anyone who has got the community's best interests at heart, it's those ladies.'

Mia looked at him sideways. 'I thought they were a bunch of old gossips when I was a kid.'

'And you'd be right, with some of them. Not all,' he answered mildly, looking around. 'So where is Marty?'

'Out with the sarge,' Mia answered.

Another glance at the map and Dave shifted back towards the door.

'I see. Well, we'd better get out there and find out what Senior Sergeant Tyler would like us to do.'

Mia stared, then started to shake her head. 'No. No, I can't. I'll get into trouble again. I'd better—'

'Constable Worth, it's my understanding that you've been trained in this type of search?'

She glanced at Dave quickly, who was staring down at her. 'Yes, Sarge, I have been.' She looked away, thinking about Zach's implied words after she'd arrested Ben. Do as you're told. 'But I've been told to stay here.'

Dave raised his eyebrows slightly. 'To my way of thinking, every available body should be involved in a search like this. We're looking for a child and we have family members to comfort and look out for as well. So, all hands on deck.' He paused and looked at her. 'That's unless you would rather stay here, of course.'

CHAPTER 20

'So, tell me a bit about yourself, Mia. This your first posting?'

Mia nodded. She felt excitement, along with the heaviness of responsibility. They had a child to find and she had a strange mixture of emotions. This missing girl was her first real case.

'Yeah, I was so glad when a vacancy became available. As soon as I saw it, I applied to come here.'

'Oh? It's an unusual posting. Not too many young women want to head out bush.'

'My nan has dementia and is in the home here. I wanted to be closer.' She swallowed.

'If that isn't a mongrel disease,' Dave said. 'What sort of stage is she at?'

Mia looked out the window, trying to hide the tears that unexpectedly sprung to her eyes at his kindness.

'Sounds like it's nearly at four,' she said. After a moment she turned towards him. 'Did someone from your family have it?'

'No one close, but I've had a couple of mates whose parents were diagnosed. Heard them talk. Pretty tough for all involved.' Dave leaned forward and fiddled with the radio, making sure the volume was up high and he could hear what was going on. There hadn't been any comms from anyone in the field during the time they'd been in the vehicle.

'I feel really powerless.'

'Yeah, I could only imagine.'

There was a silence and then Dave flicked on his blinker to turn down Lake Moore Road. 'Have you met this family? The Chellows?' he asked.

Mia shook her head. 'I haven't been here long enough to meet many people. Just the doctor and the few people Richie and I pulled over on my first day. I don't think you can say that I actually "met" them either. A licence check doesn't really equate to a "Hi, how are you?" at the pub.'

Dave agreed. 'Look here,' he said. 'See all the vehicle tracks into the gateway? Always a good way to tell that there's something going on. We're in the right spot. Gravel roads give a lot of information if you know what to look for.'

Mia absorbed that piece of information. For a moment, she wished that Dave was her sergeant not the grumpy hulk, Zachery Tyler.

'I stuffed up yesterday.' The words were out of her mouth before she could stop them. Embarrassment shot through her and she looked away quickly. She'd never usually open up to someone so quickly, and it wasn't the done thing to rat out the people you worked with, but Dave . . . there was something easy about him. Easy to talk to, easy to like.

Again, there was silence. Like he was waiting for her to tell him, but it was okay if she didn't want to.

Quickly, before they pulled up at the tent that had been erected at the Chellows' farmhouse, she told him what had taken place with the two young lads the day before.

Switching off the engine, Dave looked at her. 'Bugger of a thing to happen,' he said mildly. 'It's always hard when you start at a new station. Local knowledge doesn't happen overnight. These blokes here, they've been in Broad River for a while. Still, not to worry. You'll be surprised at how quickly you work things out.' He gave her a comforting smile. 'Nothing that a bit of time won't fix. Come on, let's see what we can find here.'

Mia looked around as she stepped out onto the squelchy, wet ground, bolstered by Dave's presence. He hadn't said he supported her, but she felt like he did. And Mia took actions over words any day.

A big shed, filled with red and green machinery, was to the left of the house, while the homestead featured an expansive green lawn, a swing set and wide garden beds filled with roses, honeysuckle and wisteria. Another shed was to the right. Mia noticed yards behind it and clocked it as a shearing shed. She wondered if it was still used, considering she hadn't seen sheep in any of the short distances she'd travelled since she'd arrived in Broad River.

Wide paddocks surrounded all sides of the house. She could see the orange dots of men and women from the SES walking every paddock in a grid-like search. Their voices, calling 'Tahlia!' drifted through the air and gave Mia a prickly feeling in her stomach.

Zach strode across the gravel when he saw Mia and Dave. A brief smile for Dave and a glare for Mia. A phone rang somewhere from the depths of his pockets and he ignored it.

'Dave, thanks for coming. Got your offsider with you?'

'Jack? No, DTS called his name.'

Zach nodded. 'Unfortunate. One-man band now?'

'I'd imagine so, but I haven't heard anything from up the line. What have we got here?'

Without answering, Zach turned to Mia. 'I thought I left you in the office.'

'I, ah—'

Dave interjected. 'I brought her out. The more the better in this type of situation, don't you agree, Zach? And there were a few tricky questions coming through from the media and CWA. We've diverted the phone and stuck a note on the door with your mobile number. Now, what can we do here?'

Mia watched Zach's face turn from red to an ugly shade of purple. 'For fuck's sake, is that why this bloody phone won't stop ringing?' He turned and stomped back towards the tent. 'I'll give you a team in a minute, but perhaps, just for once, you'll refrain from taking over this search and investigation as you seem to do in every situation that I find you in.'

'If you're referring to the search in Wilpena Pound for the missing tourist, you were out of line then, Tyler,' Dave snapped back. 'That's my turf and I knew the lay of the land. You didn't. And your fucked-up instructions almost cost that woman her life. If I hadn't overruled you, she would have died out there on Saint Mary Peak.'

'And this is my turf, Burrows,' Zach retorted. 'So I know the lay of the land here.'

Mia's curiosity had been piqued at Dave's words and she noticed that Zach didn't flinch at the accusation. She studied both men for a moment. Her sarge had a vein throbbing on the left-hand side of his temple; Dave seemed pumped and keen to get on with the job. She hoped her instincts hadn't been wrong about this friendly detective. He hadn't been met with open arms by Zach, that was for sure. Perhaps aligning herself with Dave wasn't a good idea.

'This isn't a pissing competition, Tyler,' Dave said. 'We've got a young girl to find, so perhaps you could brief me?'

Dave gave her a pointed glance and then tipped his head towards the tent. Mia turned to head under the tarp, frustration sweeping through her. Who should she trust? She didn't know the pecking order, nor the politics or history of the coppers stationed around the area. What she did know was that jostling egos in police stations were rife and she didn't want to be caught up in any of it. Just get on, do her job, protect the community and spend time with her nan. That's all she wanted.

Still, she couldn't deny the excitement that was seeping through her at the thought of getting on the ground and helping look for Tahlia.

Near the hills, the grey curtain of a shower of rain moved towards them and began to fall gently. Mia turned up the hood of her jacket and quickly made her way to the tent.

Zach was speaking to Dave, his tone clipped. Mia listened as she turned slowly, taking in the yard, shed and haystack.

'Tahlia Chellow, four, was last seen by her mother on the swing set just before midday today. When she called her daughter for lunch, she discovered the front yard was empty and the child wasn't anywhere in sight. She's searched the compound.' Zach stretched his arm out, indicating the sheds. 'The Broad River and Kalagyne SES volunteers are searching. I've been on site for . . .' He glanced at his watch.

Mia was distracted by the gentle drip, drip, drip from the roof of the canvas onto the ground.

'Two and a half hours, and there has been no sign of her.'

So much had happened in such a short space of time, but to Mia it felt as if only half an hour had passed.

His phone rang, and again, he ignored it.

Mia's stomach flipped with nerves.

The wind picked up and the tent flapped, almost drowning out Dave's words. 'Any indication of a family problem? Stepmother or father?'

'No. Parents are happily married and Tahlia is their only daughter.'

'Any people who are upset with them and could have taken her?'

'The parents don't think so.'

'Is there a family liaison officer with them?'

'Not at the moment. If you're talking about Marty, he's helping Richie search.' Zach hardened his voice. 'Like you said. The more the merrier.'

Dave nodded and Mia watched them both carefully, trying to glean any knowledge she could.

'Sarge?' she began, heading back towards them. 'Did her parents actively discourage her from leaving the yard? I noticed that there is a fairly solid fence around it. Either the gate was left open, was opened deliberately or she's climbed out.' Mia pointed to the cement pillared fence that had been painted white. There were pillars every two metres and what looked like wrought-iron bars in between. 'Those bars could have acted as handholds,' she said.

Dave turned to Zach and waited.

'The gate in the front yard was always shut,' Zach answered, eyeing Mia. 'If you go and check, you'll see it's like any country gate that's never used—it's imbedded in the dirt. You wouldn't be able to open it. The gate to the side was open as that's the way they come in and out. There is no access from the front yard to the side.'

'So, she climbed?' Dave asked.

'At this point, that's our assumption, however . . .' Zach paused and indicated for them to follow him. The phone rang a third time. This time, he swore and pulled it out, switched it to silent and put it back in his pocket without looking at the screen. 'Climbing is something she's never done before.'

The ground was muddy now and the rain persistent. The small drops were seeping through Mia's police-issued jacket and she pulled it tighter, the urge to find this little girl getting stronger with each drip. 'The lake . . .' Mia's voice trailed off. 'Is it full?'

'Yes.' The three stood sombre, hoping what they were all thinking wasn't going to be the outcome.

Shifting slightly, Mia turned her attention to the sheds. 'And the sheds? They've all been searched thoroughly? The house? Is there a cellar she liked to play in or a cubby somewhere?'

Zach bristled. 'I don't know who you think you are, asking those sorts of questions. You're a new connie, the lowest rank, you don't get to question me.'

Mia wished the ground would open up and swallow her. The SES volunteers working the radio were pretending not to listen and had their heads over a map, with a protractor and pencils in hand, marking off where the search teams had already been.

'Sorry,' she muttered. 'I wasn't trying to be smart—'

Dave interrupted her. 'Whoa, hang on, mate,' he said to Zach. 'They're reasonable questions.' Dave was holding his hands up towards Zach. 'The more information we have, the better we can search. That's what happened with the search in Wilpena, I—' Dave stressed the word I '—I kept asking questions then found out that one of the other campers had seen the woman heading up the mountain.

'You know as well as I do, Zach, when a search starts everyone is keen to get out in the bush and sometimes the closest areas get skipped over. I could imagine how that might happen here with the lake being so close.

'Mia wasn't casting any aspersions, and neither am I. We're gathering facts so we can make informed decisions.' Dave wasn't backing down. 'Who searched the sheds, house and around the compound?'

Dave had drawn himself up even taller than what his six-foot frame usually seemed, and the two men were eye to eye. Mia took a couple of steps back. She knew she was absolutely able to ask those questions. New to the search ground, she had to understand what had been done and what hadn't.

'Of course these areas have been searched. Not only by my men, but by the family as well.' Zach inhaled so sharply, his nostrils sucked in. 'I do know what I'm doing.'

'Look, I know these types of searches are highly emotional,' Dave said. 'But being all het up isn't going to help anyone, Zach.'

Peace-keeping seemed like a good idea to Mia right now.

'I don't need someone constantly telling me how to do my job.' Zach still glared at Dave. 'You seem to like interfering.' He turned to Mia. 'And you, a new connie, need to know when to keep your mouth shut and follow instructions.'

The sarge took a few more deep breaths and turned to look out across the landscape. The misty drizzle had turned into rain and the low cloud now shrouded the hills and paddocks. Lake Moore couldn't be seen, and neither could the searchers. Still, their voices calling out Tahlia's name came from within the mist and bounced off the hills. The atmosphere was eerie and still. Mia shivered.

Zach dug in his pocket and thrust a mobile phone at her. 'Here's my mobile. You can answer all the questions, and if you don't know the answer write the callers' names down and I'll get back to them.' Striding away, he slipped on the wet gravel and seemed as if he was going to fall. Waving his arms slightly, he managed to regain his balance but fury radiated from his whole body. He strode on, pretending it hadn't happened, without looking back. Over his shoulder, Zach called back, 'Go speak to the mother too. You can be family liaison—that's a good job for you. Until I come and find you, stay out of my way. I'm a busy man. Burrows, here's your team.' An orange bus with more SES volunteers turned into the drive. 'Now both of you bugger off and do your jobs. And just an FYI, Burrows, I've got water police on stand-by because there's every chance that she's gone into the lake.' He stomped away, stopping only to wave at the bus.

'God, I'm so sorry,' Mia rushed to say as soon as Zach was out of earshot. 'If I'd known me coming here was going to cause so much trouble, I would have stayed back at the station.'

'Don't worry about it. He's under the pump; a kid going missing is never good and the pressure takes its toll. My advice? Be around. In earshot, but stay out of his way for a little while.' Dave turned and looked back up at the house. 'Kids always take the path of least resistance. This compound is pretty open, so there's no obvious direction she could have gone . . .'

Dave seemed to be speaking to himself so Mia gathered Zach's phone and went to speak with Tahlia's parents.

CHAPTER 21

Mia could hear the sound of sobbing even from outside the house as she walked down the path, letting her hands brush over the lavender bushes on either side. The droplets splattered on her fingers and left a lingering smell.

Knocking gently on the front door, she waited, her eyes raking over the garden for any little hidey-hole that could have been missed or any sign of the little girl.

Any footprints would have been washed away by now, so the searchers would have nothing to work with. Just open plains, grass-covered paddocks, muddy soil and a lake.

The door opened, a loud squeak sounding from the hinges, and an older woman with fuzzy, short grey hair looked out.

'Have you found her?'

Mia shook her head. 'Not yet, I'm afraid, but they are doing everything they can to bring Tahlia home safely. I'm Constable Mia Worth. Could I come in? You are?'

The door opened more and inside, Mia could see a large, freshly painted kitchen, bright pictures on the wall and a fridge full of a child's drawings.

'I'm Carol. Tahlia's grandmother. Tate and Naomi are in the lounge room.'

Mia thanked her and shook off her coat, leaving it on the verandah, before taking off her shoes and going inside. She'd never forgotten the rules of the bush. Before going into a house, take your shoes off. Anything could be on the bottom of them.

'Thanks,' she said, looking around. 'Is this Tahlia?' she touched a photo in a silver frame on the wall. A little blonde girl with green eyes and a thin smile, showing missing teeth to the side of her front teeth. 'Could I take this?'

'Such a pretty girl, isn't she?' Carol's voice caught in her throat. 'I guess you can. You'll want it for media, I suppose?'

Mia didn't answer. She didn't know if the sarge had contacted the media to put an alert out for a missing child. But even if he hadn't, the photo would help the searchers. She just smiled and took the frame from the wall.

'Anyway, come through. I guess you've got more questions. Can I make you a cup of tea?'

'Oh no, thanks. You've got enough on your plate.'

Mia followed the older lady into the lounge room where Carol introduced her to Tahlia's parents.

Tate stood up and shook her hand, but then seemed at a loss. He looked down at his wife, who was staring at Mia. The shock seemed to have rendered both incapable of doing anything much.

'Tell me you've found her,' Naomi pleaded, reaching her hands up.

Mia took the woman's hands and squeezed, before sitting alongside her. 'Not yet.' She repeated the information she'd given to Carol. 'But I would like to ask you a few questions. Would that be all right?'

Naomi nodded, her eyes never leaving Mia's. Mia felt the weight of Naomi's hope and sagged a little.

'I'd love for you to tell me a little about Tahlia,' Mia said. 'She liked to play outside?'

'The front yard was her favourite spot,' Tate said, perching on the arm of the sofa. 'She'd play with imaginary friends out there, make cups of tea with the little toy tea set she was given for Christmas. Under the bushes, she made cubby houses for her teddy bears and dolls.'

Naomi took up the commentary. 'Every morning when she wasn't going to kindy, we'd go out and feed the chooks, then she could have a play on the swing set. In the afternoon, sometimes she'd have a sleep, but other times she was happy to roam around outside. Never outside the fence though. We had very clear rules about that. I've always been frightened . . .' Naomi shuddered and closed her eyes, as Tate leaned over and rubbed her shoulder. 'Always been frightened that she'd get run over by a tractor or header, or something else. Tahlia knew from a very young age never to climb the fence.'

Tate spoke. 'And she never did, which is why we can't understand what's happened. She'd stand at the fence and wave to me as I drove past in the ute or whatever machine

I was in.' His voice cracked a little and it was Naomi's turn to comfort him, placing a hand over his.

'Okay.' Mia was about to ask another question, but Naomi rushed on.

'The door, you would have heard it squeak when you came in. We never oiled it because that was how I knew if she'd gone outside. It's the only door we use, unless I'm hanging out the washing and I go out the laundry door. You can hear that screech from anywhere in the house.'

'Great alarm system.' Mia smiled. 'And you don't have any other children?' She'd been told no, but it was always good to hear the answers for yourself. At the question, she heard Carol suck in her breath, but Mia kept her eyes on Naomi.

The woman's shoulders slumped and Tate ran his hands across his face, Mia heard the rasp of stubble.

'No,' Naomi answered in a low voice. 'No other children.'

The fire threw flames into the chimney. Mia leaned forward. 'What happened?' she asked.

Tate and Naomi looked at each other before swallowing hard. They didn't seem to have any tears left.

'Chelsea, she was our first. Our little angel. She never got the chance to take a breath. She died before she was born.'

'I'm sorry.' Mia's heart ached for the parents.

Tate stood and moved across to the window. 'Normally, I'd be thrilled with this rain, but not today,' he said. 'We've got to do something more to find her. Tahlia will be cold and frightened and—'

'I know.' Mia brought her voice down a level and tried to sound confident. 'We are looking as quickly as we can, but we need to search thoroughly. We can't leave any stone unturned, so to speak, so it can take a while to cover the ground we need to.' The phone buzzed in her pocket. It was her turn to ignore it.

'Has Tahlia been talking about any friends or animals lately?' she asked Naomi. 'Does she have a pet, other than the chooks?'

'When doesn't she! That child has the most active imagination, always rattling on about her friends. They've even got names! Hannah, Abigail and Jemima —they're three that I can remember.'

'Okay and does she have a cubby house. Other than the ones she makes under the bushes. You know one made out of wood or something else?'

'I've been promising to build her a tree house, but I always seem to be busy on the farm,' Tate said miserably.

Mia looked around the room. 'This is an old house. Do you have a cellar?'

This time it was Carol who answered. She got up and indicated for Mia to follow her. Through the hallway and toilet, to the laundry.

'Down here.' Carol showed Mia the enclosed stairs leading under the house. 'She can't get in though. It's enclosed and the door is always locked.'

'Has anyone checked down here in case she slipped through?' Mia asked.

'I don't know. Do you want to go down?'

'Please.'

Carol opened the laundry door and reached for a key hanging on a board just inside. 'Surely we'd hear her?'

'Yes, most likely, but I want to see for myself.'

Mia felt for the torch on her belt and turned it on. Its light shone down into the darkness, picking up the old steps. They looked like they were made from a mixture of stone, wood and cement and reminded her of the ones in the haberdashery shop.

She gingerly made her way down the stairs, watching her footing until she got to the bottom.

'Tahlia,' she called out. 'Tahlia, my name's Mia. I'm a policewoman. Are you down here?' She used her torch to flash up and down the walls, looking for a light switch. She found it and pulled the long cord that hung from the ceiling. A naked bulb spread a yellow glow across the small room.

Shelves lined one wall and a cupboard was on the other.

Down on her hands and knees, she made sure the shelves were empty and then opened the cupboard door.

Empty of Tahlia. Full of jams and preserves.

Clenching her jaw, she turned off the light and went back upstairs.

In the lounge room, there were now cups of steaming tea, although Mia was sure neither of the parents had touched theirs.

Even in the minutes since she'd arrived, she could see the increasing toll Tahlia's disappearance was having on Naomi and Tate. Red eyes, pale faces, hands that couldn't stop moving.

Again, she felt the pressure. It was a good pressure because it kept her senses sharp and galvanised her into action.

'Tahlia's not down there,' she said. Probably unnecessarily, but they were words and noise and Tahlia's name. 'You have a good relationship with your neighbours?'

'Yes, of course. Abby and Karl are some of the nicest people we know. Why?'

'With an investigation like this, we need to know there aren't any people who you've upset or . . .'

'No one would have taken her, if that's what you're implying.' Tate's words were emphatic. 'She's wandered off somewhere. That's all.'

Mia nodded. Sometimes when people were so certain, the opposite had happened.

'Let's just quickly have a chat about the lake,' Mia said, rushing her words. She was loath to bring up the subject and she saw Naomi blanch at the comment.

'Tahlia knows it's dangerous down there. She'd even have to cross the road and that's just something she wouldn't do.' Naomi's voice was strained.

'I agree,' Carol said. 'She never—'

'But you didn't think she'd wander off either,' Mia said gently. 'We have to look at all possibilities. Did she have her shoes on?'

'Rubber boots. They're pink. And she was wearing a pink puffer jacket.' Naomi smiled, looking at the image in her mind. 'She was so cute.'

Mia stilled. '*Was* so cute?'

Tate rose to his feet. 'We have had nothing to do with the disappearance of our little girl,' he said loudly. 'How dare you—'

Mia stood too. 'I'm not implying anything, but Naomi said "was" as in past tense. I . . . I . . .' She cast around for someone to help her out of the hole she had dug herself.

Naomi stared at her, then a realisation dawned on her face. 'Oh, I was thinking of when she was wearing it earlier this morning. She wears different clothes all the time and that particular clobber is gorgeous on her.'

Mia apologised again. Leaning forward, she picked up a cup of weak tea; they all seemed to be made the same and neither milk nor sugar was on offer. She took a moment to gather her thoughts. 'Is there anything else you want to tell me about Tahlia?' The urge to get outside and look through the sheds was overwhelming. She had to be out there doing something useful. Sitting with Naomi, Tate and Carol was important, but she was thinking about when she was a child. All the places she'd made cubbies and hid from the adults.

Her fantasy world of imaginary friends and pets had kept her company for the long hours that Nana had been at the shop, and she suspected this little girl may have a similar imagination.

'We do go to the lake,' Naomi said suddenly. 'Together as a family. We catch yabbies there.'

'Is there a certain area you go to?'

'Yeah, across the road and to the west a little, there's a two-wheel track in there. Only locals know it's there. But I don't know if she'd know where to find it.'

'I'm going to go and give that information to the team. I'll be back soon,' Mia said. 'If there's any change, I'll let you know straightaway. I promise.'

'Please find her,' Naomi said, grasping towards Tate. 'Please.'

CHAPTER 22

Outside the rain had reduced to a drizzle, but now there was a gentle breeze winding its way in between the sheds and trees. Pulling her jacket close around her body, Mia looked out across the grey land and gave a heavy sigh. That poor little girl.

She could understand Zach's angst now. She felt it too, building in her gut. Fear of the unknown. Fear of what they could find. Fear of not finding anything.

Mia wondered if there was any CCTV on the start of Lake Moore Road, then instantly dismissed it from her mind. Of course, there wouldn't be. As Zach had so succinctly reminded her after she'd chased the boy in the green hoodie, this was a country town. A *quiet* country town. And they were on farmland now. Still, she wondered if any of the farmers might have security cameras up. After all, diesel was so expensive she knew there were people driving onto farms and helping themselves.

She made a note in her book to ask Tate and Naomi about cameras.

The radio on her hip came to life, with distorted voices telling the headquarters they had finished searching grid A and would be starting on grid C.

No sign of the little girl yet.

Another heavy sigh and Mia put her head down, walking quickly towards the tent. She took out Zach's phone and looked at the screen. There were fifteen missed calls with just as many texts. She scrolled through, noting the names. Most were from Campbell Duncan, the journo, who had already tried to speak to her. A couple from Shirley.

The CWA are more than happy to help out with food, Zach. Just let me know. I spoke to your young constable a while ago, and she was going to get back to me. I haven't heard anything. That poor family.

How does any of this get around town so quickly? she wondered again. Then she realised that Naomi and Tate would have rung their neighbours to ask if they'd seen Tahlia, who in turn would have rung others to gather people to help search.

'How are you all getting on?' Mia asked the two men who were huddled under the tent.

'Better than Tahlia,' one of them replied. 'At least we have walls around us, no matter how thin.'

At that, the canvas walls rattled with another gust, and the water that had pooled on the roof splattered to the ground.

'Has anyone asked about security cameras on the farms?'

The two men looked at her.

'Yeah, Zach said there weren't any here.'

Mia nodded, a sinking feeling in her stomach. What a bloody shame. 'Do you know if anything has been organised for meals?'

'Not that I know of,' the younger one replied. He had dark hair and a scarf wrapped around his neck, while his companion was ginger with freckles standing out against his pale skin. A dark blue beanie highlighted his fair features.

'What would be the protocol?' She pulled up a folding chair and sat down at the makeshift table. It was covered in radio equipment, maps and notes. 'And how many do we have on site?'

Freckles referred to his clipboard. 'Twenty SES searching and you coppers. I'd reckon we should get some food in. They've been out there for four hours now and it's going to get dark soon.'

There was an ominous tone to his voice. They all knew what that meant.

'Okay, I'll ring this Shirley lady from the CWA. I'm assuming we're too far out for HQ to send food trucks?'

Scarf man looked at her as if she'd lost her mind. 'I reckon you could be right there,' he said dryly.

Wanting to snap back, to tell him that she'd only been here for less than a week and was still finding her feet through difficult circumstances, she tossed a haughty look towards him and turned on her heel.

She walked towards the machinery shed, holding the phone to her ear.

'Zach?' Shirley answered. 'How are you getting on? Any sign of that little girl?'

'Ah, it's Constable Worth here, Shirley. I'm ringing on behalf of Zach.'

'Oh, you're the new girl.'

'New constable, yes,' Mia corrected gently.

'Has she been found yet?'

Without answering the question, Mia said that everyone was still out in the field. 'But we would love some food and coffee, if you were able to get enough together for about twenty-five people.'

'Of course. Consider it done. I'll get the ladies together and we'll bring it out. It's the Chellow property off Lake Moore Road, isn't it? Young Tahlia.'

Not wanting to confirm, but having no other option, Mia said yes and hung up.

The phone rang with a blocked number.

'Senior Sergeant Tyler's phone, Constable Worth speaking.' She continued her slow walk towards the machinery shed, looking under the bushes and tapping on the silos as she went.

'Water Police. Constable Ryder here. Any updates?'

Mia cast her eyes around for Zach, knowing he wasn't in sight.

'Ah, I haven't had any updates, Constable Ryder. But my senior sergeant is still out searching. I'll touch base and get back to you.'

'Fine. Quicker the better, we're four hours away.'

He rang off and Mia put the phone back in her pocket. She rested her hand on the large header tyre she was standing alongside and felt the rough rubber under her fingers.

If she was a kid, where would she make a cubby? Climbing up the ladder, she opened the door into the cab and looked in. There was very little space for a child to hide. In fact, the driver's compartment wasn't capable of hiding anything—it was so small that if there had been two adults inside, they would have been touching thighs.

Back out on the platform, she looked into the grain bin behind the cabin. To get in there, you would have to clamber up the side without the use of a ladder, then swing your leg over and climb down inside. A dangerous thing to do, unless everyone knew you were inside.

There was a boy about three years behind Mia when she'd been at school. During a game of hide and seek, he'd hidden inside. The driver of the chaser bin had arrived and started emptying his load of wheat into the open-top storage. The boy was smothered to death by the grain.

She'd only been young when it had happened, but the waves of grief and ripples of guilt and blame that had gone through the community were still fresh in her memory.

Climbing down the ladder, she realised she had another question for the family.

Retracing her steps, she once again knocked on the door and Carol answered.

'Could I just ask Tate a quick question?'

Carol held the door open wide and indicated they were all still where Mia had left them.

'Tate,' she asked, standing in the doorway. 'You haven't been shifting any grain around recently? Swapping it from one silo to another or something similar?'

His head snapped up.

'Um, yeah. This morning. I unloaded the leftover barley seed from the truck into the storage against the machinery shed.' His face paled as he glanced towards Naomi. 'What time was that?' he asked in a strangled voice.

Mia's heart kicked up a notch. God, surely not!

Naomi couldn't speak. Her mouth was open, but no words could be heard.

It was Carol's calm and soothing voice that answered.

'No, that's not an option. You were doing that when I arrived just before morning smoko.' Carol turned to Mia. 'I came to take Tahlia to dance lessons. She was on the lawn when I first arrived. Came up and gave me a kiss and a cuddle, but I'd come early to spend a little time with Naomi. See how she was doing.' Turning back to her son-in-law, she said, 'You were just finishing that job off, Tate, because you came in for a cuppa and Tahlia was there then.'

Both parents sagged with relief as they remembered.

'Sorry. I couldn't work out the timing for a sec,' Tate said.

Mia nodded. 'It's hard to remember when you're under stress.' Her phone buzzed. Not Zach's.

'I'd better take this,' she said and gave them a smile. 'I'll be back.'

Hitting the accept button, she walked outside quickly. It was Dave's number and there could be only one of two reasons he was calling her.

'Dave.'

'Mia, I think we need to call the water police in.'

Mia's heart thumped in her chest.

'It's getting late and it'll take a while for them to get up here. There's no sign of her anywhere down here so we might have to drag the lake.'

'Okay. Zach knows about this?'

'He's standing alongside me. You've got his phone, remember.'

'Yes.' Mia felt the back of her throat close over and no more words came out. 'I'll ring them now,' she finally said. 'Do I tell the parents?'

There was a muffled discussion and Dave came back on the phone. 'Let's get the water police on their way before we do that.'

Hands shaking, she found Zach's phone buried deep in her jacket and opened the contact list. Ryder had been his name. Finding the number under Water Police, she dialled.

He answered immediately.

'Right, I'll get the team mobilised,' he told her, his voice resigned but still professional. Every single person was affected when they were searching for a missing child. 'Will text with an ETA.'

After Ryder had hung up, she tapped the phone to her mouth, unable to ignore the sinking feeling in her stomach.

Another text on her phone.

Chris.

Heard the news. You okay?

We're searching now. Nothing yet.

Shitty day.

The whole thing is awful.

There was nothing more to say. Mia walked towards the hay shed this time, smelling the fresh scent of newly baled oats. The straw was scratchy as she ran her hands over it and she bent down to take a deep whiff. There had to be positives in times like this and a simple pleasure such as this was one.

The rain on the iron roof drummed with a relentless beat. A brush against Mia's arm, and she shot up from the hay bale and squealed.

Stupid, stupid, stupid! Of course there will be mice and snakes in here. It's a freaking hay shed, you idiot!

Then she heard a soft meow and turned to see a ginger cat, teats hanging from beneath her. She looked balefully at Mia and tried to rub against her again, but Mia took another step back, watching her. Wild cats were usually mongrels, although this one didn't seem that fierce.

The cat meowed again and took a couple of graceful jumps towards the top of the haystack and looked around. Mia ignored her. There was no way she was climbing that stack, even with the promise of cute kittens at the top.

She walked back to the entry—the rain seemed to be easing now. The shearing shed stood lonely and abandoned. Maybe that was another place to look. Not that she expected to find any evidence of Tahlia. After all this time, the lake seemed the most obvious place she would have gone if you went with Dave's theory of kids taking the path of least resistance. No gates, no fences, no bush. Only a wide dirt driveway, a bitumen road and then a track leading down to the wide expanse of water.

The rain had stopped again, and silence strung out through the shed.

She heard the cat meowing again.

Turning to look, she realised the cat had disappeared towards the roof, where willy wagtail birds were darting in and out, diving towards the hay as if they were trying to scare something away.

The kittens, she supposed.

Mia frowned at a thin sound, trying to work out what the noise was. Walking quietly back to the hay, she raised her eyes to the tin roof.

Listening hard, then realisation filtered through.

'*Pussy cat, pussy cat, where have you been . . .*'

Mia ran to the haystack and leaped onto the bottom bale. As she climbed as quickly as she could, towards the roof, the voice became louder.

'*I've been to London to visit the queen.*'

Mia's breath caught in her throat. *This area has been searched*, kept echoing in her mind. *This can't be her.*

A swoop of wings and a breath of wind passing the back of her head. She swiped at the willy wagtail who was dive-bombing her now.

Not wanting to call out and frighten the little girl, Mia could hear her own ragged breath and a drumming in her ears as she climbed the bales.

Finally reaching the top, she peered into the dimness. Far towards the back of the shed, she saw the outline of a little girl, sitting on the hay, holding something to her chest.

The ginger cat was weaving her way around the child, rubbing against her back and stomach. A hand reached out to pat the cat.

'S'all right,' the girl said quietly. 'I'm just playing with your baby.'

Mia had to hold in the sob that had formed in her throat. The little girl was the exact image of the girl in the photo frame she had taken from the wall earlier.

Mia finally spoke. 'Hello there. What's your name?'

The little girl looked up, quizzical at first. Then she smiled. 'I'm Tahlia and this—' she held out a kitten with ginger and tan markings, just like its mum '—this is Jemima.'

'She's very cute,' Mia said softly. Heaving her body over the corner of the bale and onto the flat surface of the summit, she asked another question. 'Does she have any brothers and sisters?'

Tahlia nodded enthusiastically. 'Hannah and Abigail. There're more babies, but I haven't named them all yet.'

Jemima, Hannah and Abigail! They were the same names that Naomi had said Tahlia had been talking about recently! They'd thought they were Tahlia's imaginary friends, but there was nothing imaginary about these kittens. Mia could hear the high-pitched snuffles and squeaks.

'How many?'

'One, two, three, four . . .' Tahlia's voice trailed off. 'What comes after four?'

Mia shook her head, a crazy smile spreading across her face. A bubble of excitement and happiness welling in her chest. When she spoke again, her voice caught. 'Is this your cubby?'

Tahlia looked around. 'Sort of. Ginger showed me where she had her babies, so I made a cubby. Do you like it? I brought this blanket up so the kittens wouldn't get cold.' She touched the red woollen blanket she had wrapped around the nest.

'I do and I love those kittens. They make very good friends, don't they? I had one that looked like Jemima when I was your age.'

'I love them too,' Tahlia declared, hugging the one she was holding even tighter.

'Tahlia, your mummy and daddy are very worried about you. Do you think you'd like to come home to see them?'

A sad look crossed the little girl's face. 'Daddy said he didn't want any kittens.'

Finally, Mia understood.

'I think Daddy will let you keep the kittens, honey.' She held out her hand. 'Come on, let's go and find them.'

CHAPTER 23

Mia took the little girl's hand and helped her to the edge of the haystack.

'What about the babies?' Tahlia asked, tears filling her eyes. 'I don't want to leave them.'

'They'll be here when you get back. Mummy and Daddy might even let you move them to the house later tonight. Should we ask them?'

Nodding her head with vigour, Tahlia said, 'I'm hungry.'

'I bet you are, baby, I bet you are. Now can you climb down safely?'

She nodded and started to scamper down with the ease of an acrobat.

Mia pulled out her phone and dialled Dave.

'The water rats on their way?' he asked in way of greeting.

'I've got her.' The words tumbled out of her mouth and this time the tears flowed. 'I've got her,' she repeated.

'Jesus, what? Where?' Dave's voice was loud in her ear when he yelled, 'Mia's found her. Call the teams in. Mia's got her!'

'In the hay shed. At the top. There are some kittens.'

Dave's voice softened. 'Is she okay?'

'More than okay.'

'Well done, Mia. Good job. See you back at HQ.' He hung up and Mia stared down at the little girl, her pigtails bouncing as she reached the ground.

Tahlia waited until Mia hit the ground too, looking at her curiously as if taking in her uniform for the first time.

'Are you a police lady?' she asked.

Mia took her hand and started walking towards the house. 'I am.'

'Why are you at my farm?'

Mia told her again how her parents were worried.

'But I always go to the haystack,' Tahlia said. 'I like to climb on the bales.'

'Do you? That's pretty dangerous, isn't it? I thought hay bales could fall.'

'They never have.'

'They're big bales. I think they'd squash a little girl like you. And that wouldn't be fun, would it? Maybe you should stay away from them until you're bigger.'

'It's like a playground.'

Mia didn't get to answer because just then a shriek echoed around the compound. Naomi, Tate and Carol were running across the yard, their arms outstretched.

'Tahlia! Oh my god, Tahlia!'

Mia let go of the little girl's hand, only seconds before Naomi caught her up in a tight hug, tears streaming down her face. Tahlia looked confused but gave her mum a hug back.

Later, when the search team's vehicles arrived back at the house, their lights slipping through the darkness, the three were standing in a circle. Tahlia in the middle, her parents' arms around her as if they would never let her go.

Richie hurled himself out of the first vehicle, striding across to Mia, who had moved back to the tent where the SES volunteers were gathering, leaving the family to their privacy.

'Where was she?'

Mia looked at him steadily. 'Hay shed.'

'She wasn't. I looked.'

Mia shrugged. She wasn't going to be drawn into this.

Zach was in the next vehicle. He was less quick to exit the car, but he offered his congratulations. 'Well done, Worth. Unexpected, but well done.' He turned to Richie. 'I thought you searched that area.'

Richie had his arms crossed. 'We did. She couldn't have been there then.'

Marty arrived. 'We had a bit of a poke around in the shed,' he confirmed. His face was a picture of both concern and relief. Richie just looked angry.

The weary SES troops started to fill the area and dismantle the makeshift HQ they had set up. Tents, radios and chairs were all packed away.

Mia noticed Dave was helping them, laughing and joking, relief covering everyone like a balm. The grim atmosphere from the start of the search had been replaced with a buoyancy. A slightly hysterical happiness.

Naomi and Tate came over, Tahlia between them.

'We can't thank you enough,' Tate said.

Naomi didn't seem to be able to speak yet.

Zach squatted down, smiling at Tahlia and putting out his hand to shake her tiny one. 'Well, Miss Tahlia, I have to say, I'm very happy to see you. Those kittens must have taken your attention for a very long time!'

'Do you want to see them? Daddy says they can come and live in the house. That police lady said he would.'

'I think the house would be a great place for those little ones now,' Zach agreed. 'You must be very tired?'

'I'm hungry.'

Zach laughed loudly as did so many of the SES volunteers. 'What's your favourite dinner?' he asked.

'Pizza.'

'Do you know, the CWA ladies are bringing us all something to eat and I reckon they'll have some pizza. I think Mum and Dad will let you eat as much as you like tonight!' He touched her face with his pointer finger before standing up. Mia saw a surprising look of tenderness on his face.

The Chellow family wandered off to talk to the volunteers, Tate and Naomi shaking their hands and thanking them for their efforts.

Zach turned back to Richie, his face closed. 'You obviously didn't search that area well enough. You and Marty head back to the station and I'll talk to you shortly. I'll finish up here first. Don't leave before I get there.'

Richie opened his mouth to contradict Zach, but Zach shut him down with one glance.

'Yes, Sarge.'

Richie turned, casting his own glance—one that would kill—to Mia.

Mia let her head fall back onto the headrest in Dave's car as they headed back towards Broad River. Her legs were aching, and she had the start of a headache thumping near the back of her neck.

The initial adrenalin of finding Tahlia had worn off and she was bone-achingly exhausted.

'You did good today,' Dave said. 'Difficult being your first search and all. Especially as it was a child.'

Mia caught Dave's eyes, his face illuminated by the soft glow from the instrument panel.

'What made you go into the hay shed?'

She shrugged. 'The whole thing was a bit fluky really. I'd checked out the machinery shed and then went over there. I had a horrible thought she might have been smothered by grain at the bottom of the silo.'

Dave didn't say anything, his eyes on the road, but she noticed a slight tic in his cheek when she mentioned her thoughts. Pushing the horror of that idea down, she went on. 'When I was a kid, Mr Marshall used to bring hay bales into town on the back of a Dodge truck and unload them at the stock and station agent's business. That was right next to my nan's place in the main street of Barker.' She kept her eyes to the front, looking for any kangaroos that might stray from the bush on the side of the road into their path. 'I always loved the smell and I used to make a cubby there sometimes. There weren't many other places that I could go and have some privacy.' Rubbing her fingers along the seam of her police uniform, Mia kept talking. 'I didn't think she would be anywhere in that compound. Richie said he'd searched everywhere, and the lake was looking like the only option. Then that cat turned up and I heard her singing. I was in the right place at the right time.' She paused then whispered. 'Too bad for Richie.'

Again, that twitch in Dave's jawline.

'But you searched all those sheds and went inside every piece of machinery?'

'Yeah.' Mia nodded. 'It was the grain bin on the back of the header that got me thinking about the other scenario. Tate said he'd been moving grain around that morning. The only reason I didn't ask him to go and auger the silo out was because Carol put the timeline together and we knew Tahlia hadn't been anywhere near the silos or shed before smoko.'

'Well, Mia, you've done a sterling job today and that family will be forever grateful. I know Tahlia would have come down in the end, but it was you who found her and that deserves a heap of praise.'

Mia didn't answer. She'd seen Richie's look towards her as he was leaving, and she'd hung around at the house for as long as she could before returning to Broad River. Zach had left not long after Richie and Marty had. The station wouldn't be a pleasant place to be for a few hours.

For a while all she could hear was the rush of the car and road noise, and she felt her eyes begin to droop. She thought about Tahlia—her voice singing the nursery rhyme—and Naomi's tears and Tate's fear.

Dave's voice cut across her thoughts. 'I know we had a bit of a chat about this on the way out, but how are things going at the station? Anything you want to talk through?'

Mia twisted in her seat, trying to get comfortable. She remembered Zach's cutting remarks about Dave interfering and her indecision on who to trust. 'There are a few teething problems. Maybe this good outcome will help.' She already knew any optimism she felt on that front was misplaced.

The lights of Broad River had come into view and they were already passing the machinery dealership, a few houses and the pub.

Richie's death stares and Zach's crappy comments about her being a wet-behind-the-ears connie weren't going to get any better. If anything, they'd get worse. Still, this was her job and she loved it. A couple of idiotic blokes weren't going to stop her, even though her stomach was turning in circles at the thought of seeing them. Hopefully, Richie would have headed home already.

Dave came to a slow stop in front of the station. 'You'd better go and finish off the last of the paperwork and head home. Been a big day.'

'My mate Chris is over at Burra. On his first day, he was on the scene of a fatal car accident. Now I've had this. I wonder what the rest of the crew had for their first week?' Tiredly, she reached for the door handle. 'Thanks for your support today, Dave. And the ride.'

'Hang in there. Things will get better.'

Mia kept her thoughts about that to herself.

The lights from the front office filtered out onto the street. Her watch told her it was nearly nine o'clock at night, although she could have sworn it was later. Pulling open the door, she fell inside to be greeted by Marty's wide smile.

'Here's the hero of the day! All bow to Constable Worth.' He raised his arms and bowed towards her a few times.

Mia giggled. 'Stop that. Just doing my job, same as you.'

Zach appeared from his office and Mia noticed the lines pulled tight around his eyes.

'Ah, you're back, Worth. Good job out there today. Credit where credit is due.' He nodded towards her, unsmiling, but at least he didn't look grumpy. Just tired.

'Thanks, Sarge,' she said, brimming with pleasure at his words.

'I'll leave you with Marty. I wanted to wait until you got back before I left.' He headed for the door. 'Good job again. See you in the morning.'

'Morning? That feels too soon.' Mia slumped into a chair beside Marty.

He grinned again and put his foot on the arm of her chair, rocking it slightly. 'Get yourself a coffee and let's finish up this paperwork, so we can go home.'

In the kitchen, Mia heaped coffee into a cup and grabbed the milk from the fridge, while waiting for the kettle to boil.

Hearing Marty behind her, she turned. 'Do you want one?'

'Nah, I've had a couple.' Marty didn't move from the doorway and the expression on his face was hard to read.

A shot of fear ran through Mia. 'What's up?' she asked.

'Zach ripped us new arseholes when we got back,' Marty finally said.

A little shudder of relief ran through her. Turning back to the kettle, she poured her coffee and stirred in the milk. Marty was still a good guy.

'Oh?'

'Tore into Richie like I've never seen before. Richie swears he searched the hay shed, but I'm not sure he did. I walked through the shearing shed, and I checked the chutes that lead outside and all the nooks and crannies there. But to be honest, Mia, we were all so focused on getting to the lake that I'm damn certain we didn't search that compound area properly.'

Mia wondered what she was supposed to say. Well done for telling me you stuffed up? 'I guess the lake was the scariest option, wasn't it?'

Marty shook his head. 'We all know that kids don't stray that far from home. As the first ones there, we should've searched the house and yards before going anywhere else. But we didn't. We took the word of the parents. I heard about your grain smothering theory.' He looked straight at her. 'That never even occurred to me.'

Marty sighed and sat down at the table. Mia joined him.

'Richie can be a bit sloppy sometimes, and today wasn't the day to be slack. We both stuffed up, but Richie? Well, he flat-out lied to Zach when we got back here. Said he climbed up and looked in the top, but he didn't because I saw him walk to the front, look up and then walk away.' He held Mia's eyes. 'You need to watch your back now. He's a vindictive SOB and he's had it in for you the minute he heard you were coming here.'

Mia held her hands out. 'But why? What have I done?'

'Absolutely nothing,' Marty said. 'He doesn't like new coppers.'

'Something to do with being a woman?'

Marty shook his head. 'It's all new connies. From what I know, he was partnered with a green bloke a few years back and there was a mistake made that put Richie in a bad spot. Got the shit beaten out of him. Since then, he's never wanted to work with anyone new.'

'Oh right.' Mia got up angrily and walked the length of the room and back, then sat down again. 'So, that makes it okay for him to treat us all like shit?'

'Like I said, he's an SOB. A weak one at that.'

'No, he's just a bully.'

Marty rubbed the back of his neck. 'You can use that word if you like, Mia, but everyone seems to get upset by it these days.'

'If the caps fits,' Mia said and got up again, ending the conversation.

CHAPTER 24

Mia let herself into her house and closed the door behind her, leaning against it with a huge sigh. 'Wow,' she said aloud. 'Just wow.'

She wanted to crawl into bed with a Milo, but her stomach was rumbling. Somehow, she'd missed out on the dinner the CWA ladies had brought. All ten of them, bustling around, making sure everyone was fed and watered, and talking nineteen to the dozen.

Zach had been right—there had been pizza, and Tahlia had eaten her fair share.

Mia was still leaning against the door and she smiled at the memory of the little girl eating dinner while pushing eight kittens and their mum in a doll's pram. Her face had been a picture of contentment and happiness.

Naomi and Tate hadn't let their little girl get too far away from them, their hands constantly straying to touch her head or give her a kiss on the cheek. To reassure themselves she was still there.

Mia's phone rang and she groaned. She'd had enough of people for the day.

The screen told her it was Chris.

'I can't talk, I'm too tired,' she said as way of greeting, pushing herself off the wall and going into the bedroom. She put the call on speaker as she stripped off her uniform, hoping the new gas bottle had been delivered.

'Too bad! You're the hero of the hour, I hear. Tell me everything. I've got to know!'

'Ha. I'm no hero if you ask Richie.'

'Oh yeah? Steal his limelight, did you?'

Mia didn't even have the energy to laugh at Chris's disdain. She imagined him in a chair, his feet swung over the edge, a beer resting on his stomach.

She carried the phone into the bathroom and turned on the shower, holding her hand under the water. It didn't take long for the heat to come through and she smiled with relief. 'Marty pulled me aside at the station tonight and told me to watch my back. Richie's vindictive, apparently. Said that he had a bad experience working with a newbie and he didn't trust them. Not that that's any excuse. Tell me what's been going on with you while I shower quickly.' Mia walked into the shower and quickly ran the soap over her body, rinsed and got out, listening as Chris told her about his day, full of footy practice and mind-numbing paperwork to do with a boundary fence in the wrong position.

All Mia wanted to do was have a feed and get into bed. Let her tired eyes close and aching legs rest.

'Deskwork is nothing but a brain drain,' she agreed, towelling herself dry. She gave him a quick summary of what had happened over her day and how Richie had been caught out not doing his job properly.

'Make sure you don't take any of that shit on board,' Chris said. 'He's just a tosser.'

'I know.' Mia dragged on her trackie pants and a jumper, before heading into the kitchen and checking what was in the freezer section of the car fridge.

There was bread, which she could turn into toast. Two slices in the toaster and Bob was the uncle that everyone wished never turned up at Christmas.

'But I've embarrassed him. That won't end well for me.' She fossicked in the cupboard and brought out a jar of peanut butter. Crossing her fingers there was butter in the fridge, she opened the lid and found it.

'New blood in the station—some people cut too much slack, and some don't cut any. This Richie is obviously one of the latter. But there sounds like there is more to it. What about requesting a transfer?'

'No! You think I'm going to let him win? I'm staying. He can have me.' Her voice dropped as if she was narrating a horror novel. 'The best of me.'

'All he's going to do is make your life hell.'

'Maybe Zach will step up to the plate.'

'Jury is still out on that one,' Chris said wryly. 'He hasn't convinced me he's much better.'

Mia was silent, wanting to agree but for some reason feeling a loyalty towards her sarge. Then she laughed just as her toast popped up, loving that Chris was indignant for her.

But she knew she was the only one who could fix the situation, or stop it. On the trip back with Dave, a plan had started to form in her mind. 'I'm not saying—'

Suddenly the kitchen was plunged into darkness and Mia heard the fridge switch off. She was left standing with the toast in her hand and her phone tucked in between her shoulder and ear. 'Argh!' she said crossly.

'What's happened?'

'Power's out. Hang on.' Tapping the speaker button, she turned on her phone's torch and put the toast on her plate. Brushing the crumbs from her hands, she went down the hallway, checking the bedroom.

'Everywhere? You'd better report it.'

'Not sure, but nothing would surprise me with this house.' She pulled open the front door and glanced out.

The street and house lights were on across the road.

'Oh. Weird.' She shut the door and looked back down the passageway. Inky blackness.

'What?'

'I'll ring you back. I have to check the fuse box. The lights are still on everywhere else.'

'Don't hang up,' Chris said. 'I'll stay on the phone.' There was a tightness in his voice.

'It'll be fine,' Mia said. 'I bet it's only a short-circuit. Like the gas the other night. It's an old house, and I don't think the real estate checked it properly before I moved in.'

'Hopefully that's all it is,' he said.

As he spoke, the lights lit up again and Mia blinked with the sudden brightness.

'Ah, there we go, they're back on.'

'Strange,' Chris said.

Mia opened the door again and stepped out onto the porch. Did she imagine that sound of thudding feet? Or the rustle of branches near the fence? A little quiver in her stomach. Her intuition on high alert.

The phone was still to her ear, although she jumped when Chris spoke again.

'Mia, you still there?'

'Shush a moment,' she said quietly, making her way around the side of the house to the fuse box.

She held the torch up and searched for the galvanised tin box. There it was, right near the gas bottles. She flashed the torch to the ground. No footprints she could see. Still, it was cement and it was wet from the rain.

The squeak from the box's hinge seemed to echo through the whole town, while rain pitter-pattered on the leaves and pavement. A gentle, reassuring sound. Or was the curtain of droplets hiding something?

'What have you found?' Chris wanted to know.

'Nothing yet . . . Oh.'

'Mia?'

'Lots of spiders and heavy cobwebs,' she said. 'Dust everywhere.'

The relief in Chris's voice was clear. 'Well, that's good, isn't it?'

'Everything except the mains switch. That's clean, Chris.' Her heart thundered now, and she glanced side to side to see if there was anyone approaching.

Silence.

'What else can you see?' he asked.

'Broken cobwebs, an outline on the switch that looks like a rag has been used to turn it off and back on again.'

'Hiding fingerprints. You think someone is playing games?'

'What would you think?'

'Richie,' Chris said immediately, but Mia didn't agree.

'No. He's a bully and a wanker but not petty. If he was going to do something, it would be bigger than this and out in the open.'

'Take photos, Mia. And tell the sarge.'

Mia put the phone back on speaker and opened the camera app. A few clicks later and she'd documented the whole area.

She considered what Chris had said as she shut up the box and made sure the catch was tight. 'Nah, I won't tell the sarge yet. Someone is trying to spook me. I'll buy a padlock for the fuse box tomorrow and maybe get a couple of security cameras.' She went back inside, shutting the front door firmly behind her, checking the locks.

Funnily enough, she wasn't frightened or angry, she just wanted to know who had decided to target her. And why.

'You don't need to put up with this,' Chris was saying. 'I'll call Zach myself. He has to know.'

'No, you won't, Chris. I've got to fight my own battles. I can't run to people about every little thing! I have to live here.'

By the time she was back in the kitchen, the toast was cold, but she buttered it anyway, spreading peanut butter from side to side and finally crunching down. The cup she'd got out earlier was still on the bench with Milo inside. Slumping at the table, she decided she'd wait until she was on her way to bed to boil the kettle and make the comforting hot drink.

'What if it is Richie?' Chris asked. 'This could be some serious shit. You need to start documenting it. He could get kicked off the force for this.'

Exhaustion hit her like a brick. 'I can't talk anymore, Chris, I'm too tired. I'll ring you in the morning, okay?'

'What time do you have to go into work?' he asked after a silence.

'I'm not ignoring what you're saying, I promise.' She knew he thought she was brushing him off. 'I'm just too tired. I'm not working until the afternoon shift.'

'Good. Make sure you draw your curtains tight and don't wake up with the sun the way you usually do.'

'Yes, Dad,' Mia said with a smile in her voice. 'Night. And Chris? Thanks.'

Gently she put the phone on the table and leaned forward with a groan. She stayed there for a few moments, then, leaving her half-eaten toast, she went to her bedroom, crawled into bed and turned on the electric blanket.

But sleep didn't come.

The bed felt as if rocks had been sewn into the mattress and tiny pebbles were pressing into her hips. She tossed and turned, thinking of Tahlia, the fuse box and the misplaced photo. The gun filtered into her thoughts too and she was back in Simpson's Haberdashery as a child, behind the counter with Nana.

Mr Marshall came in carrying a kitten.

'Here, young lady, I've got the perfect present for you.'

A young Mia reached up, taking the black-and-white kitten, her eyes full of wonder.

'Thanks, Mr Marshall,' she said, patting the kitten's tiny head. She giggled as a rough tongue slid across her hand.

'He's a boy, so in a few months' time you'll need to trot along to the vet and get him to remove those things there.' He pointed to some funny round-shaped things near the tail.

'I'm going to call him Blue Eyes,' Mia said. 'Nana, you talk about a singer called Ol' Blue Eyes, don't you?'

Suddenly Nana was standing, the gun in her hand. She was waving it at Mr Marshall.

'Don't give my granddaughter a kitten! They're dangerous things! Almost as dangerous as that hay you've got out there! Don't you know the bales could fall, or catch fire or—'

Mia woke with a start, her heart pounding, the doona kicked onto the floor, her forehead slick with sweat. The glowing green lights of the bedside clock read 4.22 a.m.

What had woken her? The dream, or . . .

Her brain told her not to be silly, of course it was the dream.

But her ears strained to hear if there were any unfamiliar noises in the house. The breathing of someone hiding in the cupboard, or under her bed.

She screwed her toes up tightly, not moving a muscle in case she made a sound that told the intruder she'd woken.

The next minute, there was light filtering in through the window and the sound of kids talking and laughing.

Mia lay there a moment, wondering what part of last night had been real. The lights had gone out and the fuse box had been tampered with. That was real.

Had there been a noise in the house when she'd woken in the early hours?

She wasn't sure.

Her phone buzzed with a message. Rolling over she reached for it and, through blurry eyes, read the message from Zach.

Office ASAP. You've been seconded to Barker Police Station.

CHAPTER 25

Mia held her nan's arm as they walked towards the dining room. She was still reeling from Zach's words this morning.

'HQ called and they need to replace the senior connie who was in Barker. They wanted to know if I had anyone to spare. You're it. Rest of us have families and lives here. You've only just arrived.'

Mia had opened her mouth to remind him about her grandmother then shut it again. There was no point, because he wouldn't listen, and the idea of working out of a station that was run by Dave Burrows was also appealing. Barker was only a short trip as drives in the outback Flinders Ranges went. She could pop back over and see her nan whenever she wasn't working.

The unspoken part of Zach's conversation was: 'I'll be glad to see the back of you.' Or, if Mia was being generous: 'I know Richie is going to give you shit and I'm getting you out.'

Unlikely but it was a nice thought.

Richie had been at his desk, when she'd arrived holding a brown paper bag filled with freshly baked sweet buns from the bakery. Her offering had gone ignored by him, but she'd felt his eyes follow her everywhere.

After her meeting with Zach, when Mia had gone to gather the few items from her desk and say goodbye to Marty, she'd heard him mutter something about 'Good riddance to bad rubbish', but not in such charitable words.

Mia's head had been held high as she left the station, knowing that karma always came around to people who deserved it.

'So, I'm packing again, Nana,' she said quietly as they entered the dining room. 'But only for a few weeks.'

'I think that senior sergeant you have there is a bit of a mongrel if you ask me,' Nana said.

Mia raised her eyebrows. Nana seemed to be pretty good today. Her memory front and centre.

'On the upside, I'm not starting until next week, so I'll have the weekend to get settled. And I'll get to spend a bit more time at the shop in Barker.' She found a table and pulled out a chair for her nan. 'Whoa, check out this spread!'

A plate in the centre of the table held slices of fruit cake, melting moments biscuits and scones. There was fresh cream, jam and butter next to it.

'CWA ladies had some titbits left over from something they did yesterday, so I'm told.' Clara reached out for the fruit cake and bit into it. Chewing slowly, with her eyes closed, she said, 'I think Mrs Jackson made this. When I used to judge the local shows, fruit cake was my speciality. She always added half a cup of orange juice from her own oranges. Added a bit of sweetness.' She chewed with pleasure.

Mia leaned back, still tired from the previous day's activities, and accepted a cup of tea on a saucer from Casey.

'I heard all about your work yesterday,' Casey said with an admiring smile. 'You'll be up for the local hero award on Australia Day, I'm sure.'

'What?' Mia asked incredulously. 'Don't be silly. I was doing my job.'

'You finding Tahlia like you did.' Casey gave Clara a soft nudge with her elbow. 'Your granddaughter is quite the town celeb now.'

'Doesn't seem like it to me, the way she's being treated,' Clara said grumpily, but she turned to bestow a large chalky grin on Mia. 'She's always been that way, you know. Saving the unfortunate, looking after the needy. That's why she became a policewoman. She deserves all the accolades she gets.' Reaching out her papery-skinned hand, she patted Mia's arm.

'What do you mean about how she's being treated?' Casey asked. 'What happened?'

'Nothing bad,' Mia answered. 'I've been seconded over to Barker station because they're an officer short over there. Just for a little while until they find a replacement.'

Casey offered the teapot to Clara who waved her away. 'If it's only for a few weeks, it won't be a problem, will it? Still be able to call in and see this one.'

'Yep, I'll be over as often as I can. Nana was the reason I came back to Broad River.'

Casey moved on to the next table and Mia reassessed Clara. When she'd gone into the station this morning Marty had handed her the paperwork for her firearm's licence, then snapped her photo and witnessed her signature. The gun was now back in her possession. For some reason that made her feel safe.

'Is there anything you'd like me to bring back from the shop for you, Nana? I might start sorting through every-thing. There's a lot there and you won't want to open the shop again, will you? I can't run it.'

Nana stared off into the distance, lost in memories, and Mia took another sip of her tea, waiting.

'The cellar,' her nan said abruptly. 'There should be a photo album in there. I'd like that.'

'Okay, I'll see if I can find it. Who's in it?' Mia held her breath, hoping there would be a mention of her father.

'What?' Nana looked at her and Mia knew she'd lost her to the mind thief again. Her eyes were distant and unfocused.

'Who is in the photo album? So I know if I've got the right one.'

'I don't know.' She shrugged and reached for the fruit cake again, then tapped the table. 'You know, I'm sure that

Mrs Jackson made this cake. She has a secret ingredient. I bet you can't guess what it is.'

Mia looked at the face she'd loved all her life and forced herself to smile. 'No, Nana, I can't. What is it?'

'Orange juice!' she cried triumphantly. 'From her own orchard, you know.'

⁓

Mia loaded her suitcase into the car and checked that all the doors were locked. She would only be in Barker for a short time so this house was still hers. Heading down the path to the fuse box, Mia cast around, looking for anything she'd missed in the darkness, then lifted the cover again.

Broken cobwebs, cased in years of dust. A clean smudge on the mains switch and a partial swipe in the dust on the bottom of the box.

On the ground there was no evidence anyone had been there, but inside told another story.

Back in the car, she typed a message to Josie.

Heading to Barker to work there for a couple of weeks. Want to come and stay?

She hadn't heard from Josie since her excited phone call. That was not unexpected. Josie contacted people only when she wanted to. Mia didn't mind. They'd been friends for so long that nothing bothered or surprised her with Josie. And she knew that if she called and needed her friend, Josie would be the first one there. Well, perhaps behind Chris, but she would still be there as quickly as she could.

Fiddling with the radio, Mia backed out of the drive and headed to the hardware store. Someone had deliberately turned her power off last night and she was going to find out who it was.

⁓

Barker appeared different to Mia on Monday morning as she drove past the sixty kilometre an hour sign and into the main street. Perhaps it was because she was coming home, this time, even if it was only for a short period. The street oozed atmosphere—warmth and friendliness. A couple of young kids waved at her as she drove by and there was a shaggy black-and-white dog sleeping outside of the deli.

Dave met her at the front of the house, leaning against the car, a pose that Mia was becoming familiar with. Laid-back, casual, but still aware of everything that was going on.

He gave a small wave and unlocked the door for her.

'Jack and Zara have only just left, so everything will still be working. The mice shouldn't have moved in yet. They're buggers to keep out of these old houses. You block up one place and a new draught comes in. They seem to find every place the wind whistles through.'

'Thanks for your help, Dave.' She put her suitcase in the hall and stood to look at him. 'Did you organise this secondment?'

Dave gave a laugh. 'Actually, I didn't. I found out about it the same day you did, but I think that it will work well, don't you?'

'Probably more than you realise. I really want to go through Nana's things in the shop up on the main street, so I'll have lots to do when I'm not working.'

'What's in there? That place has been boarded up the whole time I've been here.'

'It's a funny place. I remember it as a kid, all hustle and bustle. Tinned food next to material to make dresses with. Toys and the like. Something for everyone in that place! I don't remember it ever being empty; always at least one customer, if not more. It's a little mysterious now, though, because it appears that Nana just walked out. Locked up and left it all. There's so much stuff still in there. I don't know if much of it has any value, but I met the cafe owners, you know, that day I first met you, and they were keen to lease it.' Mia shrugged. 'The shop won't be mine until Nana dies, but with her dementia advancing, I might be able to work something out with the lawyer who manages Nana's financial affairs.'

Dave nodded. 'Sounds like a great idea. It would be nice to see it cleaned and open.' He rubbed his hands together. 'Right, what do you want to do first? Unpack or come to the station?'

'I'll come down with you now, if that's okay?'

'Righto, jump in, it's only around the corner. We've got a case, ah, I—' he gave her a rueful glance '—I still have to get used to the fact that Jack isn't here.' He started again. 'I've got a case on the go at the moment. Jack and I did an interview the day before he left, and then we had Tahlia missing, so I haven't had a chance to do any follow-up. I'll let you read the file, then perhaps we can start the follow-ups together.'

Mia felt a rush of excitement run through her. This was already so different from Broad River Police Station. 'I'd really like that,' she said.

Dave pointed to a large woman with curly blonde hair coming down the driveway of the house opposite. 'I'll introduce you to my wife first. A word of warning: she'll feed you as much as you can eat, if not more.'

'Oh, you live there?'

'Too close?'

'No. Just surprised. Don't know why.'

'Hello, both of you,' the woman called as she approached. 'I'm Kim.' She kept walking until she stood in front of Mia. 'Kim Burrows.'

'This is the new Jack,' Dave told his wife. 'Mia Worth from over at Broad River. I told you about her when I got home last night.' Dave put his arm around Kim.

Mia put out her hand and shook Kim's. 'It's nice to meet you,' she said.

'Likewise. Dave will be glad of the company now that Jack has left,' Kim said with a large smile. 'Not that Dave would ever admit it, but he would have got lonely in that office all by himself, wouldn't you, love?' She turned and flashed Dave the most brilliant smile.

Mia wanted to take a step back and hold a tea towel in front of her face. The way these two interacted told Mia they were very much in love.

Dave laughed. 'Maybe that might have been the case, but Mia has turned up almost immediately, so that's not going to happen.'

'It'll be lovely to have a policewoman here,' Kim said. 'Dave will make sure everything is okay for you, I promise. Won't you?'

Dave held his hands out, palms up. 'Mia will have to pull her weight the same here as in any station,' he said, until Kim gave his arm a little whack. 'Anything you say, honey.' There was a teasing tone to his voice.

'That's right, take the mickey.'

'I'm glad to be here,' Mia interrupted, hoping the banter between the two of them would stop. 'Looking forward to getting my teeth stuck in.'

Kim turned the full force of her attention to Mia, reaching forward and putting a hand on her arm. 'Now, Mia, tell me. No food allergies or anything I should know about? I'll cook a couple of meals up for you while you settle in. That way you don't have to worry when you get back after your shift.'

'No, no,' Mia stuttered. 'That's fine. I can look after myself. You don't need—'

'Mia, just go with it,' Dave said in a resigned tone. 'It'll happen whether you want it to or not. My wife often feels the need to feed the whole town. You should see our grocery bill some weeks!' It was all said with another great smile as he looked down at Kim. 'That's what Kim is known for. Food and local knowledge. She's been here all her life so she can usually tell you about anything that happened here in her lifetime.' Dave winked at Kim as he spoke. 'She's my secret weapon sometimes.'

'He's right, you know,' Kim said, laughing. 'I'll just cook something up and leave it on the step for you. I did that for Zara the first couple of days she was here. So you might as well just go with it.'

'Oh, well, thank you very much. No, no allergies.'

Kim beamed this time. 'Wonderful,' she said. 'It'll be nice to have someone in the house across the road. I don't like seeing empty houses.'

'Anyway, we'd better go,' Dave said. 'Come on, Mia, I'll introduce you to Joan, who's been here longer than all of us, and then we'll get on the road.' He turned to Kim. 'At the risk of getting you talking again, Mia's family was originally from here. They owned that boarded-up shop in the main street.'

Kim was silent for a moment, and just as Mia started to say Simpson's Haberdashery, Kim said the same words. 'I remember your grandmother. And,' she wrinkled her brow, 'maybe your mum.'

Mia could see Kim was thinking hard. The words were out of her mouth before she could stop them. 'My father?'

Kim's frown deepened. 'Hmm, let me get back to you on that.' Another brilliant smile and she twirled on her heel. 'Right, must fly. Got a few meals to cook for Catering Angels. Enjoy your first day, Mia.'

Dave watched her leave and shook his head. 'Such a whirlwind,' he said affectionately. His face sobered as he turned to face Mia. 'Okay, let's get on. This case I was telling you about is an odd one. Rhys Martindale is a local farmer. He's organically certified and it appears that his crop has been sprayed out by chemicals that can't be used in an organic rotation. We're testing the plants to see what type of substance it is, but I'm suspecting the paddock may have been sprayed with something that has a residual in it.' He indicated for her to hop into the police four-wheel drive.

'So it was sprayed before the crop was sown?'

'I believe so but I'm waiting to hear back from the agro. Hopefully there might be an email with all that information when we get to the station.' He turned onto the main street.

Mia couldn't help but glance towards the shop as Dave made a beeline for the police station. From the outside, the place looked unloved. Hopefully, Josie would be over on the weekend and they could start fixing it up. Maybe Chris might come too, although he'd texted this morning and said his dad was in hospital so he was heading to Mildura to be with him. The timing couldn't be worse from a job perspective, he'd said, but I'll only ever have one dad.

Mia had felt the absence of her father strongly as she'd read her friend's text. What would it have been like to know him and have him in her life rather than a large blank space.

'Big shop,' Dave said, following her gaze.

Mia nodded. 'It's full of spider webs and dust. And things—material, toys and clothes—and that's just for starters! It'll take me forever to clean out.'

'I reckon if you say the word, Kim will help. She's always looking for something else to do.'

Dave pulled the car up outside the police station and got out. 'Let's meet Joan and then you can read the file. Barker is a pretty big council area, but it doesn't have too many people in it. Perhaps about fifteen hundred, including the surrounds. I'll get you a map of the district for while you're here.'

CHAPTER 26

Dave watched Mia as she worked at Jack's desk. She was lost in the file of Rhys Martindale's crop.

Occasionally, she made a note as she read, and he could see there was about half a page of questions already there.

A fresh pair of eyes wouldn't hurt on this one, for sure. He'd been surprised when Jack had turned the questioning of John Manson to the argument between Rhys and John. It wasn't something he'd heard about but he knew even minor incidents could cause lifelong enemies in these parts.

Max, the agronomist, had forwarded an email from the lab. The summary of the soil test results read: *Traces of Atrazine found. Almost completely diluted. Seeding can resume within another two weeks.*

Yes, it could if this had been on a farm that was able to use chemicals. Dave suspected it would be closer to two years before Rhys could sow a crop in that paddock again.

He glanced over the list of people who had bought chemicals that weren't Atrazine and ruled a line through them.

Harley and Natalia Stokes had bought one thousand litres of Atrazine last month, he was reading when his phone buzzed in his pocket. He took it out, expecting it to be Kim. Instead, it was Jack.

Unpacked. There was a photo of a small brown-brick house in the middle of a paddock, and a line of shrubby bushes running along the fence.

Looks great. Settled? he texted back. The words took him and his thick fingers a little while to type.

Jack's reply was instant. *Yep.*

Housewarming soon then?

I start in two weeks, so before then. You'll be down?

Wouldn't miss it.

Dave wanted to tell Jack about the search for Tahlia yesterday and Richie's treatment of Mia, and how suddenly he had a new offsider, but there was no way he could put all of that in a text. The words would take him all year to type.

No, that discussion would involve a phone call and some beer. One night on the verandah when he'd finished work. He'd put his feet up, crack a stubbie and ring.

There was no doubt that Kim and Zara had already exchanged a zillion text messages—Kim could type as fast as she could talk and Zara was even quicker. It made him dizzy just to imagine the speed of the messages passing in mid-air between the two. Kim would have brought Zara up to date with Mia's entrance, so Jack would know soon enough. He might even ring later tonight.

The lack of Jack's presence was like a pain pressing in his chest. Something akin to how he felt when Spencer Brown, his old partner, had died. A longing, a missing, wanting to change something that couldn't be.

Jack had his own life to live now and didn't need to be crowded by an old has-been like Dave. Still, Dave missed his mate.

'Uh, Dave?'

He looked across the room and saw Mia with a question on her face.

'What have you found?' Dave asked, leaning forward.

'This argument between these two, Martindale and Manson. Over a fence?'

Dave stretched back in his chair, ready to explain country life. 'I guess that might seem a bit odd . . .'

'Oh no, I understand the reasoning behind it. But what I find strange is why Martindale wouldn't have fixed his fence. Surely keeping his stock in is to his benefit. He won't lose valuable animals that way—especially if they're rams. I read the *Stock Journal* and last year's sales results for rams were pretty high. Up around the fifteen-hundred-dollar mark.'

Dave looked suitably impressed. 'You're right. Rams are worth a lot and so are merino ewes. Good breeding lines are making in excess of one hundred and fifty dollars. Some even nearing two hundred.'

'Why then would Martindale be happy to have his expensive animals roaming around the countryside?'

'I can't answer that. Could be financial strain, can't get a fencing contractor, that type of thing. Perhaps that's a question we need to ask.' He leaned back and thought. 'It's not illegal to move sheep or cattle down a public road if they've got all the right signs and notifications but we certainly would rather stock weren't taking themselves for a walk down a public road. If there was an accident, say someone hit a beast, we can prosecute the owner. In saying that we can't enforce fences being stock proof. The *Dividing Fence Act* is there to keep animals out, rather than inside the paddock.'

Mia was quiet for a moment, and she looked back at her notes. 'We could ask about that, though?'

'Absolutely you can.' Dave stood up. 'Let's go and do it right now.'

'Yeah, okay, but hang on, I've got a couple of other questions here.' She tapped on a photo. 'You've got tyre tracks. Do we know what type of vehicle these are from?'

'Toyota LandCruiser ute.'

'Did you or Jack do a search to find out who owns them in the district?'

Dave sat back down and gave a laugh. 'Only every second farmer in the area. They're the most popular ute there is. But I have pulled the records and there is a list here.'

Mia rolled her eyes. 'I had a feeling you were going to say that.' A rare smile split her face.

For such a serious girl, she was pretty. Dave wasn't surprised she'd copped so much shit at Broad River. None of those fellas were known for their chivalry. Except Marty.

He thought for a moment, wondering if it was the right time for what he wanted to say. He'd seen it so often: a policewoman judged by her looks. There were four different kinds of blokes in the force when it came to women. One, a protector. The woman represented their sister or mum and they felt they needed to act like a father.

Two, the ones who think the women are gay or a man hater. Perhaps they'd try and come onto her and she'd turn them down. Humiliated, they'd call her frigid.

Three, the ones who underrated a woman's ability.

Four, the ones who just got on with the job and judged their fellow cops on their ability rather than gender.

Dave always took people as he found them and knew he was in the last category, but he wanted to tell Mia that if he accidentally went down the path of being a protector, she needed to make sure he knew to pull his head in. It had been a while since he'd worked with a woman.

He was lucky that Kim was welcoming to everyone. There were some coppers who received no end of grief from their wives when they were working with women. Those people must be insecure in their relationship.

'What we haven't done is follow up on Sophie, the woman who was working in the pub the other night,' Dave said. 'I made a note in the file at the back.'

Mia flipped the pages over and was quiet while she read.

'Okay, so there was a woman in a John Deere tractor looking for Rhys Martindale's farm.'

'If the tractor was owned by a contractor, they would have had their business name on the side, but Sophie said that wasn't the case. So we need to try and work out who it was.'

'Description of the woman?'

'For either you or me to ask when we talk to Sophie,' Dave said.

Mia smiled.

'The other thing is to find out if anyone else wanted to buy the Harcourt's land,' Dave said. 'This investigation will start to have legs once we ask a few more questions. Unfortunately, you'll find it a little hard to get your feet with this investigation because of your lack of local knowledge.'

Mia nodded. 'But I can ask questions? Maybe the real estate agent who listed the farm could help us too.'

'Sure. Two heads are always better than one.' He paused. 'Mia, I will take you at your ability. Nothing else. You have my word on that.'

Colour flamed around her face. 'Good. That's the only way I want to be taken.'

'I won't make any comment about Broad River, but I was aware what was happening there . . .'

Mia held up her hand. 'We don't need to have this conversation, Dave. I'm a big girl and can handle most things on my own.'

'I've got no doubt about that.' He grinned. 'But, hey, if I get annoying, just let me know!'

'You think I'd let you get away with it?'

'I hope not.' Dave meant every one of those three words.

Mia returned to the notes she'd made. 'And this guy Rhys hasn't upset anyone? Shifted a boundary fence or something silly?'

'Not that I know of, but we haven't questioned the other neighbours yet. We can do that today.'

'Okay. What about the tracks in the paddock? If the earth had been worked, which it would have been since he's organic, surely you could have seen the outline of tractor impressions in the dirt.'

'Yeah, except the marks we can see are Rhys's. He would have run over any others that were there.'

Mia was quiet while she scratched herself a couple more notes then gathered the file. Dave waited until she was ready before heading out the door and calling goodbye to Joan.

In the car, Dave gave her a bit more background about the town. 'I like to do a run east and west once a week, get the speed camera up, just to remind people we're not sitting on our hands. Then, on the way back from that, I do a few community visits. There are some older people out on farms by themselves who I check on, just to make sure they haven't had a fall or other misadventure.

'As quiet as this place seems, there's always something going on. Whether it's a ring-in causing some trouble, or a local giving another local a bit of grief. What I have learned living here is that you must stay on top of everything and not let anyone get too out of control. Otherwise, people think they run the town, and they don't.'

He took the road towards the Martindale farm and pointed out a couple of landmarks. 'That's the rodeo ground, and once a year there is a rodeo. That's how I came to Barker in the first place. The treasurer was car-jacked and I came to investigate. Kim and I had been together when we were teenagers and we reconnected, so at the end of the case I asked to be stationed here.

'Heaps of people come into town over the rodeo weekend and camp on the grounds. We get in a few more coppers, usually from Broad River and surrounds, just to help keep the peace. Much like you did when Tahlia went missing. Things can get a bit over the top sometimes.'

'I've never been to one,' Mia said.

The grounds slipped by—the buildings, light towers and white tyres surrounding the arena were quickly out of sight.

'Pretty amazing to watch all the guys and girls riding. It's a display of sheer skill and athleticism.'

'What else happens during the year?'

'Footy grand final—that can always cause a bit of trouble. Then there's the agricultural show and the Christmas pageant. They're both minor compared to the rodeo and footy final.' He glanced over at her. 'Ever gone to a country final?' he asked.

Mia was looking out the window but turned back to him. 'Nah, not really my thing. I played netball for a while, and I thought about trying to get into a team when I arrived at Broad River.' She shrugged. 'But I haven't had a chance yet.'

'A country footy final can make an AFL melee look angelic,' Dave said. 'There can be bad blood from the year before, especially if the winning team has won a couple of years in a row.' He pointed out the window. 'Add alcohol and you've got a recipe for disaster sometimes.

'This is the paddock.' He pulled the car to a halt. 'Did you want to get out and have a look?'

'Yep, let's do that.'

Mia got out, bringing the file with her. She dug out the photos and held them up to compare what she was seeing now to then. Out in the paddock, she squatted down and looked at the ground, outlining something with her finger.

'Can't have been any rain up here since seeding time. I can still see the wheel tracks.'

Dave stuck his hands in his pockets and wandered over. 'According to Rhys, these aren't his. I picked up a cigarette butt here too, and neither Rhys nor his wife smoke, so I think the impressions belong to whoever has done this. That rain they had near Broad River yesterday didn't make it this far north.' He took in the dry soil and blue sky. 'Reckon these blokes could do with a bit soon though.'

'Check out the dust coming up the road.' Mia nodded to a plume that seemed as large as a small hill.

A white Toyota LandCruiser came into view and slowed when it saw the police vehicle on the side of the road. As it pulled up to a stop, Dave recognised the driver.

'Here we go. Mr Manson himself. Come on, I'll introduce you.'

Mia stood up. 'Thanks, Dave,' she said softly.

Dave pretended not to hear her. Raising his hand, he called out a greeting to John, who got out of the car.

'I see you're back at the scene of the crime,' he said. 'Talked to Martindale yet?'

'Just following up on some further enquiries, John,' Dave said. 'This is my new offsider, Constable Mia Worth.'

John's gaze slid across to Mia and for a moment he went very still. Dave wondered what caused his reaction and was about to ask if they already knew each other, when John spoke.

'Worth, you said?'

Mia held out her hand. 'Yes, Constable Worth. Mr Manson. Nice to meet you.'

They shook hands.

'Mia's family is originally from Barker,' Dave said.

John seemed to appraise her. 'Your parents, were they Alex and Nicole Worth?'

This time it was Mia who froze. Dave saw her try to speak.

'You look like Nicole,' John said.

'Yeah,' Mia answered. 'They were my parents. Did you know them?'

CHAPTER 27

John Manson shifted uncomfortably. 'Well, no. Not really. I knew Clara and remembered she had a granddaughter.'

Mia nodded. 'Oh, of course.'

'I recall you used to be in the shop with her at times.' He stuck his hands in his pockets and rocked back and forth on his heels. 'Your father, well . . . hmm.'

Mia frowned. John gave the distinct impression he hadn't liked Alex. He looked about her nan's age. Perhaps he'd known her. His face was heavy with wrinkles and his eyes drooped like a Saint Bernard dog. But, unlike her nan, the energy that radiated from him was young. She had more questions. Lots of them. If remembered Clara, then maybe he would remember her dad! Perhaps the more she asked, the more people she would find who knew him, and they might have photos! But now wasn't the time.

Unwilling to have the conversation in front of Dave, who was openly watching them, Mia tried to shift her thoughts back to the job at hand. 'Well, it's good to make the connection,' she said, glancing across at Dave, who seemed to take her hint.

'How are things at your place, John?' Dave asked. 'No problems of any kind?'

John dragged his gaze away from Mia and refocused on Dave. 'Problems? Nope. None that I know of.' He nodded towards the crop. 'Certainly did some damage here. Pretty malicious.'

'You can see why we'd like to find the person who has done this. Actually, I've got another question for you, John. A witness tells us they saw a John Deere tractor about a month before seeding started. The driver was asking for directions to Rhys's place. Female driver. Did you see anyone matching that description?'

John's eyebrows shot up. 'A contractor?'

'We're just trying to find the woman so we can ask some questions,' Dave said.

'No, I can't say I saw her. Just trying to think who has John Deere machinery around here . . . I'll have a think and let you know what I come up with.'

John nodded to the road, and they all turned.

'More company,' he said as another white LandCruiser rounded the corner and started to slow. 'Ah, my old mate, Martindale.' John crossed his arms and widened his stance as the ute came to a halt.

Rhys wound down his window and perched his elbow on the frame.

'Morning all. Looks like you've got a stop work meeting. All you need is a thermos and a shovel.'

Dave laughed, but John didn't. He watched Mia stand back, trying to learn the local knowledge that he'd talked about.

'We'll have to stop meeting like this,' Dave said. 'People will talk.'

'You got your fence fixed yet, Martindale?' John asked.

'Not yet, John. Can't hurry a good job.'

'My ewes would be grateful if you did.'

'All in time.' Rhys turned his attention to Dave. 'Got any information about who did this to my crop?'

Dave noticed Rhys didn't look at John when he asked.

'Not yet. Following up some enquiries. In fact, we were coming to see you to ask a few more questions.'

'Go your hardest.'

John shifted and kicked at the dirt a bit. 'I best get about my business,' he said. 'Don't want to interrupt the great work you people do. You should encourage this young buck to do something about his fences, Dave. Wouldn't want some poor person colliding with a sheep and hurting themselves, would we?' He threw another glance at Rhys and then one at Mia, his weathered face pale under his hat.

'Catch you round, John,' Dave said.

They waited until he'd left, pulling out onto the road slowly. They could see his eyes in the rear-view mirror as he drove away. They were on Mia still.

'So, what can I do you for, Dave?' Rhys raised his hand a little at Mia. 'Heard you had a new partner.'

Dave introduced them. 'We've been told you had a bit of an altercation with John a while back. Something about a fence?'

Rhys nodded. 'Yeah, my rams got out onto the road and in with his ewes. He was most put out. I offered to organise the vet to come out and abort them all but he wouldn't have that.'

'Are you going to fix your fence?' asked Dave.

'I'll get to it. You got any idea how hard it is to get a contractor around these parts? They're booked up months in advance.'

Dave nodded and glanced across at Mia.

'Sir, I'm wondering why you won't make the fences stock proof yourself, considering the value of the animals,' she asked.

Rhys did a double-take. 'You shitting me?' he asked. 'They are stock proof. My boys just liked the green pick on the side of the road and got a bit boisterous. Can't stop a ram when he can smell the ewes cycling, you know.'

'Well, the fences can't be stock proof if the rams got out.' Mia stuck to her guns. 'Bad blood between neighbours doesn't always end well.' She indicated the crop.

'You think the old bloke did it? I don't reckon. Yeah, he gets a bit cranky sometimes, but he wouldn't have it in him.'

'What about the fact you bought Harcourt's? We understand John was very keen to purchase too.'

Rhys glanced across at Dave then back at Mia. 'Whoever fronts up with the money buys the land, you know.'

Dave interjected. 'I guess what we're looking for here, Rhys, is a reason for someone to do this to you. I've got the report back on the soil and the plants and it was Atrazine. Someone deliberately sprayed it. There has to be a reason. A motive. So when we hear that you and John have got a bit of a beef with each other, we wanted to ask you about it, because we've already asked John.'

Looking from one to the other, Rhys shifted in his seat. 'Not sure why you're questioning me like this when, like you just said, it's my paddock and crop that's been affected, but I'll answer your questions.

'Yeah, John gets a bit annoyed with my fence and my rams. I am making plans to get it refenced, but I can't get a contractor for a few months. I've belted in a few steel posts to make it a little sturdier than it was. To be honest, I was winding him up in the stock and station agent the other day, saying I wasn't going to do anything because I'd already been along the fence line and done what I could.

'And as for buying the Harcourt's farm, well, when he found out, John rang up to congratulate me.' Rhys looked towards John's land. 'We have our moments, but mostly we get on fine.'

'Why would you want to wind him up?'

Rhys shrugged. 'For fun?'

Dave let the silence fill the gap in the conversation before changing the subject. 'You like coaching at Barker?'

A grin spread across Rhys's face. 'Oh yeah. It's only my first year but I think I'm getting the hang of it. Reckon there are a couple of blokes who don't like my style, but they don't argue. Just get on and do what I ask of them. I think—' he leaned out of the window '—I shouldn't say anything, because I'll bloody jinx it, but I *think* we might make the finals.' He looked excited but also nervous.

'Been a while since Barker has made it that far,' Dave said.

'Yeah. And I'd like to be the one who gets us there.' He gave a self-deprecating smile. 'I'm pretty competitive when I get going.'

'Why do you think some blokes don't like your coaching style?'

'I'm not sure if they don't like my style, or they're just a bit lippy. That young Craig Johnston and Mark Waters, they always give me a mouthful when they don't want to do something. Easy enough to fix. Get 'em to run another ten laps when the others have finished and having a beer.' He shrugged. 'They'll work it out soon enough. They don't seem to understand you can't make it to the top without hard yards. Always got to put in the ground work and you'll be rewarded. That goes for everything in life.'

Dave nodded and looked over at Mia. 'Any other questions, Constable?'

'Mr Martindale, you realise that if someone hits one of your animals, we are able to prosecute you?'

'They're rarely on the road. I'm doing my best to get some contractors here and—'

'Yes, I heard all of that,' Mia said, interrupting. 'I'm just making you aware you can be charged.'

'I see. Well, thanks for the heads-up.'

'Have you spoken to the accrediting company about this?' Dave asked.

Rhys nodded. 'I can cordon this paddock off for the year. Has to be out of the program for a whole twelve months though, then the soil retested.'

'Have you seen a woman driving a John Deere tractor with a boom spray in the last couple of months?' Mia asked.

'Whereabouts?'

'Along this road. Near here.'

'What? No. Was there someone . . .'

'We're not sure,' Dave said, then explained what they knew.

'I haven't seen anyone and I didn't book any contractors to come and spray my own bloody paddock out, if that's what you're insinuating.' Rhys crossed his arms and glared at them both. 'Look, this has cost me money! I told you, Dave, I've lost the use of this paddock for twelve months, at the minimum. Why would I do this to myself?'

'We're not saying anything like that, Rhys,' Dave soothed.

'Mr Martindale,' Mia spoke quietly, 'can you insure against this sort of damage?'

Both men turned to look at her.

'What?'

'Are you able to insure for an overspray?'

'Yes, you are, but I don't spray in the first place so why would I have that type of insurance?'

'Who is your insurance agent?'

'That's in the file, Constable Worth,' Dave said. He gave her a quick glance to let her know she was pushing a bit too hard.

Rhys turned his attention to Dave. 'Are you getting anywhere with this or just driving around talking to people?'

Dave pushed himself off his car and took a couple of steps towards Rhys. 'Asking questions is usually how we get answers to things, Rhys,' he said mildly.

Rhys held up his hands as if in a sorry gesture. 'Just another *question* then,' he said, putting his car into gear. 'Finished with me today?'

'We'll be in touch.' Dave and Mia both gave him a wave.

Back on the road, Mia was watching the countryside go by, but Dave could see she was deep in thought. Probably not even taking in the scenery.

'You had a good line of enquiry back there,' he said.

'Hmm.' Mia didn't turn to face him. 'He's got a bit of a temper, doesn't he?'

'No one likes being put under the spotlight. Especially when it's unofficial, like today. We were fact-gathering. It always helps if you can make your questions sound like you're having a conversation, rather than firing questions, one after the other.'

'I was out of line?'

'Not quite, but he was getting agitated and once the person of interest gets his or her back up, you won't get anything more out of them.'

'Okay.' Mia nodded and this time looked at him.

Before she could say anything more, Dave asked, 'Ever come across John Manson before?' even though he already knew the answer.

Mia seemed to rouse herself. Shaking her head, she wiped her hands along her uniform. 'Nope, but I'd like to talk to him a bit more.' There was a pause as if she were weighing up whether to say something.

'I didn't know my dad and know nothing about him. Nana won't talk about him at all. I've always wondered why. I'm interested in finding out a bit more about him.'

Without making comment, Dave pointed at a sign on the side of the road. 'This is Rhys's other neighbour, Abel Keegan. We might just pop in here and have a yarn too.'

'He bought some of the Atrazine, didn't he?' Mia asked, flicking open the file.

'Yeah. Now, just a heads-up, when I go out to visit farms, I usually take a paper or milk or something because these people don't get to town very often. Obviously, I haven't got any with me today, but that's what I'd normally do. I'm also going to ask to see his firearms cabinet. Just a routine check, then we can ask some very general questions about Rhys and how they get along. Okay?'

'Sounds good to me, boss.'

Dave grinned. He was pretty sure they were going to work well together, and her enquiries had been thoughtful and intelligent, if not a bit gung-ho, which was normal for most new recruits. They were always full of energy and enthusiasm.

'This might be out of left field, Dave, but has Rhys ever had any charges laid against him?'

'Not that I've found. Why do you ask?'

'Just that temper of his.'

'Hmm. While we're here, keep an eye out for a John Deere tractor.' Dave pointed to the ute parked next to the shed. 'We'll try there first, not up at the house. Out here, if you see a ute, you head for that. You'll rarely find a farmer at home.'

'Oh look,' Mia said, 'another Toyota LandCruiser.'

'They're like arseholes out here—everyone's got one. Told you that,' Dave said with a laugh. 'Excellent, here comes Abel.' He leaned out of the car; his arm outstretched. 'G'day, Abel. How're you getting on?'

Mia and Dave both got out.

Abel was wiping his hands on a rag, oil and grease covering his arms and a spanner stuck in the back pocket of his jeans.

'Not too bad, Dave. Just finished seeding and now I'm cleaning up. Got a few minor things to fix before the old girl goes back in the shed.' He shot the seeding rig a fond glance. 'Almost spent more time with her than my wife over the last month or two.'

The tractor was red and the word Case was branded across it. Not John Deere. 'Seems to be how it is at this time of year, doesn't it? How'd you get on with seeding? No hassles?'

'All pretty smooth really. No breakdowns for once. Diesel prices are a bit high for my liking, but hopefully we won't have to worry about them for a while. Harvest is another six months away.' His eyes flicked curiously to Mia, and Dave introduced them.

'I guess you're not here to find out how seeding went,' Abel said. He looked at them expectantly.

'We were out this way and thought we'd come by and check your gun cabinet. Gotta do that once in a blue moon. Can we have a look?'

Abel nodded. 'Sure, it's in the shed here, right at the back.'

'Mia, you can check that for me.' Dave looked around the shed, then leaned against the workbench.

'So how's the footy team going?' he called to Abel's back. 'Your young Luke is in the A grade this year.'

'He sure is. Making not a bad fist of it either.'

'I went down and watched them play Broad River a few weeks ago. Looks like Rhys has got the team all gelling together.'

'Hmm, I wouldn't be so sure. Now I used to coach a few years back, and I still think Rhys has a thing or two to learn.'

'Heard that they might make it to the finals, so he can't be too bad.'

'Might do. Probably a bit too early to tell yet.'

'Yeah, well, I guess you're right. We're not halfway through the season and if a couple of the key players get taken out with an injury . . . who knows.' Dave spread his legs and crossed his arms, rocking on his heels. 'You don't like Rhys's coaching style?'

'I don't dislike it,' Abel said, looking across at Dave. 'I go down and watch some nights. He's a bit Jekyll and Hyde, if you ask me. Doesn't work well when you need to get everyone coming together as a team.'

'Be tricky being a coach. Take some skill,' Dave said. 'Be good to see Barker get to at least a quarter final. Been a long time. Is there anyone he has a crack at all the time?'

Abel shook his head. 'Not really. Anyhow,' he changed the subject, 'I saw his paddock. What a bloody mess.'

'Yeah, been making a few enquiries but can't seem to find a reason anyone would want to do that to him.'

Abel took the spanner out of his pocket and hung it up on the shadow board. 'Dunno either,' he said. 'Someone sprayed it out though?'

'Yeah. Used Atrazine. Do you guys use that chemical at all?'

Abel nodded. 'Yeah, we use it as a pre-emergent to get rid of the broadleaf weeds before we plant canola or lupins. Real handy chemical to have.'

'Did you use it this year?'

'Sure did. Got a couple of hundred hectares of canola in. Atrazine gets rid of all the capeweed and dock we have. Annihilates the clover and we've got a good clean paddock to seed into and nothing to compete for moisture.'

Dave nodded as Mia came back to stand alongside him. 'Got any left over?'

'Nope, I always work out exactly what I need and buy that. Too expensive to have any just lying around.'

'Mmm.' Dave rocked on his heels again, thinking.

'Do you know who has John Deere machinery around here?'

'Something more to these questions, Dave?' Abel asked as he put his hands on the workbench.

Dave made his tone questioning. 'Yeah, we've had a report of someone asking for directions to Rhys's place. They were driving a tractor with a spray rig behind it.'

'Ah, the old trailing boom,' Abel said. 'There're heaps of people who still have them, but the bigger operators—the ones who have to get over a lot of land quickly—usually have self-propelled boom sprays.'

Realisation spread through Dave. Of course! He'd seen these all-in-one machines that had booms that folded in against the cab. When they were extended they were so large they looked like a prehistoric dinosaur, the wings waving as they raced over the paddocks.

Well, he thought, *that rules out a contractor.*

CHAPTER 28

Mia held up her phone to Dave as they got back into the car.

'Is this what he's talking about?'

Dave glanced over and saw a picture of a Hardi Rubicon sprayer. The tyres were like a tractor's and the booms folded in against the cab.

'Yep,' Dave said. 'That's a self-propelled one.'

'Would I be right in thinking that contractors usually have new equipment?'

Nodding, Dave gave a distracted smile. 'I've just had that exact same thought. I think we can rule out any contractors.'

'So we're looking for a farmer with older machinery?'

'Not necessarily. Trailing booms are still a thing, for sure, and not everyone upgrades their equipment without reason. So yes, in a way, that's a possibility, but no, as they're not the only people to look at.'

'Okay. Perhaps farmers who aren't making much profit or . . .'

'Farmers who are older and not willing to change.' Dave started the car and tapped his fingers on the steering wheel before pulling out of the driveway. 'The list is endless. Can't afford them, country doesn't suit.'

They were quiet as Dave turned the car and headed back towards Barker.

'Guess I don't need to research contractors around the district then,' Mia said. 'Is there anything more I can do to help on this today?'

Dave glanced at his watch. 'Nah, by the time we get back, it'll be knock-off time and you've got to get unpacked. I'll drop you at your place and I'll see you down at the station in the morning.'

'Sure?'

'Yeah, you need to get yourself organised.' Dave wrinkled his brow as he thought again. Maybe he'd go back into the pub tonight and see if Sophie was on. There were a few more questions that needed to be asked.

'Have you got any thoughts on this?' Mia asked.

'One thing you need to recognise as a copper is gut feelings, and you need to learn to trust them,' Dave said. 'Right from the start, I've thought there was something really vindictive about this. Whoever has done this has tried to take away Rhys's livelihood. They want to hurt him or his family. That screams personal. I think we need to be looking close to home.'

'How do we work out where to start looking?'

'I'll do a bit of digging around tonight. See what I can find. We know there's been the altercation between Rhys and John.' Dave wiggled his head from side to side as he thought. 'That's certainly worth pursuing. But other than that and the footy team, we don't have anything.'

'Should I check the records and see if anyone has filed a complaint about Rhys? I know there're no charges, but a complaint . . .'

'Yeah, and perhaps do all the neighbours. I'm sure I'd know, but not if something's happened in a different district. Maybe even see if Rhys owns land outside of the Barker Shire.'

Dave motored into Barker and headed towards Mia's house.

'Could you leave me in the main street?' she asked. 'I'm going to have a quick look inside the shop. Nana asked me to pick something up for her.'

'Easy as.' He changed direction and drove around the median strip before pulling up out the front.

'Thanks for today, Dave,' Mia said, unclipping her seatbelt. 'It's been the most fun day I've had on the job since I started.' She grinned. 'I'm very glad Zach sent me here.'

'I think Barker will be good for you and you will be good for the town . . .' He paused. 'For the few weeks you're here. I guess you shouldn't get too comfortable.'

Once she was out of the car, Mia unlocked the shop door and reached for the light switch. A soft sound and the store was lit up with the glow of warm light. Good, the phone call to the electricity company had restored the power. That would make things easier.

The door clicked behind her. The wonder and magic she felt every time she stepped into the shop seeped through her, erasing the anxiety and stress of the last few days. The silence was only broken by the scratching of a mouse somewhere in the wall. Making a mental note to buy some baits, she moved deeper into the shop.

This time, she looked at the stock in a different way, wondering if it would be worth holding a garage sale or if there was an organisation she could donate it to. There was certainly more than enough clothes and materials. She'd have to make sure that none of it was damaged by mice or moths, or any other pests that may have found their way in during the years since her grandmother had left.

Back at the counter, she looked underneath for anything she'd missed the first time. A clue about her father, or the gun.

Her nan's reaction when Mia had showed her the gun had sent her policewoman's antenna up. It was more than the weapon being her grandfather's, but Nana was either not going to share, or couldn't remember. If Nana hadn't had dementia, Mia would have thought it was the former.

The weird conversation with John Manson today had unsettled her too, and she wanted to know how he had established so quickly that she was Clara's granddaughter. Her looks, he'd said. Well, possibly. More likely from her name 'Worth'. Clara would have been well known throughout the town. John's reaction to her father was confusing. Why hadn't John liked him? Then that made her ask the question again: why didn't her family speak about Alex?

Coming back to Barker had heightened her interest in her father. She'd grown up knowing he was dead, understanding her family didn't speak of him. She'd never wanted or needed to know about him before. Even when her mother had died, Nana had loved her enough for both of them, so she'd never questioned what had happened to her father.

Nana's reaction to his name was also a reason never to ask. Mia didn't want to cause her grandmother any hurt, and for some reason, that's what Alex's name did.

But now she was here—in the town he grew up in—and his ghost was tapping on her shoulder, asking to be heard.

There was nothing of interest underneath the counter, so she went to the corner of the shop where the trapdoor was for the cellar. Pulling the mat back she found the large ring attached to a bolt and put her fingers through it. The steel was cold to touch. How long had it been since someone had been down here?

Mia pulled hard and gave a squeal as the door came up, a lot more easily than she'd anticipated after her struggle trying to open it last time. Overbalancing, she landed on her bum once again and gave a groan, the wind slightly knocked out of her.

Getting to her knees, Mia peered into the gaping mouth of blackness, before switching on her torch and pointing it into the abyss. More cobwebs and dust. Simpson's Haberdashery had shares in those bloody things! More shelves lined with tins of food and bottles of beer. Christmas decorations and . . . Mia squinted. Bullets? Were there boxes of bullets down there? Like the packet under the counter?

288

Searching for the stairs, she tested the first step and found the rail to hold onto. Her torch tucked in under her neck, she slowly descended.

The air in the cellar was musty and damp, although none of the products looked like they'd been affected by the lack of airflow.

A meat safe was in one corner and homemade heavy wooden shelves lined one wall from the ceiling to the floor. Every inch was crammed with something: packets of crayons and sketchpads, two old suitcases and a box of children's skipping ropes.

Mia drew one out—they were the old-fashioned type with wooden handles and thick rope. She remembered skipping with something similar at primary school. Maybe Nana had taken one of these with her when she left.

There were wooden crates branded with Winchester across the top. Mia turned one box over in her hand and the lid slid off. Inside was a cardboard box completely intact with bullets for a .22 Long Rifle, the sort that most farmers had. Mia hadn't known that Clara had sold bullets. Maybe that's why they were kept down here. Out of sight, out of mind.

Thirty boxes in total. Hundreds and hundreds of bullets.

She'd have to get Dave to help her take them back to the police station and lock them up. Good thing none had exploded while they were being stored.

Turning her attention to the suitcases, she wondered if that's where the photo album that her nan wanted was. The first suitcase was brown with silver latches, dotted with small patches of rust. A thick layer of dirt lay on top, but she could still see a silver plate. Her fingers swiped the dust away and she tried to read what was inscribed. *CAS*. That was pretty straightforward. Clara Alexandra Simpson—Nana's maiden name. She tried the latches. One opened but the other was stubborn and wouldn't reward her with the sound of a click. She pulled at the top and managed to get it half open.

It seemed to be filled with papers and diaries, but in one corner was a small brown hardcover case.

'Come on,' Mia growled, tugging at the suitcase lid even more, but it wouldn't budge. What could she use to prise the latch open? Of course! The nearby tins of . . . Spam! She grabbed one of the rectangular tins and used the bottom of it to hit the latch.

Nothing.

Again. And again.

With a cry of triumph, Mia saw the latch spring open. Gently now, she pulled the lid up, her gaze drawn to the case in the corner. It was almost like a binocular case but bigger. A couple of sheets of paper on top told of daily takings and orders but her fingers drew out the object.

She opened the clip and the top pulled back to show an old-style camera with a winder and film. The front said it was a Kodak and around the lens were the numbers for the exposures. Turning it over, she looked at the back and realised there was still a film inside. Who developed old films these days, she wondered. What treasures could be on here that her nan would love to see?

A surge of excitement ran through her. She put the camera on the ground to take with her when she left.

The rest of the suitcase didn't hold anything exciting. The diaries were just to do with the shop.

July 5th 1968—Sales: Two tins beans, half a pound of sugar and three bags of SR Flour to Mrs Grant.

Two lengths of pink cotton to Mrs Forbes.

One pair of socks and one set of blue overalls to Mr King.

She glanced through the ledger filled with Nana's neat, cursive handwriting, the same as in the diaries. The looseleaf sheets of paper only pertained to orders Nana needed to put in to suppliers, or from customers who were coming in from out of town.

No photo album.

Mia turned her attention to the next suitcase, which opened easily. A cloud of dust slid off as she lifted the lid and peered inside. This one looked more likely to hold a photo album. Books filled the inside.

She took the first one from the top and looked at the red cover. *What Katie Did* by Susan Coolidge. The pages inside were thick and luxurious, the type almost smearing into the softness. On the inside was beautiful cursive writing, which Mia didn't recognise, saying: *Hammond Public School, 1924. Presented to Gwen Simpson. First prize. Grade V.*

Mia's fingers traced the page, thinking how precious it was to have a memento of her great-grandmother. Closing the cover, she carefully placed it to the side and dug in a little further. There were first-edition copies of Famous Five and Hardy Boys novels, then later novels of the Adventurous Four and Banjo Paterson's poems.

Hauling out a Henry Lawson book, she opened it and a handwritten page floated out. On one side there was the poem 'Unknown' by Henry Lawson, written out in a man's handwriting. It was about the death of an unknown man in the middle of the scrub. One line had heavy black markings under it. *Or the shame that had sent him here.*

The reverse side held a message:

To Clara, Fear not the shame that comes with this, because in time no one will remember. I wish I could change your mind, but I know I can't. That's one of the things I love about you, your clarity. Still, I will love you until my dying day. Remember that. P.

Mia read the poem again and then flicked back over, wondering who P was. Her grandfather's name had been Dougal, so it wasn't from him.

She looked closer. Maybe it was a D, just a badly written one. Or was it even T? T was Mr Marshall. Theo Marshall.

Finding other letters within the poem, she tried to compare them, but most were in lower object.

Goosebumps spread across her skin. *Fear not the shame* ... The shame of what?

Placing the sheet of paper next to the camera, she looked for the album, finding one right at the bottom. She opened the first page and saw that it was the sort where the photo was stuck to the page and a clear piece of plastic held it in place. The first image was of a house and garden, men and women lined up against the wall holding tennis racquets. Then there were photos of shearing and men sitting around tables with their hands in front of them, clenched into fists. Not dissimilar to the way that footy players posed for grand final pictures.

But Mia didn't recognise any of them.

Another page—wedding photos of Gwen and her husband; then babies in long christening gowns; then kids in shorts with knee-high socks and shoes. Mia thought she recognised Clara.

Then there was Clara and Dougal and that was the end.

Disappointment filled her. She'd really been hoping to find something about her father in there, but once again, there was nothing. It was as if Clara had decided to wipe any indication that he'd ever been alive from the face of the earth.

CHAPTER 29

The air was frigid when Mia stepped outside and locked up the store.

Her watch told her it was 8 p.m. She was tired and her body ached from hunching over the books for so long.

The search for anything to do with her father had been fruitless, but she'd decided to start taking the stock from the shelves and do a stocktake. Then she'd know what was there and what she could do with it all.

Josie had answered the text message she'd sent earlier.

I can be there on the weekend.

Bring your old clothes, Mia had replied. *Everything is filthy.*

That had been met with the thumbs-up icon and a smiley face.

The past few days had been surreal. It seemed imposs-ible that it had only been last week she'd been stationed in Broad River. Now, here she was in Barker, after a day in the car with Dave and a few hours in the shop. Tonight she'd sleep in a new house and eat some dinner prepared by her sergeant's wife.

The difference from her experience in Broad River was extreme.

Mia walked along the main street, stopping to look at the shop windows. The cafe had a few tables and chairs at the front. The IGA had standard checkout counters at the front and lollies lined up on the counter's edge ready for little fingers to convince their parents they needed something to eat on the way home.

Across the road and over from the soldier memorial was a tourist shop, with postcards and history books lining the window.

Some of the names on the memorial were familiar: Hack, Harper, Smith and Tooper. She thought that there may have been a lady called Mrs Harper who had taken Nana's ironing on when she got too busy to do it. And there had been a Reverend Tooper in the Uniting Church. Nana had talked about him. Not pleasantly.

There was no listing for Marshall. Mia thought about Nan's friend Mr Marshall as she wandered the main street. Was he still alive? If he was, did he live here, in Barker?

A spotlight lit up the real estate agent's window and drew her towards the listings. Searching for the Harcourt's farm, she finally found it with a sold sticker over the photo. The farm was five thousand acres of prime red loam soil and was suitable for livestock operations and cropping. In the drier parts of the Flinders Ranges, those blocks were worth a small fortune and highly sought after. There would have been more than two farmers trying to buy that block for sure.

Could someone have been so annoyed they missed out on it that they attacked Rhys's paddock? The gut feeling that Dave talked about earlier was mixed for her. Yes, missing out on a farm could be heartbreaking but would it be something you'd take personally? Surely it was more of a business decision? Still, she mused, not being able to buy a farm impacted on the business's future income and whether there was enough land for the kids to come home and eventually take over. To support three or four families.

Laughter rang out from the pub and suddenly Mia wanted a beer. It was late and she should go home, but her mouth was watering. From outside, she could see a fire dancing in the corner and a few men sitting in a row, staring at the TV hung high above the bar. A bloke was behind the counter wiping it down and talking to another couple of men at the northern end.

Taking a breath, she pushed open the door and went inside. The talking stopped as everyone swung to look at her.

Silence.

Finding her courage, Mia waved at them all. 'How's it going, fellas?' she asked, taking a step over the threshold. As she did, she noticed her shoe—a black work-issued boot.

Shit, she was still in her uniform.

Recovering quickly, she flashed another winning smile. 'Don't worry, I'm off duty. Just here for a beer.'

A couple of the blokes laughed. 'You allowed to do that in uniform?'

'I won't tell if you don't,' she said, knowing full well she would get a warning for doing something so stupid.

The man behind the bar leaned over and offered his hand. 'I'm Hopper. You're taking Jack's place, right?'

'Yeah. Mia Worth. Only here for a couple of weeks while the powers that be work out who's going to be stationed here permanently.'

'Well, welcome, Mia Worth,' Hopper said with a grin. 'First beer's on the house. What'll it be?'

Mia checked out the beers on tap and chose one, hoisting herself up onto a bar stool. She looked at the man sitting next to her and introduced herself. He grunted and shook her hand, not telling her his name. Everyone in the bar had started to talk again and Mia was left alone, hoping someone would be interested enough to come and say hello.

Hopper put the beer in front of her.

'So, where you from?' he asked, leaning on the counter.

'Funnily enough, here originally. My nan used to own Simpson's Haberdashery, but we left when I was really small. Nana's in the nursing home at Broad River now, so once I finished at the academy and I found out there was a vacancy, I applied. I wanted to be closer to her as she got older.'

The man to her left shifted slightly to look at her. 'You're Clara Worth's granddaughter?'

Mia took a sip of her beer and savoured it for a moment before answering. 'Yeah, I am.'

'Ah.' He continued to appraise her for a few more seconds then went back to his beer.

It was a loaded look, like the one John Manson had given her earlier in the day. But why? A little feeling of uncertainty filtered through. Perhaps saying her grandmother's name wasn't a good idea around these parts.

'Did you know her?'

'Oh yes.'

Mia waited but it became apparent there was nothing more coming. Deciding to bite the bullet she asked his name.

He turned slowly and looked at her. Deep lines ran around either side of his mouth and wrinkles around his eyes indicated he'd laughed a lot in his life. His dark brown eyes seemed slightly faded and didn't fit with the shock of white hair that stood up in patches on his head. He looked like someone needed to give him a comb.

Instead of answering her, he put down his beer. 'I'll see you anon,' he said to Hopper and left the bar.

Mia stared after him, wondering what on earth she'd said to upset him. Her eyes wide, she followed the man's path before looking to Hopper.

'Don't worry about him,' Hopper said with a little flick of his wrist. 'Bit odd in the head.' He tapped his own for emphasis and nodded towards her glass. 'Another one?'

As he spoke a woman about the same age as Mia walked through the archway from the dining room, an older, stooped man at her side. Mia recognised John Manson.

Against her better judgement, she agreed to another drink and got out her phone to pay. In the mirror she watched John and the woman walking together, deep in conversation. The woman was dark-haired like Mia and had the same body type; short and slight. John was shaking his finger at her, while the woman smiled and brought up a hand to wrap around his gently.

'Now, Papa, I don't think that's very fair, do you?' she heard the woman say, a smile in her voice.

'I don't care what you think, young lady. It has to be fixed.'

'Of course, but is that the way, I wonder?'

'Have you got a better idea?'

'Why don't we ring the council . . .'

Her voice faded as they walked out the front door. Moments later, lights from a car hit the back wall of the pub and the sound of the engine started, then died away as they drove off.

'Who was that?' Mia asked Hopper as he held out the EFTPOS machine and she placed her phone over the screen.

'John Manson and his granddaughter, Jayde Tonkin.' He gave a fond smile. 'Such a good girl, that one. Brings him in here every week for dinner, without fail. Comes all the way from over Mount Remarkable to do it. Don't know how she gets the time because she's always running after her mother and husband. That bloke of hers, he's one tough taskmaster, but she seems to manage him and get everything else done too.' He cocked his head to one side. 'Must be about your age, I reckon.'

'She sounds like a great family person.'

'She is that.' He gave a bark of laughter. 'A few nights ago she ran fair smack bang into Dave. He gave her a bit of a to-do. Must've almost run him off the road in her rush earlier in the day. They had a laugh about it afterwards.' He shook his head, still smiling at the memory.

Mia wondered what it must be like to be judged on the way you treated your family and how hard you worked. A small town's opinion could weigh heavily on shoulders, she was sure.

'John lives by himself?' she asked.

'Yeah, his wife's been gone for years now. Died before I bought the pub.'

'Must be a lonely life out there by himself. Dave and I went out that way today and I know it's only an hour or so drive from here, but the country feels like it's out bush somewhere. Really isolated.'

'I know what you mean, but it's just a feeling. There are actually a lot of families living out that way. And the land is so vast and hilly, you can't always see the houses from the road.'

Mia leaned forward and glanced around before she spoke softly to Hopper. 'Do you know anything about this crop damage out at Rhys Martindale's place?'

'I know that when it happened it was at the top of everyone's conversation list.' Hopper opened the dishwasher and a cloud of steam hit him, fogging up the glasses he wore. He swore and pulled out a glass and started polishing it.

'Is Rhys accepted well within the community?'

Hopper looked at her for a moment as if he was wondering whether he should talk or not. Publicans always knew what was going on in town and Mia assumed it was a fine line whether they told the cops anything in case they upset their patrons.

'Ah, what the heck,' Hopper said, confirming her thoughts. 'Mostly, but he can put people off with his manner sometimes.'

It was a compromise. Enough to make her come back while not betraying any of his patrons.

Mia smiled and nodded. 'Thanks, Hopper.'

CHAPTER 30

Mia dinged the silver bell on the front desk of the real estate agent and waited for someone to serve her.

'I'll be right out!' A male voice from deep in the back of the office called out and she heard a door slam.

While she waited, Mia looked at the houses that were for sale to see if she recognised any of them. The town felt so familiar and yet she couldn't remember a lot about her life here. The shop and Nana were clear but other memories were murky. A lady who patted her head at church; a flower garden where she liked to stop and smell all the different coloured flowers and try to catch the bees.

'Hello! How can I help?'

Mia swung around, not having heard the man enter the office. His step was sprightly and he was thin, with wispy grey strands of hair across an otherwise bald head. 'Hello,' she introduced herself while the man took off his glasses, fished around for a hanky in his pocket and rubbed them clean.

'Aiden Galloway. Well, well, well, a police lady. Haven't had one of them in Barker ever, I don't reckon. When'd you arrive, love?'

'Mr Galloway, I wanted to ask you a few questions about the Harcourt's property,' she said, ignoring his condescending tone. 'Do you have some time?'

'I don't seem to be run off my feet, so I guess the answer is yes.'

Mia assessed him, trying to put the sarcasm aside. 'Great, thanks. Would you be able to tell me how many people made offers for the Harcourt's place, please?'

He stared at her, openly curious, and Mia kept her face deadpan. 'Let me think,' he said. 'Yeah, two. Martindale and John Manson.'

Mia watched him. 'Two?'

'Yep.' Aiden reached up and brushed an invisible stray hair away from his forehead. 'Anything else you need to know?'

'I'm surprised, that's all. That type of land seems to be highly sought after.'

'Can be. But there's this little thing that's needed called moolah! You have to have money to be able to buy a farm.'

Annoyance flicked through her. 'I realise it's been difficult to get loans approved since the banking royal commission,' Mia said, staring straight at him. 'However, my understanding of the families around the area is that they've been there for generations. I would have thought there would be little debt.'

'Assumptions are dangerous. How could you know who owes what?'

'Mr Galloway, it's an offence to obstruct an enquiry. Would you like to come to the station and answer my questions? I'm more than happy to let my sarge know I'm bringing you in for a chat.' Her eyes hardened at the slim man, wondering whether he didn't like her because she was a woman, a police officer or just that she was new and not Jack.

'I'm not obstructing you. Ask away.' He spread his hands out and smiled, showing a dead front tooth. Mia liked him even less.

'I'm just surprised there were only two offers.' She stared at him. He started to fidget, and she knew she'd got through.

'I can't tell you why the place didn't have any more offers on it,' Aiden finally said. 'I was as surprised as you are. There were another three families I thought might have a look, at least. Whether they decided to place an offer, well, that would have been their call, but I was shocked they didn't even come for a look.'

'I see. So, there were only two who inspected the place?'

'I don't think I can make it any clearer for you. Two inspected, two offered, one bought. Martindale and Manson. Martindale and Manson. Martindale.'

Mia wanted to give him a slap around the head, but she just smiled sweetly and took a step towards the counter, as she dug in her back pocket. 'Well, now Mr Galloway, thank you for being so helpful.' She put her card on the counter, still holding his eyes. 'Perhaps if you think of some further information, you'll give me a call.'

Aiden picked up her card and looked at it. 'Constable Mia Worth.' His head snapped up, finding her gaze.

'And next time I need to talk to you,' she said, 'you'll forgive me if I take you straight to the station instead of having an unofficial chat.' She turned on her heel. 'That would give the town something to talk about, wouldn't it?'

Outside, her heart was beating rapidly and she took a few breaths to calm herself.

'Prick.'

She picked up her pace and headed back towards the police station, nodding to a couple walking down the street. Why was it, she wondered, that women had to work harder than the blokes to prove they could do the job? She'd bet her left ball, if she had one, that Dave wouldn't have been treated like that.

Flinging open the door, she marched in, still frowning and muttering under her breath.

Joan looked up. 'Oh dear, what's happened? Someone upset you?'

Mia heard Dave's chair roll over to the door and he stuck his head out from the office, listening.

'Nothing that I shouldn't expect. Sorry. I had such a great day with you yesterday, Dave, and I didn't expect to be on the receiving end of attitude today, that's all. I shouldn't have let it get the better of me.'

'Aiden Galloway?'

'Yeah.' Mia punched in the code and let herself in. 'Anyway, that's a dead end. Only two people looked at the place and they're the two we already know about.'

Dave leaned back on his chair. 'Only two?' he replied slowly.

'To quote Mr Galloway,' Mia said, wobbling her head side to side in an agitated way. 'I don't think I can make it any clearer for you. Two inspected, two offered, one bought. Martindale and Manson. Martindale and Manson. Martindale.'

Dave bit his lip to stop himself from laughing.

'What?' asked Mia. 'He was a prick!'

'I'm not saying he wasn't, but you'll have to get a bit more of a hard case around you if you're going to be a country cop, sorry to say.'

'Stuff him,' Mia said. 'I told him next time I'd bring him into the station instead of bothering with a visit.'

Dave winced. 'Well, you've probably got him offside forever now. I know, I know . . .' He held up his hand as she opened her mouth to defend herself. 'You can't let people walk all over you. You're new and, sorry for pointing out the obvious, you're a woman. Being a cop is going to be much harder here for you than it is for me. But my old partner, fella called Bob Holden—I worked with him in the stock squad for a few years—he always used to say that you catch more flies with honey than vinegar.'

Dave used his feet to roll his chair back inside the office.

The fight left Mia and she sagged, dragging a chair next to Joan. 'Ugh,' was all she said, letting her head drop on the desk.

Joan patted her back. 'You know the best piece of advice I can give you,' she said softly, glancing towards where Dave sat.

Mia looked up at her. 'What's that?'

'Don't get too emotional.'

Mia's face went red as memories of Richie's comments flashed back. 'I didn't—'

'Dave can't say that to you, but I can. Take a breath and remember you are a policewoman and you'll be setting an example for everyone—man, woman and child. Prick, Prick-ess, Prince or Princess. One day you might even inspire another young girl to do what you're doing.' She patted Mia again and turned back to her computer.

'Right, well, I guess that wipes out that line of enquiry,' Mia said to Dave when she sat down opposite him, ten minutes later.

After Joan's cleverly chosen words, she'd taken herself outside for a quick walk to regroup and then quietly let herself back into the station. She knew she was walking a fine line.

Dave leaned back in his chair. 'I phoned Sophie last night. She was trying to remember exactly when she saw this tractor, so she went back through her diary.' He flipped open his notebook. 'She thinks it was the second weekend in April. They had a birthday party to go to on the Saturday night, and she drove over on the Friday. Now that would fit with the timing. I've been back and looked at the weather records for the two weeks around that weekend. During the first week there was twenty mils of rain. An unbelievable start.'

'Because of the amount of rain?'

Dave nodded. 'Very unusual to get such a large amount in one fall. I rang Rhys this morning and he seeded that paddock during the third week of April.'

Mia understood. 'The tractor was seen during the second weekend so there was time to spray before it was seeded.'

'That's right. Given that the germination might have taken three or four days, the timing is spot on.'

'So we're looking for a female driving a John Deere tractor with a trailing boom behind it.'

'Nothing like a good old-fashioned needle in a haystack investigation.'

'I talked to the guy behind the bar last night. Hopper, is it?'

'Yep, sure is.' Dave leaned forward. 'And what words of wisdom did Hopper have for you?'

'Only that Rhys is liked by some and not by others.'

'I think we'd worked that out, hadn't we?' He pushed a piece of paper with some names written on it over to Mia. 'Can you run backgrounds on all these, please? They're the people who've bought the right amount of chemical this season. Once we know what we're dealing with, we'll go and have a chat.'

The phone in the outer office rang and Mia heard Joan answer it before calling out to Dave that it was Rhys Martindale.

Mia straightened as Dave picked up the phone. She tapped a few key words into the computer as she listened.

'No, mate, sorry, we're not any closer to finding out who did this. We're still in the early stages of our enquiries.'

Silence.

'I know this is a game changer for you.'

Pause.

Mia began checking Cranky Joe Newman's background. His real name was John Newman. He didn't have a record that she could see. Not even a speeding charge. His driver's licence was clean.

'Rhys, Constable Worth and I are working on this as quickly as we can. I can issue an incident report for your organic certification agency if you like. Would that help? Ah, I see.'

Mia glanced up as Dave tucked the phone in between his ear and shoulders and wrote a couple of notes.

'Right, I'll be in touch as soon as we have any news. And again, all I can do is reassure you that we're working on it.' Dave hung up the phone and kept writing in his notebook.

Mia waited for him to tell her what Rhys had said but before he could a voice called out from the front, 'Yoohoo!'

Mia saw Dave's face light up.

'Kim,' he said, like he needed to confirm for her. 'She will have brought smoko or lunch or something.' He got up and went to the door.

'Hey, honey,' Mia heard Kim say. 'Joan must have stepped out, she's not at her desk. Can you let me in?'

Kim was carrying a wicker basket and she put it on the desk, smiling at Mia. 'How was your first night in the house?' she asked.

'Well, I was later than I expected to be,' Mia said. 'I went to the shop then on to the pub.' She gave Kim a smile. 'Thank you so much for dinner. I put it in the microwave when I got back. Chicken curry is one of my favourites.'

'That's what I fed Jack when he first arrived and he liked it too.' Kim brought out a couple of plastic containers and one wrapped in alfoil. 'I made some beef pies and there're a few biscuits and cupcakes in these.' She tapped each container as she spoke.

'You spoil us,' Dave said, giving his wife a kiss.

Mia looked down at the desk, hoping they'd move apart soon. She had some questions she wanted to ask Kim, and maybe now was a good time, but it would distract the happy couple.

'Kim, can I please ask you something?'

'Of course.' Kim peeled the alfoil back and handed her a beef pie. 'There's sauce in that container there.'

Dave took his pie and sat back down, his eyes straying to his computer screen. Mia noticed he typed something then turned back to the conversation.

'Did you remember if you knew my dad?' she asked.

There was a long silence and Kim and Dave exchanged glances. Clearly, she did.

'What is it?' Mia asked. 'I'd really like to know. There was a bloke in the pub last night who asked if I was Clara Worth's granddaughter, and when I said yes, he walked out. I'm starting to think Nana must have done something awful and there are still people around who remember what it was.'

Kim put down the plate she was holding and reached for Mia's hand. 'I do remember your dad,' she said. 'Not well, but I remember he played cricket and worked as an orderly in the hospital.'

'None of that sounds too bad. Do you know how he died?'

Kim licked her lips. 'Did your grandmother not tell you anything about your dad's death either?'

Mia shook her head, fear seeping through her. She wasn't sure she wanted to know what Kim was about to say.

'Well, honey, I don't know much about how he died, I'm sorry. There was a bit of mystery around the happenings and I wasn't old enough to make much sense of what was going on.'

Mia's heart gave a heavy thud as she stared at Kim. 'Mystery?'

'Oh well, at least a bit of good old country town chat around his death. Whether you can class that as mystery or not, I don't know.' She rustled in the basket again and brought out some paper serviettes. 'Sorry, I can't help more. It's a while ago.'

'Oh.' Mia blinked a couple of times then turned away so they couldn't see the tears on her cheeks.

'Honey, his grave is out at the cemetery, here in Barker. If you wanted to go and see him, and needed company, I could go with you.'

'I don't know,' Mia said softly. 'I honestly don't know if I want to.'

'You don't have to make that decision today,' Dave said quietly. 'He's not going anywhere.'

CHAPTER 31

'Burrows?' Dave answered his mobile and pointed to Mia to take a left turn at the T-junction.

They were heading to Cranky Joe Newman's place. Dave had let Mia behind the wheel because he wanted to get a handle on how competent she was. He'd need to know in an emergency.

As Bob Holden had always told him, there are ways around finding out what people know and how good they are at the job, without putting them through their paces.

Mia was handling the dirt roads well.

'Is that right?' Dave asked his boss and listened again. 'Right, well shoot me the details and I'll keep an eye out.' Pause. 'Yep, yep.' Pause. 'No trouble. Righto, catch you later.'

He tapped the screen to end the call and looked at Mia. 'Well, our quiet time out here might be coming to an end. There's a BOLO out on a white Mazda. Be on the lookout.

Fella took off from Melbourne after shooting a cop. Got family links up here apparently.'

Dave saw Mia glancing across at him then back at the road. 'Got vision of him heading this way?'

'Nope, they've lost him. They're just giving us notice in case he turns up. Still, I'd be surprised. No crim in their right mind would go where family is. They know that's the first place we look.' He glanced over at her. 'Sorry that Kim couldn't help you with more information about your dad. How are you feeling?'

'No, it doesn't matter. I just thought she might remember him. I'll have to do some more research and see what I can find out.' There was a wry grin on her face as she shrugged. 'Like you said earlier, he's not going anywhere and a few more days or weeks won't make much difference since I've waited this long . . .' Her voice trailed off.

'Quite right,' Dave said. 'There'll be someone around here who knows. Ask questions. A bit of detective work.'

'Yeah. Yeah, I could. And I might. In time.'

Dave cleared his throat and leaned forward to check the radio volume.

'You haven't told me what Rhys wanted yet,' Mia said.

'Just wanting to know where we were at with the investigation. The organic certification people said that he can keep that paddock out for the year and every other paddock is fine to use, but he's wanting to get legal advice. When we can prove without reasonable doubt who did this, then we'll charge them, but Rhys wants to know where he's at, in a legal sense.'

'But we can't help with that, can we?'

'Well, Rhys can supply the lawyers with the testing information, but we can't give him any evidence we've gathered as yet. I think he was hoping I would.' Dave paused, got his bearings then said, 'Here's the turnoff to the driveway.' He pointed to a microwave on a pole on the side of the road ahead.

'What's that?' Mia asked, suddenly laughing. 'A microwave?'

'Mailbox,' Dave said with a grin.

'Of course.' Mia chuckled and Dave noticed with satisfaction that she handled the slippery gravel driveway with ease.

Cranky Joe was waiting for them, sitting on the railing of a set of sheep yards. Behind him was a mob of full wool ewes and some lambs in another pen. Another two blokes and one woman was standing around the cradle with lambs in it. The noise of the lambs reached them before Mia switched off the engine.

'Lamb marking by the looks,' Dave said, even though he knew it was unnecessary. He glanced at his watch. 'Afternoon smoko. Good timing, Ninety-nine. You asking the questions, or am I?' He could see she wanted to and was surprised but pleased when she shook her head.

Perhaps Joan's little chat had helped. He'd pretended that he hadn't heard, but he knew everything that went on in that police station.

She was a quick learner if Mia had realised already that there was no way she could come into a town—a small country town at that—and expect people to trust her and

315

tell her what she wanted to know, just because she was wearing a uniform.

⌒

Mia followed at a distance and watched the way Dave interacted with Joe. He'd set the man at ease straightaway by his casual demeanour. She got out her notebook and waited. She would scribe.

Seeing them chat, Mia remembered what Dave had said on the day they'd been searching for Tahlia. 'It takes time to get the local knowledge.'

Mia had heard him, but she hadn't listened.

'How's the percentage of the lambing?' Dave asked, leaning against the fence. 'Looks like you've got close to one hundred.'

'Yeah.' Joe pushed his hat back, scratching his head as he answered. 'Yeah, one hundred and ten per cent. Been a good year so far.'

'Did you wet and dry the ewes?'

Mia had no idea what that meant, but it would be something she needed to learn. Policing wasn't all about investigating and locking people up, chasing cars or speed checks. She was going to need to add more to her armoury. The language of farming.

She watched as Dave leaned against the yards and talked to Joe about farming, first getting a few laughs out of him before he hit him with the questions.

'Joe, I'm sure you would have heard that Rhys Martindale had damage done to his crops the other week.'

'Yeah, been the talk of the town. Don't know who did it, but.'

'What crops have you got in this year, Joe?'

'Oh, bit of canola, barley and wheat. Wanted to put some oats in to make some hay, but I wasn't sure if we'd get enough rain to make it viable.'

'Do you use Atrazine?'

'Sure do. Can't grow canola without it.'

'And you bought,' Dave referred back to his notebook, 'two hundred and fifty litres this year?'

Oh. That question was a game changer.

Joe stared at Dave, his eyes narrowed now. Mia took in his stance; feet planted firmly in the dirt, arms crossed. He radiated suspicion.

Mia was surprised when he answered mildly. 'Yeah, that seems about right for the amount of canola we planted. Just had to do the figures in my head.'

'What we've ascertained is that Atrazine was used before Rhys seeded his crop. Of course, as a pre-emergent it kills the barley.'

'Yeah, it would do that, for sure,' Joe agreed.

'What type of sprayer do you have?'

'Self-propelled Nitro. Millers.'

'Know anyone who still uses a trailing sprayer?'

'Oh, fair few of us still do. Not everyone can afford these big monsters!' He gave a grin and nodded his head towards the machinery shed. 'Take a look if you like. Do you know what type you're looking for?'

'Only that it was towed by a John Deere tractor, driven by a woman.'

Joe shook his head. 'I'm getting the feeling this is a roundabout way of asking if I have a rig like that. No, I don't. And I don't have a woman who would drive it either.' He threw a look over his shoulder at the people around the lamb marking cradle. He nodded towards the two young blokes and woman. 'That's my workforce. Two sons and a ring-in. All three are handy.'

Mia made a note.

'Have you heard that Rhys has fallen out with anyone lately?'

'I don't get off the farm too much. Always busy, but my two lads play footy. You want to talk to them?'

'I would,' Dave said. 'But before that, can you tell me where you were during the second weekend of April?'

Mia thought Joe might give Dave a mouthful, but he didn't. Instead, he took out a notebook with the logo of the local farm merchandise store on the front from his pocket and flipped back through it. 'I was seeding canola. My young fellas were running around behind me, with the fuel cart, seed and fertiliser. Along with checking the lambing ewes. Our AI lambs were about to start dropping. We were all on the farm.'

'Thanks,' Dave said.

'Look, if you're wanting to know who has John Deere equipment, why don't you ask the machinery dealership over in Port Augusta? They'd have a list.'

'Yeah, but that doesn't help us with the privately sold ones.'

Mia made a note to follow up with the dealership.

Joe turned and called out to the men behind him. 'Hey, Kane, Darren. Can you come and talk to Dave, please?'

The two boys finished each lamb they were working on and downed tools, ambling over casually. Mia hid a smile as each bloke put a hand on the rail and jumped over, seemingly effortlessly.

'G'day, Dave,' they both said. Their hands were covered in engrained dirt and blood so they didn't offer to shake Dave's. The one named Darren gave Mia a once-over— curious more than anything else. He was about her age.

Dave repeated his questions, then asked where they'd been during the second weekend of April.

'That was the weekend the AI lambs were dropping,' Joe reminded them.

Darren leaned against the fence and looped his thumbs through the belt links of his jeans. 'Oh yeah, yeah,' he said, turning to his father. 'That's the bloody weekend I heard that plane, remember? It scared the ewes and a few of the lambs got mismothered because it sounded like it was flying so low.'

Joe nodded slowly. 'I do remember you talking about that, son,' he said.

'What sort of plane?' Dave asked, leaning forward.

'Well, I didn't see it,' Darren answered. 'Just heard it, but it sent the ewes everywhere. Kane and I spent a good half a day fixing the fences the buggers went over, didn't we?'

'Yup, pain in the arse,' Kane said, adopting the same stance as his father.

'Which direction was the noise coming from?' Mia asked.

They all turned to look at her then Kane waved his hand to the west. 'Over near John Manson's place.'

CHAPTER 32

'Get on the blower and find out where the closest contractor aerial sprayer is,' Dave said as they settled themselves in the car.

Mia nodded, a thrill of excitement running through her.

'Are you thinking what I am?' she asked. 'No tracks in the paddock.'

'Exactly. No one would take a second glance at a plane flying overhead. They'd all look up and assume their neighbour or someone in the district had employed the contractor.' Dave slammed his palm into the steering wheel. 'I should have thought of that! It makes so much sense. But it still doesn't explain who this woman is and why she was looking for Rhys's place.'

Mia got out her phone and googled agricultural aerial sprayers.

'There's two. One based at Broad River.' She looked over at Dave. 'There's an airstrip right on the outskirts of town with a few hangars. And one in Port Pirie.'

'Okay, give 'em a call and see what you can find out.'

Dave was jazzed and, in turn, Mia was too. Her fingers were shaking as she dialled the number for the contractor based in Broad River.

'Good afternoon, my name is Constable Mia Worth and I'm with the Barker Police Station. Could I speak to whoever takes your bookings, please?'

There was silence while she was transferred. She could hear the engine of Dave's car humming and the small stones pinging up as they drove quickly along the gravel roads.

'Yes, I'm looking for information on a job that you might have been given during the second week of April over near Barker. Can you help with that?'

'Got the name of who made the booking?'

'No, I don't have, but it may have been under Rhys Martindale.' She flicked the phone onto speaker so Dave could hear.

The woman speaking said, 'We don't usually give out information about our clients.'

'I understand, but this is part of an ongoing police enquiry. We would come to see you in person, but we're a couple of hours away from you, in Barker.'

'This seems highly irregular. How do I actually know you're the police and not some kind of scammer?'

Dave leaned over to be closer to the microphone.

'Good afternoon, my name is Detective Dave Burrows. I'm in charge of the Barker Police Station. If you're uncomfortable with answering questions over the phone, I can get my colleague from the Broad River Police Station to come in and ask on our behalf. His name is Senior Sergeant Zach Tyler.'

Mia looked at Dave. She didn't want that to happen.

There was a silence across the line then a clicking of keys.

'I know Zach,' she said. 'He coaches my son at footy. You must be legit if you know him.' Another silence.

'Thanks very much for your help. What did you say your name was?'

'Michelle. Michelle Green.'

'And what's your position in the business, Michelle?'

'My husband, Dean, and I own it. Dean's the pilot and I run the office and organise the ground crews.'

'How long have you been in business for?'

'Eight years. Okay, so you're looking at the second week in April, right?'

'Yes, please,' Mia said.

'We flew a job on the Friday for the Carters over near Spalding and then on the way back we dropped in on the other side of Broad River for a small job at Spencers'. They were both knockdowns. Let's see about the Saturday . . . Hmm. No, nothing there. But Sunday, ah, yeah, we had a job for Martine?'

'Martindale,' Mia corrected. 'Rhys Martindale.'

'Might be my writing. GPS co-ordinates . . .' She reeled them off and Mia wrote them down quickly. 'Spraying Atrazine.'

Mia did a happy dance in her seat and looked at Dave, who had a large grin on his face too.

'That's great information,' Dave said, keeping a steady tone. 'Could you tell me who you sent the bill to?'

'Hang on.' The sound of more clicking. 'It's just a company with a PO box number. Jancarter Pastoral Pty Ltd. PO Box 1942 in Adelaide.'

Mia quickly thanked Michelle and hung up. 'How do we find out who this company is owned by?' she asked Dave.

'I'll put a request into the finance squad, see what they can come up with. Have you got that list of who bought the chemical with you? That name rings a bell.'

'Of course!' Mia leaned over to the back seat and grabbed the file, flicking through it until she found the page she was looking for. She ran her finger down the printout and took in a breath. 'Here,' she said. 'Jancarter Pastoral Pty Ltd. We haven't investigated them yet.'

'Is the printout of the original invoice there? Has somebody signed for the chemical or is there an order number perhaps?'

Mia flipped through again, this time more slowly. 'No. I haven't got any of that. Should I ring—'

'We're about fifteen minutes away from Barker. Be better to go and see Max face to face,' Dave said.

Dave's phone rang and he punched at the screen.

'Joan.'

'Dave, I've got Max Cooper, the agronomist, in the office wanting to see you. Are you far away?'

'That's interesting,' Dave said. 'We were just talking about him. We're only about fifteen minutes from you. Make him a coffee and tell him we'll be there shortly.' He disconnected and looked over at Mia. 'Did you run a check on Max?'

'No, he wasn't on my list.'

Dave snatched up the radio and called HQ asking for any information available on the agronomist.

Mia wanted to ask what he was thinking, but she didn't dare. Dave had pushed his foot down on the accelerator and was focused on heading back to Barker as quickly as he could. The purple and red hills passed by with speed and she found herself trying to link Max with anything she knew.

She had nothing.

When they arrived at the station, Joan pointed to the interview room that she had led Max to minutes before.

'Any idea?' Dave asked her, but she shook her head.

'Just asked to see you.'

Dave pushed open the door and ushered Mia inside, closing the door behind them. 'G'day, Max, need anything to drink or are you right? Joan make you a coffee?'

The man shifted uneasily in the seat and then shook his head. 'G'day, Dave. Let's just get this over with.'

'What would you like to get off your chest?'

Max clenched his fists, which were resting on the table in front of him. 'It's not Aussie to dob people in,' he began.

'I think it's okay if you're helping solve something illegal,' Dave said.

Nodding, Max swallowed. Mia watched his Adam's apple bob up and down. There were beads of sweat on one side of his forehead, a sure sign, in Mia's mind, that he was nervous. Guilty? Perhaps, but definitely nervous.

'Hear you're looking for a female in a John Deere tractor with a trailing boom spray?'

'Do you know someone who fits the bill?'

'Yeah. Jayde Tonkin.'

There was a silence while Mia and Dave processed his words.

'Jayde Tonkin?' Dave sounded as if he had to be sure he'd heard correctly.

'Yeah. She was on the side of the road, checking the tyres, that's how I know it was her.'

'Did she talk to you?'

'I stopped to ask if she was okay, but she was, so I drove on. Rhys's main drive was just a couple of ks from where I saw her.'

'And you saw her get back in the tractor?'

'When I looked in the rear-view mirror, I could see the tractor moving away from Rhys's.'

Dave nodded and turned to Mia. 'Have you got that company name?'

'Jancarter Pastoral Pty Ltd,' Mia said, checking her notes. She glanced up at Max. 'Do you have anyone with an account at your shop who is known by that name?'

Max nodded slowly. 'It sounds familiar, but I can't place it. Want me to look it up when I go back?'

'Yes, please. I'll come around in an hour or so and pick up the information. Just got a couple of things to tidy up here first,' Mia said. 'I've also got a couple of invoices I'd like you to check for me, if you don't mind.'

Max shifted in his seat. 'I know this sounds all TV-like, but do you need a warrant?'

'Not if you're happy to give us the information, Max,' Dave said.

'It's my business so I can do what I like, can't I?'

'Sounds about right.' Dave stood up and held out his hand. 'Thanks very much for coming in, Max. You've done the right thing. Any little detail can blow a case wide open.'

When he was gone, Mia turned to Dave. 'I've put those GPS co-ords into Google Maps and they come up with the paddock that's been sprayed on Rhys's place.'

'So we know how it was done, just not why or by who. But this Jayde Tonkin information has thrown a bit of a curve ball, hasn't it?' Dave leaned back and crossed his arms, dropping his chin onto his chest, while Mia watched.

'Joan?' Dave called.

The older woman appeared at the doorway. 'Yep?'

'What do you know about Jayde Tonkin?'

'Jayde? Her mother is Emily Rose and she married a guy from the other side of the ranges—that's about all. I don't think she's got any kids yet. Oh, but she's John Manson's granddaughter.'

'Yeah, I think I knew that.' Dave frowned hard. 'There's something here we're missing,' he muttered.

'Yeah, I saw her at the pub with him last night. Hopper says she takes John out to dinner once a week and that her husband is a bit of a hard taskmaster.'

'Aha,' Dave said, staring into the distance.

Joan gave a small smile and raised her eyebrows at Mia. 'You won't get much out of him now, not until he puts all the pieces of the puzzle together.'

'That's okay,' Mia said. 'I've got a couple of things to do.'

'Take off and get some lunch before you go and see Max,' Dave said. 'Give him a chance to find the information we're looking for.'

Mia opened the door into her new house, picking up the container that had been left at her front door. Kim had obviously been busy again. On the top was scrawled *roast lamb and veg with gravy.* The perfect lunch for a cold day.

Putting the meal into the microwave, Mia stopped at the kitchen table and stared at the diary she'd found in the shop the night before.

With all the chaos of the missing girl and moving to Barker, Mia hadn't had time to open the box she'd picked up from the shop on her first visit. She'd carefully gone through the contents of the box, now minus the gun, and piled up the three diaries, one on top of another.

There had been notes, which she'd put in a different pile, and invoices in another. The box seemed as if it had been deliberately concealed under the windcheater material. It was so close to the entrance of the cellar, Mia wondered if Nan had been going to take it down there when she'd been interrupted.

From the first quick flick through the diaries, Mia had seen there were pages torn out.

She got out a new notebook and dated the top of the page, before starting with the invoices. They were made out to Clara, from a doctor, but they didn't say who was being treated. Just a number and the date.

Every invoice was the same: CT08050714; the amount, $1405.

Back in 1994, that was a lot of money to be going out—Mia checked the dates—monthly.

She counted up twelve invoices: $16,860.

Opening her computer, she brought up Google and typed in CT08050714.

Even Google didn't know what the numbers meant. It was the first time she'd seen a page saying, *There are no results . . .* Frustrated, she searched the invoices again, hoping to see something she'd missed, but there was nothing.

Putting them aside, she turned her attention to the notes. Most were in a hand she didn't know. A strong hand, heavy lines indenting the plain white page.

My life is full of horror.

This is nothing but a prison.

My head hurts.

Mia didn't understand what she was reading, but she could feel the force of the pain coming from the pages. Whoever wrote these seemed to be in agony.

Again, she typed in one of the sentences to Google, but the long list of hits for *Where have you gone?* was too long to even try and make some sense of. Even with her grandmother's name and the word Barker included, there wasn't any joy.

Mia groaned and forked a piece of lamb into her mouth, before piercing a carrot. She chewed hard, her mind whirring, while her notepad stayed blank.

Her phone rang and she glanced at the screen. Dave.

'I've got something. The owner of Jancarter Pastoral Pty Ltd is Aiden Galloway.'

CHAPTER 33

Mia ran through the door, her coat flapping behind her. 'I still don't know what the link is,' Mia puffed as she pulled out her chair and sat down at her desk.

'Max found the information really quickly, so he brought it straight back,' Dave said.

He pushed over the documentation for the company listing, then a printout from the farm merchandise shop. Aiden Galloway's signature was plain to see.

Mia blinked then looked up at Dave.

'Can you explain this?'

'Nope. But it's nothing that asking a few questions won't fix.'

'Are Aiden and John Manson related in any way?'

'I've just flicked a text off to Kim to ask that. She'll know, I think. But look at this.' He walked over to the whiteboard on the wall, where he'd drawn connecting lines to names. 'We've got Rhys Martindale, whose property neighbours onto John Manson's. Then,' he followed the blue line, 'Rhys has bought the Harcourt's property that John wanted to buy. And here—' a red line connecting John to Jayde Tonkin '—our tractor driver. Now, over here, there's Aiden. The bloke who sold Rhys the farm that John wanted.'

Mia stood up and crossed her arms. 'To me it all points to John. He's the one who had the most to lose. Has he somehow blackmailed Aiden to help him? Or does Aiden owe him something?'

'Good question. But if that's the case, why would Aiden have sold the farm to Rhys? Surely he would have made some excuse not to put Rhys's offer forward to the vendor?' Dave tapped the circled word *Harcourt's*.

'I think, legally, they have to put any offer they get to the seller,' Mia said.

'Legally, yes, but what if Aiden knew a way around that.'

They looked at each other, then Dave's phone dinged with a text message.

Sorry, honey, I can't help you with John and Aiden. They're older than me!

'Bugger. Who else would know?' he wondered.

'Can we just ask them?'

'I like to know what I'm going into. Detecting isn't always asking questions. Sometimes it's good to know the answers to the questions, so if the person-of-interest tells you a lie, you know it. Come on, let's go.'

'Where?'

'You'll see.'

They shut and locked the station door behind them, hanging up the printed sign that said the office was unattended and if urgent help was needed to ring the mobile number listed.

In the patrol car, Dave explained that many of the churches kept family trees in their archives.

'I've got a hunch these two surnames are from Ireland, so they might be Catholic. I know it's a long shot, but let's see what we can find out. I already rang Father Doherty and he had agreed to let us look at the births, deaths and marriages in the Catholic church.'

Mia's brow crinkled. They didn't teach this sort of thing at the academy.

In front of the church were some old graves with wrought-iron fences around them, the headstones looked like monuments rather than the small headstones of today. A shaded cement path led to the church doors, which were open, and a small, wiry man was standing in the middle of them.

'Dave. Good to see you, my friend.'

'Father.' Dave nodded. 'This is our new constable, Mia Worth.'

'I'm glad to know you,' the priest said, clasping Mia's hands in his soft ones.

'Hello.'

'Come through into the hall. I've got the books spread out.'

'I solved an historical crime once by using the diaries from the Uniting Church minister,' Dave said, his voice echoing up to the rafters.

Mia was astounded. 'How?'

'He had everything written in the diary. Just had to trace it back and verify everything as best I could. Luckily the last member of the family was still alive.'

'Here you are,' Father Doherty said, waving them towards three large books. 'Births, deaths and marriages. You do realise, this will only help if the people have been born here, got married in this church and/or had their funeral conducted here?'

'Sure do, thanks again for getting these out for us.'

'I hope you find what you're looking for.' He left quietly without any questions.

'Got the birthdates of Aiden and John?' Dave asked, slipping his glasses from their pouch and putting them on. The book he opened had a heavy cover and the pages were thick. They were a yellowed colour, like they had been left out in the sun.

Mia unfolded a piece of paper and handed it to Dave, then opened another book.

Dave ran his fingers down the index. 'Manson, Manson, Manson . . . Yeah, here: John David.' He quoted the birthdate then checked the notes. 'They match. Married . . . You'll need that book there for the marriages.' He pointed to the green-covered book that Mia had opened. He gave her the dates and Mia flicked through, trying to find the information.

'Married Janice Taylor. I need the births book to check if Emily Rose is their daughter.' She put her notebook under the lines of writing to make sure she was reading the correct information.

'I've got a sister to John,' Dave said. 'Suzette Manson. She was born in 1947, so that would make her seventy-five. Is there a marriage for her?'

'Hold on a moment.' Mia turned more pages, running her eye down the margins looking for surnames. 'Yeah, there is. Oh Jesus.'

Dave's head snapped up. 'What?'

'John Manson's sister, Suzette, married Aiden Galloway.'

They stared at each other, wondering how it all fit together.

'They can't be, can they?' Mia asked Dave. 'Be related, I mean?'

'The one thing I've learned in this business, Mia, is to never make assumptions. And I don't like coincidences! Might be something, might be nothing, but we have to see which way it is.' Dave grinned. 'This is the interesting part.'

'Interesting?'

'Or fun. I always get excited when I know I'm getting close, and I think we are. But if they were brothers-in-law, why wouldn't Aiden help John to get the farm he wanted? Do Aiden and Suzette have any kids? I've only been in Barker seven years and Aiden has been alone the whole time that I've known him.'

Mia checked through the pages again. 'A boy, Jason. Looks like he'd be about forty.'

'Where is Suzette now?'

A silence while Mia looked. 'I can't see her mentioned, so either they're still married or divorced. But she hasn't been buried here in the Catholic cemetery.'

Dave closed the books and pushed them away, indicating it was time to leave. 'Thanks for your help, Father,' he called then gave a wave into the gloomy church, before leaving by the side door, Mia struggling to keep up with his long strides.

'We've got enough to go and start asking Aiden some more questions,' Dave said.

'G'day Aiden,' Dave said, leaning on the counter. Aiden Galloway sat across from him, while Mia perched against the counter's other end.

'What can I do you for, Dave?' Aiden asked. He pushed his chair away from the desk and leaned back. Smoothing the few wisps of hair down on his forehead, he waited.

Mia noticed he was avoiding looking at her, focusing on Dave only.

'Things busy in real estate?'

'They come and go. The last month has been a bit slow. Was glad to have that Harcourt's sale. Keeps the wolves from the door for a bit.' Aiden continued to stare at Dave.

Mia tried to read him. He was acting very casual, but he was alert. Like a cheetah ready to run if a deer crossed his path.

'When does that settle?'

'Settled last week.'

Mia's eyes flitted over the desk, trying to see if there was a photo of a woman or young family. Perhaps he had grandkids.

The desk held a newspaper, looseleaf paper, a notebook and some glossy files with the real estate company's branding on them. Right on the edge was a brown leather wallet. Worn and well used.

Mia glanced back at Dave to see what he was going to ask next.

'Who did you take around Harcourt's?'

'I told your constable here there were only two. Rhys and John Manson.'

'Known John Manson long?'

Aiden snorted. 'I was married to his sister.'

'Oh, I'm sorry,' Dave said. 'Was? She's passed?'

'Yeah.' Aiden shifted in his seat and finally got up, coming to stand opposite Dave. 'She died fifteen years ago. The big C. What can you do, you know? She tried to fight it for a couple of years, but she got tired and it kept coming.'

'You weren't here then?'

Aiden shook his head. The fight had gone out of him. 'No, we were in Ardrossan, over on the Yorke Peninsula. Our family was there; our son, Jason. We moved there when he was a little boy, and he grew up and fell in love with a local girl, so he stayed. Once Suzette died, I came back here. But I don't know . . .' He stared through the door into the distance.

Mia was sure he wasn't seeing anything, only memories.

'She's in Ardrossan cemetery because Jason was living there and I didn't think he'd ever leave. Sometimes I wish her grave was here so I could visit more, but I go back to see Jason and his family often enough.'

Dave cleared his throat.

'Sorry to hear that. I know how scared I was when we thought Kim had breast cancer. Frightening times.'

'What's this all about, Dave? I know you're looking for something.'

'This spraying on Rhys's property has got me all concerned. It's a pretty personal crime and I'm trying to work out why someone would do it. Something must have really upset them.'

Watching Aiden closely, Mia had her notebook and pen ready.

There wasn't even a twitch or slight tightening of his jaw line when Dave mentioned the spray.

'How do you think I can help you?'

'I'm not sure, but I thought I'd tell you what we know . . .'

Mia listened, observing every reaction. All Aiden did was nod and listen.

'We know it was your company who asked for the spraying job to be done and we have your signature on the invoice for the Atrazine. We can make this really easy and you can show us your bank records to tidy everything up, or I can get a warrant. I have more than enough evidence to do that.' Dave waited.

Aiden said nothing. The silence that filtered through the office was unnerving.

Then Aiden moved back to the desk and opened a drawer, taking out an old cash ledger.

'Here's the reason,' he said quietly. 'My father was the bank manager here when John's family had to sell that land. It caused a fair bit of angst between us, which pretty much broke down my relationship with Suzette. That was why we moved away from Barker.

'John blamed my dad and wouldn't have anything to do with me. Death by association.' Aiden rubbed his nose then looked up, this time at both Mia and Dave. 'John and I had been really good mates before that. I felt like I'd lost him and my wife all in one fell swoop.'

'But why did you spray Rhys's farm?' Dave asked, elbows on the counter.

'I tried to buy Harcourt's back. My company Jancarter put in a bid. I'm not allowed to buy through myself, so I got the company to put in a proxy bid. Told Rhys that it would be better if it went back to John's family. He just outright laughed at me. Said if it was on the open market, then he'd be putting in an offer.'

'And his offer was much higher than what you could afford?' Mia asked, reaching for the cash ledger. There must be evidence of the Mansons having to sell the farm in here. That could be the only reason Aiden had kept it so long.

'Yeah, and much higher than John's offer too.' Aiden's voice closed over. 'I thought Rhys would back off when I explained the situation, but he was too hungry. Too driven to see that the place should have gone back to its rightful owners.' Aiden scoffed. 'His offer was way over the top. Too high! John bragged that he could get two and a half times more for his grain than the conservative farmer and he'd have that place paid off in no time. I reminded him that if he wasn't farming in the usual way, his yields would be down, but he had another argument for that too.' Aiden shrugged. 'I couldn't keep my promise to Suzette—that I would get that land back into her family.'

Dave nodded and looked at Mia. She reached for her cuffs, but he shook his head, indicating Aiden's arm.

'Aiden Galloway,' she said, 'I'm arresting you—' Her words were drowned out by Aiden's sobs.

CHAPTER 34

We have to leave. Now. How much I'm giving up in doing this, but I need to protect Nicole and her growing baby . . . Mia was struggling to understand the words she was reading.

He did it, Clara wrote. *But I let him! Theo and I let him! The shame is beyond belief. How can I ever show my face in this town again?*

It seemed as if tears had fallen at this point because some of the writing was smudged.

Who had done what? *God, Nana, why didn't you put names in here?*

She looked up, then back down at the page. Did she really want to know what had happened?

Banging her fist on the table, she felt the prick of tears. 'Oh, Nan, why can't I just ring you?'

There was a knock on the door then a cold draught snuck up the passage and hit her face.

'Mia? It's Kim. Can I come in?'

Swallowing, Mia pulled up all the professionalism she'd been taught at the academy.

'Kim, hi. I'm in the kitchen.'

She needed to be like Dave. To have a face that didn't show what she was thinking or feeling. Her heart could be breaking on the inside but no one would ever know.

'Dave sent me to check on you.' Kim stood in the doorway, a little frown on her forehead.

'Yeah, of course. I was about to start going through these diaries and see what secrets they might hold.' She gave a small smile and a nod, hoping Kim would leave.

Kim sat down at the table. 'Mia, I've brought someone with me you might want to meet.'

The man who had been in the pub and left not long after she'd said her name followed Kim in. He was elderly but fit with clear eyes.

'Hello, Mia,' he said in his deep voice. 'You've grown up.'

Mia half rose then sat down again. Something was familiar. 'Mr Marshall?' Her voice was tentative.

'The one and the same. How is your grandmother?' He seemed hungry for information.

She glanced from him to Kim and back again. 'Nana's got dementia. She's in the nursing home in Broad River, but other than memory loss, physically she's pretty well.'

Mr Marshall's face drooped. 'I'm very sad to hear that,' he said. 'May I?' He indicated to a chair.

'Um, sure.' Mia looked around wondering what to do.

Kim was putting the kettle on, making her way around the kitchen with familiar ease. 'Think we could all do with a cuppa, don't you?'

No one answered her.

Mr Marshall reached out and tapped the invoices. 'I see you've found your grandmother's things. Did you find the gun too?'

'Oh! You know about it? Yes. Nana had a horrible reaction when I told her about it. What do you know?' Mia leaned forward. 'I know something awful happened, but she won't tell me.' Her voice dropped a little. 'Or can't. I'm not sure which.'

The elderly man nodded and he pressed his lips together, as if trying to keep the words inside.

Kim put cups in front of each of them and discreetly left the room.

'Can you tell me what these invoices are for?' Mia pushed them over.

'I can. But, Mia,' he looked at her steadily, 'do you really want to know?'

Mia just stared. How could she not want to?

'Once you hear this, it's not something you can unhear. You need to be prepared.'

'I don't have any choice,' she whispered. 'I have to.'

Drawing his cup of tea closer to him, Mr Marshall nodded again. 'Firstly, you need to understand how much I loved . . . still love, Clara. She was the light of my life. But she made me promise never to contact her again. She had to leave Barker. I didn't like it, but I agreed.' Mr Marshall took a deep breath and shut his eyes, contemplating what he had to say. 'Okay,' he said quietly as if to reassure himself. 'It was 1990 when your father was diagnosed with bipolar. There are a few categories of bipolar, and Alex was Bipolar Type One.'

'What does that mean?'

'He was prone to long-lasting depressive states. Sometimes psychosis.'

'Where you find it hard to recognise what is real and what isn't?'

'In a nutshell, yes. Your grandmother, Clara,' his face softened, 'she worked hard to give him the best care she could, but sometimes it wasn't enough.

'He heard voices. Ones that told him to do things. Ghastly things. Mostly, when he took his medication, he was a good lad. Hardworking. But he always kept to himself. Clara got him a job as an orderly at the hospital and for a few years, things were very calm. He married Nicole, she got pregnant with you and Clara was excited, but she was nervous too, because she thought you might inherit his mental health problems.

'I know Clara spoke to him about this because I had gone into the shop to buy some bullets and heard the conversation. I didn't want to interrupt, so I snuck out and went back later. Alex had been so angry after she'd voiced her concerns that he'd lost control and hit her.

'When I went back, she was bleeding from the forehead. I got her cleaned up and suggested she report it to the police. But of course, she wouldn't.'

Mia shook her head not wanting to hear any more, but at the same time, needing to.

'From then on things went downhill. Alex's medication didn't seem to be working and he had more and more psychotic episodes.

'One night I found him wandering along the street, covered in blood. The next day when I asked him what had happened, he couldn't remember.'

'Did anyone present at the hospital?' Mia asked, a lump in her throat.

'No. I tried to find out, but in the end I decided whoever he'd hurt—if in fact he had hurt them—had been an animal not a human.'

'So, what did you all do?'

'Clara and I discussed it and decided we needed to get him to a new doctor. There was a new drug being trialled, which Alex was offered.'

Mia took a sip of her tea, hoping to wet her mouth and make it easier to speak. The cooling liquid did nothing to help.

'Unfortunately, the new drug made him worse. And then he hurt someone.'

Mia just looked at Mr Marshall. The words from the pages echoing through her.

My life is full of horror.

This is nothing but a prison.

My head hurts.

'You locked him up?'

'I wish we had, Mia. That was our greatest regret. We took him out of the mental hospital and brought him home again. Trying, trying, to help.' His voice rose. 'You have to understand, Mia, people know so much more about this blasted disease now than we did then. We thought we were doing the right thing.' Silence. 'But we weren't.'

'The gun?' Her words were getting stuck now.

'Alex came into the shop, waving the gun. It was night and there was only Clara and me there. He said he didn't want to live. Thought that if he was dead he wouldn't have to listen to the voices in his head or the guilt of hurting people he loved.' Mr Marshall ran a hand over his face and took a rattling breath. 'Oh, I could have tackled him or tried to get the gun away. In fact, I moved to do that. But Clara, she wasn't having any of that. She grabbed my arm and stopped me.'

Mia held out her hands. 'No, I don't . . . I'm not sure . . .' Breathing hard and fast, she waited, while Mr Marshall looked at her, not saying anything.

'I think I know,' Mia whispered, sitting upright and completely alone at the end of the kitchen table.

A soft hand touched her shoulder as Mr Marshall began to speak again. Halting but relieved. Glad to get a lifetime of culpability off his shoulders.

'Clara said, "Alex, you need to do what you think is best." Then he shot himself.'

⁓

The cemetery was dark and a bitter wind blew around the graves as Mia walked blindly trying to find her father's headstone.

She needed to shout and scream at him. Was the story true?

Flashing the torch on each headstone, she read inscription after inscription hoping to see the words *Alex Worth*.

Name after name that wasn't his . . . and then, there he was: *Alex Worth*. His birth date and the date of his death.

And an inscription from the Bible.

Matthew 7:1 Do not judge lest you be judged.

There were no other names—not his mother's, not Nicole's and not hers.

Do not judge lest you be judged.

That told Mia all she needed to know.

A sob ripped from her chest and she fell to her knees in front of her father's grave.

'Mia.'

A voice so close to her ear, made her scream.

'It's okay. It's me, Chris.'

Mia turned, tears on her cheeks. 'Chris?'

'Dave rang earlier. He thought you might need a friend.'

EPILOGUE

Mia hurled the last bundle of paper into the fire and watched with satisfaction as it burned, the flames licking around it, the edges curling upwards.

Josie put her arm around her friend and gave her a squeeze. 'Oh my god, it's all done! What a freaking task!'

Mia covered her friend's hand with hers and smiled. 'Thank you. I wouldn't have been able to do it without you or Chris. Or Dave and Kim.'

'God, aren't they the cutest?' Josie exclaimed, glancing to the other side of the bonfire where Dave was standing with his arm around Kim. She was giving him a teasing smile and he was shaking his head.

'Sickly sweet,' Mia said.

Chris came over to stand alongside them. 'All good?' he asked.

'We made five thousand dollars and a bit from the garage sale,' Mia said happily. 'I can't wait to transfer the money across to the nursing home in Broad River. The lady in charge was overwhelmed when I rang her and let her know we had made that much and what the donation was going to be.'

They all turned and surveyed the scene. The shop was empty and quiet, waiting for the new owners to fill it with merchandise—tourist gifts and collectors' items.

The sordid history of its past would be erased when they moved in.

The floorboards, where Alex had shot himself, had been stained with blood.

'Is that where it happened?' she'd asked Mr Marshall.

He'd only nodded and backed away. Leaving her with what was left of her father; the place he'd died and his blood.

Mia had spent a few hours sitting alongside the area, trying to imagine a man with a mind so damaged that he felt there was no other option. The torture he must have felt.

The horror of Clara's words to her own son. What trauma to live with.

'No regrets, though,' Mr Marshall said. 'Not one day went by where she regretted her choice.'

A couple of days beforehand, she'd visited Nana and told her she knew, hoping above all hope, that Clara would say something. Just one small word or sign that she understood what Mia was saying.

Instead, her grandmother had looked blankly at her.

But Mia hadn't believed Clara's memory loss then. A twitch at the corner of her eye and a slight movement around her mouth, told Mia her nan knew what she was saying and, for once, she was choosing to hide behind the dementia.

'I don't have a son,' she'd said.

And that was the truth.

But with those words, once again she'd been out of reach.

Chris had helped her pull up the floorboards and replace them with new ones and now Bill and Annabelle from the cafe couldn't wait to move in.

Mia had had the photographs from the camera she'd found developed and yesterday she'd taken them to Nana. Saying nothing, she'd laid two of them in front of her nan. One of Alex and one of Mr Marshall and Clara.

Nana hadn't said anything, but she'd pushed the one of Alex aside and picked up the other one. Tears had run down her face. Mia had beckoned Mr Marshall into the room and Nana had outstretched her hands to him, smiling through tears.

'I know you,' she said. 'I know you by heart.' Her hand on Mr Marshall's chest. 'But what is your name?'

Mia hadn't been able to control her emotions and she'd quietly left the room.

Now, beside the bonfire, her phone rang and she pulled it out of her pocket, walking away from the group. Unknown caller.

'Hello, this is Mia,' she answered.

'Mia, Zach,' her sarge at Broad River said briskly. 'I've had word today that you're to stay at Barker. You are to report to Detective Burrows for your duties from now on.'

'I . . .' Her eyes flicked up to see Dave and Kim walking towards her, hand in hand. Both were smiling. They already knew.

'I . . . Thank you, Sarge. Sorry not to be under your command anymore.'

'I think you'll be happier at Barker, Worth,' he said and hung up.

'Great to know we've got you for good, Mia,' Dave said, nodding towards the phone. 'That was the news, I take it.'

'Did you organise it?' The same question she'd first asked him.

He shook his head. 'I told the boss that you fitted in here quite nicely, but the decision was his to make.'

Mia grinned. 'Thank you for everything, Dave. This wouldn't have happened without you.'

That wasn't the only thing to celebrate. Mia's idea of rigging up a security camera outside her house in Broad River had proven worthwhile. The vision had been sent through to her phone and she and Chris had watched while Ben, the young lad in the green hoodie she'd chased, lurked around the house.

When confronted, Ben and his mate admitted he had been tapping on her windows at night, even before she'd had the altercation with him. Apparently, they thought it was their job to give the new copper in town a run for her money. A bit of a local welcome. His father was the local real estate agent in Broad River, and Ben had stolen the spare key to get into Mia's house. He was getting more than a slap on the wrist now.

Zach had kicked their arses. And driven them to Barker to apologise to her face.

'I've got a bit more information for you,' Dave said. 'Jayde Tonkin was in the tractor that day because she was looking for the boundary gate between Manson's and Martindale's farms. She was taking the boom spray down to help out her grandfather, who couldn't sit on it anymore. Hurt his hips too much, so Jayde went to do it for him. See, isn't it funny how what we think could be the main piece of evidence is actually nothing?'

'Happy?' Chris asked, giving her another hug.

Mia looked around her back yard. She was in Barker permanently now, she had an amazing mentor and a new beginning. Her heart was still hurting for her dad, and her nan seemed to have taken a downwards turn in the last few days, but Mia had found a home and a new family.

Dave had been right. Local knowledge was good.

She didn't answer the question, just pulled Chris towards the fire with a grin on her face.

'I can't wait to see what happens next,' she said.

ACKNOWLEDGEMENTS

The sky is throwing down rain as hard as it can and the wind is whipping through the trees with fury, as I sit here at my desk wondering what to write in these acknowledgements. It's strange to think, by the time *Broad River Station* ends up in your hands, I'll probably be complaining how hot it is!

Life is a little off kilter today. My little companion, Rocket the Jack Russell, is no longer with us and, while I'm trying to find the words to celebrate twenty books and thank all of you readers for your continued support and loyalty, my office is feeling 'not quite right' and very lonely. As I started to put these thoughts down, I realised that Rocket had been around for the writing of every one of those twenty books. Snoring softly at my feet or standing in the doorway barking; demanding attention or to be fed, or (and why he got the name Stinkers) farting at exactly the right time and in the right space for maximum impact! Still, all good things must come to an end and Rocket's body and mind had given out on him. So, my little friend, my secret keeper, you're now forever chasing mice and sheep and yapping at anything that moves. My heart is sore, my eyes wet, as I type. I miss you and your paws clicking across the floorboards.

Okay, deep breath!

Well, here we are celebrating book twenty! It seems I say often that I can't quite believe that these books still keep coming and that no one has popped up to tell me this is a crazy joke and I can't write. So, the first and the biggest thanks must go to you, The Readers. You all are the only reason that I get to keep doing this. To you who have been there since the very first one, *Red Dust*, a very heartfelt thank you. Thanks for staying with the books all this time. For those of you who joined along the way, I'm so happy and grateful you found these novels. To all who have given them as presents, you're awesome. To librarians and booksellers who recommend them, you're all awesome too.

To everyone at Allen & Unwin—Tom, Annette, Christa, Laura, Sarah, Matt, Andrew, Jenn—thank you, thank you, thank you. What a long and lovely association we have and I'm so grateful to every single one of you. Not only do we work together, but I treasure the friendships we've formed.

Over the time I've been writing, I've worked with lots of other editors and publicists, but I want to make special mention of Amy Milne and Sarah Baker. Two women who I loved; they both taught me so much and perhaps I wouldn't have made it to book twenty without them. I wish they were here to celebrate with me—I miss you both and will for a very long time.

Also to Siobhan Cantrill, who was my first editor and is now doing lovely things elsewhere, your gentle, guiding hand 'way back when' was important and, again, you taught me so much.

I believe a writer needs an agent and I have the very best, Gaby Naher from Left Bank Literary—not only 'my agent', but friend and confidante.

Deonie Fiford—I love your edits. You make it all so easy.

DB—I always laugh when you retell the story of my first phone call to you. You remember it clearly and I must have been so nervous I don't recall it at all. What I do remember was your warmth and help and how this has grown into a great mateship. You're the best!

Rochelle and Hayden—life keeps moving on and sometimes I feel like a bystander, watching you both grow and strike out on your own. Always be brave, hard-working and 'just you'. I love you both dearly.

Carolyn—you've been there from before the start, my darling, very 'bestest' girlfriend! The one who tells me as it is and when to pull my socks up. I love you.

To the crew who have my back, the Brewery Bitches—you know who you all are and, yes, that includes the blokes! Graham and Lauren. Kay. Jan and Pete. Bev. Lachie. Shelley and Dave. Al. Tanya.

You know, I've had a very privileged forty-eight years. I've learned, worked hard and loved. I've lost people and things I never thought possible, and that has hurt. But all these things make us grow and perhaps the pain, as Stephen King once said, is what makes us good writers.

The one constant I've had from when I was a little girl, has been words. Whether they're in a book I'm reading, or one I'm writing, or in my journal. Words help me to understand who I am. They've been there through my darkest hours and happiest of days.

Words and writing taught me this:

The last paragraph in *Rising Dust*:

Bob reached out and grabbed Dave's hand. 'Any regrets?' he asked looking his partner in the eye.

This time, Dave could answer without hesitation. 'No. No regrets.'

Never, ever have regrets.

I'm not sure if I'll make it to another twenty books! I didn't think I'd make it here. All I can say is that I'm grateful for every opportunity these books have given me, to you the reader, and the way my life has played out. No regrets.

With love,

Fleur x